GHOST
BIRD

LISA FULLER

First published 2019 by University of Queensland Press
This UK edition published in 2021 by Old Barn Books Ltd
Warren Barn, West Sussex, RH20 1JW

www.oldbarnbooks.com
Find us on social media @oldbarnbooks
Distributed in the UK by Bounce Sales & Marketing Ltd
sales@bouncemarketing.co.uk

ISBN: 9781910646809
eBook ISBN: 9781910646816

Cover design by Jo Hunt
Typeset in 11/15 pt Bembo Std by Post Pre-press Group, Brisbane
Printed and bound by CPI Group (UK) Ltd, Croydon, CR0 4YY

First UK edition

1 3 5 7 9 10 8 6 4 2

MIX
Paper from
responsible sources
FSC
www.fsc.org   FSC® C020471

FSC® helps take care of forests
and the people and wildlife
that call them home

For Pop

Fire is the centre of our world. It's where everything happens: cooking, playing, laughing, family, story. Fire means so much more than just a bunch of burning carbon.

I sit and watch the embers escape, propelled by hot air swirling upwards. They dance into the sky, as the smoke moves steadily in one direction. My twin sister sits right in its way.

'What's wrong with you?' I shake my head as she coughs.

'Ay, smoke follows beauty, little sister.'

'Or, you know, the wind? Which in your case makes sense.'

'You wanna talk!'

'Are you sure we're related?' we say together.

Laughing with the same smile, same eyes, but a mirror image. A small freckle above the eyebrow on my right and her left is how most people tell us apart. Mirror twins are rare. Opposite sides of a whole, Mum says, even in our personalities. Laney is outgoing, sporty and popular. I am not.

'What are you two fightin bout now?'

Nan comes shuffling out of the dark, a big jewfish in one hand and a massive ceratodus in the other. I hop up to go help, but she shoos me away, tossing them to the ground. I stare in fascination at the ceratodus. 'Salmon' the old people call it, as old as we are in this country they reckon. Whitefullas said

1

they were prehistoric dinosaurs or something. Made sense to us. Sometimes people call them lung fish, cos that's what they had. Sitting by the river at night you'd hear them surface to gasp in air. Nan'd already whacked these ones on the head, otherwise that salmon'd be gasping now.

'You gonna just look at it or you wanna eat it?'

'Sorry, Nan.' I smile at her as she comes over with her cleaning gear. An old knife, some newspaper and alfoil.

I stay close, watching every move she makes, while Laney sits to the side acting like a big dainty thing with her 'ew' this and 'yuck' that. Nan looks at me and we both roll our eyes.

'Anyone would think you weren't black. Call yourself my granddaughter,' she mumbles in her rough smoker's voice. 'In my day you'd figure out how to clean it or you'd starve.'

Cleaning it is gross, I agree. But I'll take this over going into the shops and getting that boxed frozen fish rubbish any day.

I lean too close and Nan growls at me for getting in her light while she's working. She always smells like Imperial Leather soap, White Ox tobacco and talcum powder. Mum said the only thing that'd changed since she was a kid is the brands. It sounds like it should smell bad, but it never does. It smells like home.

'Nan, when ya gonna let me do that?'

'When I'm sure you can do it proper way.'

'But how will you know if you never let me?'

She snorts. 'I'll know before you.'

Fish wrapped, she takes a stick and digs out some coals, placing her parcels in and covering them. Stretching her back out, she lets out a big groan, then settles down onto one

2

of the blankets we'd laid out by the fire. Nan always keeps blankets in her car, those old scratchy hospital ones.

'Clean up them guts, granddaughters, and make your nan a cuppa.'

I go for the guts while Laney does the tea. We already had the billy on so it would be ready for Nan. When I get back to the fire Laney has hopped onto one blanket, wrapping a second one tight around her. She lifts one side for me and I climb in, cuddling close. We sit in silence watching the flames.

'Nights like this remind me of your great-grandmother's old humpy by the river,' Nan says, smiling into her tea.

She reaches into her massive bag that she dares call a purse, pulling out her rollies and getting a pre-prepared one that she dips into the embers till she has a nice cherry on it. She takes one deep drag, puffing smoke into the flames and watching it curl upward. Fear-tinged excitement rattles my heart to life. I know what is coming next. Laney and I cling closer, clasping each other's hands tight as we wait.

'He used to tell me the best stories, my old dad. Knew a lot of things.' Nan's gaze is lost in the fire and her memories. 'Couldn't teach us much, not language for sure, that old Protector fulla woulda taken us. But he told us what we needed to be safe.'

Sadness flows out of her then, mingling with the dirt and ash and painting the earth in pain. Another big draw, more smoke.

'Never say their names at night, daughters, or you'll call them to you. Don't whistle, don't draw in the dirt, don't sweep the ground neither. Not in the night or they'll come. These fullas ere, look.'

3

She holds her hand up, palm facing out and does that claw clenching move that we all know and are scared of, even adults.

Drag. Puff.

'If you're walking at night and you feel somethin behind you, don't look back. Don't run. Sing if you have ta.'

Drag. Puff.

'Stay out of them caves at night. And if you go in em in the day, don't never take nuthin from there. If you kick a stone loose, put it back.'

Drag. Puff.

'Keep your feet covered at night. Or you might find somethin ticklin em. Them things like children best and they'll wake ya if they can. Then they'll take ya and we never see yas again. They never give back what they took.'

We knew these things because Nan made sure we knew them. She still told us every time we were out by the river like this. It was our way.

'Have you ever seen one, Nan?' Laney asks.

'Well now,' she says, turning to look at us. The firelight moves strangely on her crinkled skin, making her beloved face look spooky. 'Sure you wanna hear them stories? Ya not sleepin with me tanight.'

Her warnings are always the same, but she lets us sleep with her anyway.

'Yeah, please Nan,' we say together.

'Good,' she says, nodding in approval and looking back into the fire. 'Because you'll need these stories one day, granddaughters.'

She looks lost for a minute while Laney and I sit, waiting to have the shit scared out of us. From somewhere behind

4

her I see a flicker in the dark, like when a wallaby jumps between trees, moving fast. A brief flash of red dances and I frown at it, trying to see. Probably light in the wallaby's eyes, but it looked too small for that. Turning to ask Laney, I have a second to register the glint of gold and a strange pendant around her neck before clawed, furred hands wrap around her throat.

We both gasp as it pulls her backwards out of the firelight.

'Laney!'

I spin to Nan, expecting her to move, but she's still looking into the flames.

'Nan!'

She finally turns to look at me with shining red pupils. Stumbling, I feel hands grab hold of my shoulders.

'Be ready, granddaughter,' she whispers as I'm ripped back, screaming into the dark.

The Day Of

Rolling out of bed is like getting a present, the morning chill a gift this time of year. Soon the world will be nothing but inescapable heat, so intense that the tar on the roads will bubble. I stretch, trying to shake off the weird unease in my heart, like I am forgetting something important. A heaviness sits in my gut that makes me fight to remember what I'd dreamt, but I give up when it refuses to come out. Stepping lightly over the worst of the creaking floorboards hidden under pancake-flat carpet, I drag my feet to the morning's most unpleasant duty.

I duck my head into Laney's room. I look over her piles of clothing, pick up the nearest, bulkiest shoe and peg it at the shapeless lump on the bed. Waiting long enough to hear the expected four-letter-filled response from under the covers, I go to the kitchen.

Finding the teapot half full and lukewarm is my first hint that Mum's already been up. The dishes in the sink say she's run a plate of food up to Pop; lately she's really worried about him getting too skinny. After rinsing out the pot and setting off the kettle, I make my way to the back steps. I sit and stare out over our neat little yard with its wonky clothesline and rusted tank stand. From here I can catch glimpses of the neighbours' places and the open paddock next door. Everything is a solid crackling brown. Trees flow over the hills on all sides of our town, holding the sun back as long as they can. The occasional car passes with a council worker on their way in, or a big truck filled with cattle. Magpies are warbling and the family of willy-wagtails that live in our shed are out waving their moondees, chirruping happily. The last of the cool air brushes my skin, running from the sun that's fought its way to the top of the hills. It reminds me of the aching pit in my stomach that I'd woken with and the dream that wouldn't make itself known. The kettle clicks and like a starting signal I'm up and off to get ready for the day.

Once I'm showered and fed I can't put it off anymore. I resist the urge to turn on the TV for the millionth time and zone out. The port goes over one shoulder and I'm out the door. I'm not in a rush because I love school, but getting there late means arriving all sweaty and gross. And dawdling for me equals running late. I'm always late, one of the few ways me and my twin are alike. Mum says Laney's too obsessed with the mirror to notice the time and I'm too much on my own planet to see the real one. She's right but I'll never tell her that.

Besides, this is it, my big year of lasts. The last first day of school, the last year of school ever, and hopefully the last I'll spend in this hole of a town. Most people are freaking out about Y2K and the world ending, but I can't wait for the year 2000. My morning funk disappears under that exciting thought and I could skip, I'm that happy.

Jogging down the front steps of our little weatherboard, I can see other kids walking but they're all primary schoolers. There's more than double the number of them compared to the high schoolers and only five other kids in my grade, but we'll be the biggest graduating class in a long time. If we all graduate.

At the mailbox I stop dead. A few houses down, right on the path that I always take to school, a hunched figure is pacing. Now that I'd noticed, I realised all of the littlies were crossing the road to go around. Stick-thin and clothed in one of those old-fashioned cream nighties that cover you from head to toe, Mad May Miller is doing her usual thing – bent forwards like she's searching the grass for something, muttering to invisible people and throwing her hands around like she's demanding they listen. Hopefully someone has rung her mob, God knows I can't. The hate our families have for each other is legend. One of those small-town things where no one knows how it started but every generation keeps it alive, me included. I've always thought most of the Millers are a waste of oxygen, but seeing May just makes me sad. Nan used to say she wasn't always that way; something bad happened to her so we should always be good to her, Miller or not. Then Nan would pinch her lips together and ignore my questions. She used to tell me a lot, but if she shut her mouth like that I knew not to push.

I hear the sound of a familiar engine turning into our street and I spot the white Corolla seconds later. Damn, should've left when I had the chance. The car barely stops in the dirt track that passes for our driveway before she's out and pointing at me in accusation.

'Stacey Claire Thomson, where dya think you're goin?'

'Umm, school?'

I think about running for it, but she'd probably chase me. Dad used to say it was like cornering a sand goanna – better make sure there was something bigger around or you'd get cut up when it tried to climb you. The reminder of Dad hurts somewhere deep, and for a moment I can see him in the doorway telling Mum to 'Leave my namesake alone, woman!' She'd sigh or yell back, 'I should never have named her after you.' She'd turn on him then, ready for a fight. He'd drop me a sly wink, waving a hand behind his back for me to sneak off. Dad was my tallest tree.

Shoulders slumping, I brush the waves of memory aside and refocus on my glaring mother. A tall, skinny woman with skin shades darker than mine, the only thing I'd gotten from her was her caramel-coloured eyes and the psychotic curly hair she'd already forced into a tight bun. Dressed in her hospital uniform, car keys jingling in her hands, she is always in a rush.

'You were sposed to wake your sister up.'

'I did, but she told me to f—'

'Watch your mouth or I'll soap it!'

I roll my eyes and see her anger spike. Better to try for reasonable. I take a few slow steps towards her till I'm back at the fence.

'What do you want me to do, Mum? Drag er up by er hair? That's the only way she's comin with me.'

Her glare morphs into the crinkles of worry I've seen more and more of lately. 'Daughter please, just try, ay? For me?'

I hate it when she talks to me like an adult; it means I have to be freaking responsible. Heaving a sigh I do my best sulky walk back to the house. As I brush past I catch Mum's grin.

Cow knows exactly what she's doing.

Heading into my twin's bedroom again, I stand and contemplate my plan of attack. Her den is cluttered, starting with clothes, accessories and rubbish carpeting the floor, working its way up the walls, and ceilings that are plastered with every single celebrity poster she can get. The ones from *Smash Hits* magazine are her favourites, especially when they're of muscled, shirtless boy bands and rappers, like Boyz II Men and Nas. I pick my way over her junk and flop down sideways on the covers, landing straight across her thighs.

'Get off, I'm not goin!' Her voice is muffled.

'Come on, Laney, you know she's gonna boss ya till ya move, might as well get it over with.' I wriggle against her legs to annoy her. 'There's only this year left and then she'll get off your back.'

'I don't give a shit about school!'

It's a morning for epic eye rolls but I hold in the sarcastic comment because it definitely won't get me my way. Maybe reasonable will work for me again?

'Yeah, but she does. You can put up with it for this year and you're home free, or you can bail and hear er whinge about it for the rest of your life.'

I climb off her, making sure to dig my elbow into her stomach on the way. There's an *oomph* then silence as I stand and watch.

Alright then, stuff reasonable.

'You got five seconds, then I start smashing lumps with my port.'

'Holy hell, Tace, that thing's heavier than you!'

'That was last year; this year Mum got me them extra books memba?' I heave it off the floor with a noise like a

11

wheezing old dog and pretend to test it out. 'It's gotta be another few kilos at least. You might be the track queen but I'm the weightlifter, sista girl. Now move!' Grunting some more, mostly for show, I heft my port over my head. 'Five. Four. Three. Two … two and a half.'

Nothing but a snort from under the covers. Oh she asked for it.

I drop the port to the ground and walk over to the largest poster in the room. The one of Tupac stuck front and centre on her wardrobe door. This one hadn't been folded in a magazine. Mum had given it to her for her birthday, ordered it pristine and new. Not a single crease on it.

'I've always loved this poster,' I say, fondling the corner.

'You wouldn't …'

'Be a shame ta have ta mark it up, ay? What would happen if I—'

Laney bolts from under the covers and pushes past me to the bathroom. She's cursing me but she's up. I stick the corner back carefully and go into the kitchen to start the kettle before getting her towel from her room. I'm standing on the other side of the bathroom door when it cracks open and a soapy head pokes out.

'Tace! Get my—'

Spotting the towel she snatches it and slams the door. I didn't really expect a 'thank you'. Putting together some toast for her and tea for both of us, her breakfast goes on the left like always. Two sides of the mirror Mum says; it's supposed to be a play on being mirror twins, we just call it gammon. Speak of the devil, Satan herself was heading towards the door on a wave, her purse over one thin shoulder.

I poke my tongue out at her and she grins. What a way to start the year. The Thomson twins, late again, but no one would expect anything else.

Sitting in detention on the first day of school, I sigh and turn another page. Detention's always in the library, right next to the staff room. A large single room, it has shelves on all the walls up to waist height and two taller stacks that divide it into spaces. At one end is an open area with all the little kids' books, while the stacks are all young adult fiction, and the other open area is non-fiction. The far wall in the non-fiction area has two-metre high shelving filled with reference materials. Triangular brown laminate desks, each with five or six brown chairs, dot the space in front of the stacks.

The librarian, Mr Wells, is our keeper today, and he takes great delight in handing out a 'random' essay topic to each of us. The catch is we aren't allowed to touch a computer. Leafing through an ancient encyclopaedia with a brown cover and Bible-thin pages, I am looking for my topic: 'Newtonian time'. When I finally get to the definition I send the old fart a glare. What a smart arse.

A spit ball hits my hand. I ignore it and my annoying twin.

'Don't be mad, Tace,' she whispers.

Irritated, I flip a page I haven't read yet and tuck my hand back into my lap. We've been giving each other the cold shoulder all morning but she'd caved after lunch and has been pestering me ever since. We both ignore the other person in detention with us.

Sam Miller had walked into the office not long after us. I couldn't help but feel bad for him. Mad May's great-nephew, he's the one who always goes to get her because he can keep her calm. The only boy left in year twelve, Sam has been in the same grade as us since preschool. Thirteen years of schooling and for most of that time we kept our distance. At school we can be civil, outside those gates he's a Miller and we're Thomsons. Sam never seemed that bad to me and Laney, but we'd never admit it to anyone else. As usual he picked the desk furthest away from us but I could see him, out of the corner of my eye, bent over his own book. It looked like he might've fallen asleep.

'It's your own fault, you know.' Another spit ball from Laney but this one hits my neck. I keep pretending to read.

'You'd have been on time if you hadn't dragged me in, Tatas.'

Right, that's it!

Whipping my hands out from under the desk, the rubber-band I've been carefully stretching goes flying. Bullseye! Direct hit fair on her forehead. Laney freezes in a second of shock and we both bust out laughing. Sam must've seen it because his shoulders are shaking.

'What's going on over there?'

Wells gives us the evil eye from his desk.

'Nothing, Sir.'

We put our heads down and try not to giggle. A few minutes of silence tick past before I feel her stare again. Looking up I cock an eyebrow and she smirks back.

'Can you cover for me tonight?' Laney asks.

'Why, what are ya doin?'

She smiles. 'Better you not know, liddle sista.'

I do my best impression of Mum's disapproving tight-lipped look. All it does is make her giggle.

'Nah nuthin, I just wanna see Troy.'

I roll my eyes. 'Gorn then, go hang around with Dickhead and leave me to Mum.'

I've told her heaps of times exactly what I think of Troy but it didn't stop her so I don't bother anymore. Didn't mean I was gonna be nice about it.

'Leave ya to your books ya mean.' Her lip curls in a sneer and all the fun drops out of the air. 'I don't know why you bother with the white man's education, sista, what they gotta teach us in ere isn't real life. We gotta fight the system, not take part in it.'

I turn my glare on her and there's no play in this one either.

'Don't start that shit with me. Next thing you'll be talkin native title. What's that ever done but tear us mob apart?'

'And what's education ever done but lifted one of us above the others? You've never been that selfish, Tace.' She hisses this at me and I can feel the four-letter words jumping up my throat.

We glare at each other, ready to go to war, but duck our heads down again as old Wells comes around from his desk to eyeball us. It's an old argument and so familiar we can keep going using hand signals, mostly rude ones. She'll never convince me she's right, no matter how much she tries.

Laney had been talking like a reject from the Black Panther Party since she hooked up with Troy last year. It'd started off subtle at first, but now there are times when I swear she hates white people. Mum never taught us to be like that. She always said we'd been through too much, had too much of that shit put on us and knew how bad it hurt to go dishing it out on someone else. Mum hasn't noticed Laney's new attitudes yet, but when she does Laney and Troy both better look out. It is a satisfying thought. Alana Thomson could send grown men running with that sharp tongue of hers.

Laney takes off straight after Wells releases us. Watching her climb into her man's car, that same bad feeling from this morning stirs my guts. A snippet of a dream flickers, something about Laney screaming. Goosebumps race over my flesh. Troy barely waits for her door to close before spitting gravel. Dickhead knows what I think of him, no way would I get in his car and no way he'd offer. Still, that feeling sits there. I almost whisper a request for Nan to keep Laney safe before I stop myself. Feeling depressed, I head home.

Walking up to the house I spot Troy's goonang-brown rusted bomb and frown. If word got out he was parked outside our place Mum'd be on the war path. What does Laney think she's doing?

I glare at the cocky moron, who has the balls to smile at me. Lip raised in a sneer I make it to the front door in time to bar Laney from leaving.

'Givin up on sneakin round?'

16

She rolls her eyes and shoves me. 'I forgot somethin. Now get out of the road before someone sees us.'

I stay where I am for a moment, trying to get her to look at me. She's out of her uniform in shorts and a t-shirt, but she won't meet my eyes. She just keeps right on shoving. In the end I have to back off. It isn't like I have a choice, I can't force her to tell me, especially on a gut feeling. Watching her run outside, something bothers me. It's only after she drives off that I realise she hadn't been carrying anything.

The churning inside worsens and for no reason I can explain I go and stare into Laney's room. Aside from the usual mess with her port and discarded uniform now resting on top, there isn't anything to see. But something feels wrong. Shaking my head at my imagination, I go to my room to change out of my sweaty clothes.

The Night Of

Turns out there isn't any need for a cover – Mum pulls another double shift at the hospital so I get to be on my own. I don't mind the alone bit, but I'm always worrying over Mum. The hospital is understaffed, staff underpaid and fast turning into an old people's home without the long-term care facilities. Mum is one of just two Assistants-in-Nursing in the town, and she always says with two teenage girls to support she has to take what she can get. It is better pay than what she'd get out on the orchards, but not by much. Some weeks, if a new nurse is in town, Mum barely gets any shifts.

If Mum knew how much Laney was off with Troy she would crack, but her crazy shifts mean she isn't around enough to notice. Mum has always been strict. We are the only kids our age with a curfew; some of the younger kids stay out later than us. Uncle Joe stepped in last year and talked her into loosening the reins a bit. At least now we're allowed out on the weekends, up till midnight anyway. Weeknights we're supposed to be home before full dark, homework done and early to bed. Even with the extra freedom Laney keeps pushing the boundaries; it's been worse since she got with Troy.

When Mum calls to check on us I'm parked on the couch watching *Charmed* and make out Laney's in her room doing her own thing. No matter the shift she always checks in. I rush her off the phone by telling her I got detention for being late. Her guilt has her hanging up the phone quick. I finish *Charmed* and do some channel surfing – all two of them we can get in this house – and give up when all they want to talk about is the Sydney Olympics next year. Boring! Collapsing into bed after a quick sandwich and some study (just to get ahead), I close my eyes and imagine all the places I'll see and waters I'll dive in once I'm a marine biologist. Stuff swimming with dolphins, I want to get out there with killer whales.

Big saltwater dreams for my little freshwater Murri, Nan had always said with pride. Rolling over to throw her voice out of my head, I pass out.

Racing through the bush, scrub whips my legs. Stepping high over the layers of leaves, branches and bark that coat everything, I can't escape it entirely. Every step sends out a scream of sound. I can't hear the others. The plan was to split up if they found us so why do I feel like they've abandoned me?

Dogs howl over the shouts of men. I'm running through ironbarks that give no cover. Torchlights flash through the trees – they can see me. A loud crack and wood splinters.

Holy shit, they're shooting!

'Go low and zigzag!' Troy's words fire through my head. It's the hardest thing I've ever done, but I double over and force myself to dodge erratically. Hurtling through the trees, I'm moving away at a much slower pace now.

The torchlights wave randomly. They've lost my position.

I duck behind a big tree and press my back to the rough bark. Gulping breaths as quietly as I can, I watch the beams of light dance in the trees around me. They keep jerking like the people controlling them are running. Straight towards me. My heart tries to fight its way out of my chest. I force myself to wait.

Listening to the crunching footsteps getting closer I stare up into the face of the nearly full moon. I told Troy we should have waited. It was too soon since we last raided this place and the light of the moon would make us sitting ducks. Bet he wishes he'd listened now.

'Where the fuck did he go?'

'He's gotta be close.'

Off in the dark the dogs set to howling and shouts of excitement ring out. My pursuers stop.

'Come on!'

'But we saw someone—'

'I told you it was just a big roo. But you can keep chasin it if ya want; I'm gettin some of the real action.'

More steps but this time in the opposite direction; the remaining man curses a blue streak. I squeeze my eyes shut. He starts running and it takes a few moments for me to realise his footsteps are moving away. Releasing a shaky, silent breath I try not to gasp in much needed air. Relief and guilt course through me. I was safe for now, but at whose expense?

Pushing it from my head, I open my eyes and wait for the sounds and torchlights to fade. The screaming dogs grow fainter. The sounds of my two pursuers soften. When I can hear only the crickets, see only the moon, I pry my hands from the tree. My crouching dash to the next one takes too long. I stop. No one calls out. Nothing gets shot. I force myself to do it again. And then again.

Adrenalin takes over and I'm sprinting. I try not to think about who they're chasing instead. Shutting it all out, it's like I'm on the track again, only this time the car is the finish line. The moon is the lights of the stadium. Just have to make it to the car and I'll get something better than gold – I'll be safe.

A glint of light on metal through trees signals the final stretch. Breaking out of the tree line onto the dirt track we'd found weeks ago when we'd last been here, I'm round the car, testing all the doors faster than I can think to do it. All locked.

Shit!

I press my head to the cold metal and watch my breath fog the window. I feel the trees press in on all sides and the eerie silence of the night finally registers. Not even a cricket is calling. Something worse than fear crawls along my skin. The bush is never silent, not like this.

Head lifting, I put the car at my back. Movement to my right as a speckled silvery body hurtles towards me. I'm flat on the ground without thinking. A whoosh of air overhead and I'm rolling under the car. There's blood in my mouth from biting my tongue. Terror rips through my gut and tries to crawl out of my throat.

A ghost bird. A fucking ghost bird swooping me.

I lie there trying to see out all sides of the car while keeping my movements silent. Tace says that all the old stories are just superstition. Tawny frog mouths aren't messengers. If she was here though I bet she'd be under the car with me. Some things are just ingrained.

A scrape on leaves to my left. Whipping my head towards it, my whole body jumps as though stung.

Like turning off the mute button on the TV, the crickets start calling, sound returns to the world and I can hear it all now.

'Psst.'

I tip my chin up so fast I whack my head on the undercarriage.

'Ya idiot!' I'm swearing but I'm still whispering it over his chuckles.

Troy grins at me from where he's kneeling at the front end of the car, bent over to see where I've squeezed myself.

'Lookin for these?' He dangles the car keys and laughs like we're not on the run.

'Keep it down!'

He laughs harder and holds his hands out to me.

'What for? We left those pricks behind ages ago. Besides, this is our land; no one can catch us out ere.'

I'm about to unleash on him when I feel hands clamp around my ankles. It's not like those horror movies you see where the girl gets dragged away — there's no time or breath for a full-on scream. All I get out is a gasp of fear as I'm yanked backwards into darkness.

I'm wrenched into semi-consciousness, fear pouring over me. I'm sure, so horribly sure, that Laney is in danger. Struggling out of the suffocating covers I stagger, right myself, wobbling my way to Laney's bedroom door and slamming it open. The bed is messy as usual and there's no way to see if a body is lying in it. I land on the thing, hands dragging through blankets and emptiness. My groggy mind screams its panic and I run to Mum's room. Too late I remember the double shift and plonk down onto her neatly made bed, clutching my head. My whole body is shaking and there's a metallic taste in my mouth.

Coming more awake, my mind whispers it's just a dream. It takes me a bit longer to remember that dreams aren't supposed to have any meaning, just the subconscious working through stuff. Still, everything inside me wants to call Mum; she'd make it all better. Only Laney isn't supposed to be out tonight. If I call Mum I'll be dobbing. Mum will lose it because Laney's out and I covered for her. Laney will probably show up unharmed and hungover, then she'll make me pay. No matter how you look at it I'll be in the doghouse with both of them.

Feeling a little steadier I make my way into the kitchen to scull a glass of water while the kettle boils. Shocked to see the clock above the toaster say it's only midnight, I pour myself a cuppa and banish the coppery taste from my mouth. Ignoring the voice in my head telling me it's blood. Doing that careful tea-balancing-shuffle into the sunroom, I sit on the massive couch. A big part of me wants to turn on every light in the house but I hold off. The kitchen light is still blazing, that is enough.

The sunroom's mishmash of frosted and clear louvered windows give a patchwork view of the night. The mostly full moon has sent the stars into hiding and the world is a silvered landscape, giving enough light to see almost every shape but no detail. Enough to hint at things moving in the shadows. With a shake, I banish the image of a charging bird.

A slight breeze shifts the trees and cools my clammy body. A car drives past out the front and from the sound of the engine I can tell it's the Brown boys doing their usual lapping around town into the late hours. Like it's the biggest place where there's something to see. Then again, they always have the best gossip, those boys.

23

It's quiet but it's never still here. Remembering the dead silence in the dream, I shiver.

The weird nightmare keeps trying to play through my head in full technicolour. I hold off most of it but bits keep sneaking in, like the scariest moments in a horror movie. Nan would probably have called it a special dream, one I should listen to. School says it is my subconscious telling me something about myself. Although why the hell I'd dream I'm Laney was anyone's guess. I can pinpoint the second I started to believe science more than my own mob. The day we lost Nan was the worst of my life but I'd kept the faith. I'd looked for the signs, waited to feel her close by, to come visit. If Nan visited anyone it was gonna be me. I'd been so sure.

I'd spent the most time with her listening to the old stories, learning the things that Nan always said would keep me safe. There were things she promised to tell me when I was older that I'd never get to hear now, and some she'd close her lips tight about, like with Mad May Miller. I love Pop and he's told me some great stories too, but not the ones Nan did. As I got older I realised men don't sit down like that with girls, and neither do the women with boys. Just like there are some things that you would never say to your uncle that you could to your aunty.

Losing Nan was bad – we all knew we'd lost so much more. But I knew she'd come see me again. Weeks went past, nothing happened, but I trusted in our bond. Then other cousins claimed to have seen her, felt her. The longer I waited the angrier I got, and one day I got done waiting. I turned my back on Nan's beliefs like she had done to me. Part of me knows it isn't logical to be angry with a dead woman, the rest of me doesn't care.

That nightmare, but. It felt so freaking real. Still, nothing to be done but wait for Laney to show, or Mum, or maybe the sun. Mum won't be too much longer but that doesn't mean Laney will get in before her. Sometimes she pushes her luck and if Mum is tired enough she'll only do a quick glance in to check that us girls are safely sleeping. There'd been a lot of years after Dad died when Mum wouldn't let us sleep on our own.

We were seven when we lost him in a car accident. He'd been driving back home late after a few days out tordoning by himself. Laney had once called him a tree-killer because that was the job – going out and poisoning trees to clear land. She'd been smacked for it and told not to eat the food it put on her plate if she was so high and mighty. It was maybe the only time I saw him look ashamed. Tordoning is something most of the men in town do for different properties, sometimes in gangs, sometimes by themselves. Dad had his own one-man team going. Which is why he was all alone that night when he went off the road right into a tree. The cops said it was tired driving. I didn't like to think about it.

My strongest memories of him are being held close to his massive chest, which was usually vibrating with laughter at something we'd been doing. He never called me by my name, I was his 'MnM', short for Mini-Me. Sometimes I think my parents were idiots, fancy naming your twins after yourselves. For seven years we had two Alanas and two Staceys in the house and one communal headache. There are times I miss

25

the other Stacey so bad my chest feels like it might implode. That's how I'd learnt that time doesn't heal some things, you just get used to the pain.

Gulping down the last of the tea I push to my feet like I'm shoving against my thoughts, rinse my cup and head back to bed. I hesitate at Laney's door, but decide not to create a realistic lump; if Laney is showing off somewhere she deserves to get in trouble. I climb into my own bed to wait and somehow fall asleep.

Day 1, Daylight

The screeching beep from my little alarm clock is the next thing I know about the world. Bleary-eyed I flip over and turn it off. The nightmare hadn't continued but there is a feeling like I'd had some kind of dream, something important that I really needed to remember. Shrugging it off, I tumble out of bed and head for Laney's room. When nothing but a rumpled doona greets me, I go into panic mode. Laney likes taking risks, but she isn't suicidal. Which you'd have to be to flout Mum's rules so badly. Busting into Mum's room I jump onto the bed, shaking her awake.

'Mum, wake up. Mum! Laney didn't come home last night!'

Mum cracks an eyelid open to frown at me.

'I know. What're you waking me up for; you know I got in late.'

My jaw might've unhinged, it drops that fast as Mum rolls back over. This woman should be angry and ranting, or worried and pacing, probably both. I'd seen her go into one of those frenzies before; this isn't the first time Laney has broken the rules. I reattach my jaw, reach out and grab Mum's shoulder for another shake.

'Mum, what's goin on? Why aren't you crackin?'

A long suffering sigh. Mum spoke to the wall.

'Your sister is off somewhere with that *boy*. The police are lookin for them.'

'WHAT?'

'A couple of his little gang ended up in lock-up last night; trespassin on some property. The cops came to see me at work.' Her apathy is starting to fade and I can feel the rising fury in her tone. 'Neither of those boys have cars and your sister was seen driving round in Troy's car with em last night. The cops think she's hidin out with him somewhere. Now go get ready for school.'

Knowing this isn't safe territory I hesitantly squeeze her shoulder. 'Mum …'

'And don't think I forgot that you been coverin for er too, girl.' I flinch, pulling my hand back. 'Get to school. And when you get home you better be ready to tell me how long this's been goin on. Then I'll decide your punishment.'

Busted! One difference between me and Laney is that I know when to beat a quick retreat. Even while I do it I know to be scared. This'd give Mum all day to stew and cook up a real good anger, and an even worse sentence.

Hopping into the shower I remember last night's nightmare and scoff at myself in the bright morning light. Dreams are so stupid and my twin radar isn't worth shit. Laney and Troy are probably somewhere hiding out trying to get their stories straight. I'll come home and find Laney back. Then we'd both be grounded for eternity. Just freaking great.

'Heard Laney ran off again. Who dya reckon she's doin now?' Cassie's nasal tones hit me.

I freeze in the doorway of the maths room; the kid on my heels bumps into me, shoving me forwards the rest of the way.

'Sorry Tace,' one of my classmates mumbles as she passes, giving me a quick glance, her eyebrows flying up at the look on my face. I'm too busy glaring at Cassie and her little crew to respond.

The verandah stretches the whole length of the 'Big Building'; enclosed on one side by the big open port racks that came to waist height. Serving the purpose of being right under the teachers' noses as well as barricading us in. Doorways dot the wall with louvred windows linking them in a chain, leading into the various classrooms reserved for us high schoolers. The Big Building has zero insulation and no air-con – just a few steel ceiling fans for each class – and no heating. Only the computer room has solid windows with blinds to try to keep the air-con in. The lessons aren't why most of us love that place, especially this time of year when it can go over 40 degrees.

Kids are spilling onto the verandah from every class; the only people who got out of those boxes faster than us are the teachers. Jaw clenched, I walk straight up to the group of girls clustered around the port rack and get in Cassie's face.

'What didja say?'

The others go quiet and stop their jostling and talking. All eyes are on me and the biggest bully in the school. Her queen bee attitude and occasional luck in a fight means she pretty much runs the high school girls, all eighteen of us.

Everyone except me and Laney, and she hates that so much she's sicced her little minions on us a few times. The fact Laney is more liked than her only gives Cassie more reason to be a giant bitch to us whenever she can and has done since year one – turning people against us, making sure we stay on the outer with as many people as possible. It stopped bothering me a long time ago, but always gets up Laney's nose. I've seen her do any number of nasty things to people over the years, especially if she thought she could get away with it. Mum said what most parents would – Cassie is just jealous because Laney and I are so close, so pretty, blah blah blah. Laney says it's because she's a dog. I agree.

Cassie smirks. 'What? Can't a person have a private conversation?'

Bullshit private conversation. She waited till I walked out of the maths room before saying that one as loud as she could. Her stooges, Jacinta and Naomi, stand there grinning. The three of them are cousins and they've been following Cassie's lead since they could crawl. Laney and I used to place bets on if they had an original thought between them.

'I couldn't care less what you and your little gang are on about, but if you're talkin bout my sister then we got a problem.'

'Oh yeah?' Cassie steps forwards, bringing us nose to nose, lowering her voice so no one else can hear. 'And what if I was? What're you gonna do about it? Haven't got your twin ere to back ya now.'

I snort, not bothering to lower my voice. 'That'd be right. Gotta double-bank ya dirty dogs cos ya know you'd get flogged in a fair fight.'

Cassie's face goes red and she shoves me. I hit the wall as she follows with her fist up and fury in her eyes. I bare my teeth and she hesitates.

'That's enough!'

The command knocks her back a step and wipes the grin off my face. We'd been trying to provoke each other into hitting first so we could use the self-defence claim. I knew Mrs Clay was still in the maths room, and the weird silence on the verandah would tip her to a fight.

'Cassie. Stacey. Down to the Principal's office, right now!' The broad woman with her stern, wrinkled face took no shit from anyone.

'But Miss, she—' Cassie tries.

'I don't care, young lady, we do not put hands on each other. Now move!'

'We saw the whole thing, Miss.' Jacinta jumps in and gets a glare for her troubles.

'And we both know whose side you'd pick. Get to your next class. All of you!'

Her voice sends the other kids hurrying to their bags, whispering. Naomi shoots me the finger behind Mrs Clay's back as Jacinta turns to join in the gossiping.

Following a few steps behind the old woman, I slouch down the stairs, through the covered area where we have parade with the littlies each morning, and down past the empty library into the office. The blame will probably get put on me with Cassie's two lackeys running around yipping, but when me and Laney got … the thought stops me in my tracks.

'Sit!' Mrs Clay barks before heading into the Principal's office.

The admin ladies eye us like we're walking dog treats and they are the bitches I've always known them to be. They try to buddy up to us and get the inside news. I ignore them and so does Cassie. They're all white women, and who knew how that shit would get twisted. No matter what we did or didn't say, the news would be out by lunch, spread by this pack of dorries.

The whole time I can feel Cassie staring at me, but I keep my eyes forwards. As soon as the office ladies get bored and go back to whatever it is they do, I hear her chair creak as she shifts towards me.

'So, do you know?'

Pretending I can't hear her, I yawn and start picking fake dirt out of my nails.

'Or maybe she doesn't tell ya everythin after all?'

Hmm, must not've washed the paint from art class out properly.

'Clinton tells me everything.'

It is harder to pretend now, but I keep right on inspecting my nails like they hold the secrets of the universe. Cassie's cousin Clinton is one of the boys in lock-up waiting for his court date. They never let anyone but 'immediate' family into those things; cops don't acknowledge extended mob so she's full of shit. Still, Clinton's mum might've said something to her.

'He told me how Laney and Troy left him and Tyrone high and dry out at that property.'

My head comes up and I stare her down. 'Bullshit!'

Cassie sits back, happy she'd gotten a rise. I could smack myself upside the head. Instead I glare straight into her smug, pug-nosed face.

'It's true. They were parked somewhere bush and when they got back the car was gone. Betchu that bitch twin of yours talked Troy into leavin em there to get flogged up. No wonder Troy dumped er.'

The roll of an office chair sounds as the admin staff drift back towards us like a bunch of magpies spotting food. They won't stop us if the fists start flying.

The Principal's door opens and we slump back in our seats. Mr Clay stands in the doorway and with a look sends the admin ladies rolling back. Mr Clay is married to Mrs Clay; neither of them are very nice people. I'm not sure if it's because they're unhappy with being dumped in our small town where they have no clue about the cultural differences of half their students, or if they genuinely don't like kids. He turns his glare on us and we go from angry to nervous.

'Right, you first, Cassie.'

My mouth opens. As the 'victim' I should be first; the guilty one always gets seen to last, everyone in the school knows that. Mr Clay is really predictable. My nerves hit a new peak, forced to watch a victorious Cassie saunter into the office. When she comes back out fifteen minutes later she doesn't look as happy, but she still gives me a sneer.

'Stacey, come on in.'

There's something weird in Mr Clay's voice, it's still stern, but it isn't his usual harsh 'you're in trouble' tone, so maybe it hasn't all gone Cassie's way. Stepping in, I shut the door, taking the only free seat across from Mr Clay. Mrs Clay sits to my right and says nothing.

'Now Stacey, would you like to tell us what happened?'

He folds his arms on the desk and gives me a stern look that demands the truth. He probably did the same to Cassie but like hell she gave him what he wanted.

'Cassie said somethin nasty about my sister, Sir, so I told er to stop an she pushed me. Mrs Clay came out and stopped er from hittin me.'

'Hurm. And what exactly did she say?'

I fidget in my chair. 'It's really rude, Sir.'

'I think I can take it.'

Oh well, he asked. 'She said that Laney'd run off again and asked Jacinta and Naomi who she was doin now.'

Mr Clay's eyebrows lifts. 'Who or what?'

'What?' I frown.

Mr Clay nods. 'I know you think you heard Cassie say "who", but she swears she said "what". As in "what was Laney doing now".'

I shake my head violently. 'No way, Sir, she said "who".'

Mr Clay sighs at my stubborn response and Mrs Clay steps in.

'It doesn't matter. The fact is Cassie pushed you and then lifted her fist to strike you. She'll be getting two weeks' detention.'

My face feels like I've been sucking on a lemon while smelling a fart. The Clays run this whole zero tolerance line, but they only ever apply it to the kids they decide are lost causes or too much trouble. Kids like Laney and me. If I'd done what Cassie did I'd have been suspended. I know it for a fact because last year Laney had been the one in Cassie's position; she'd gotten two weeks suspension for 'becoming physical' with another student and for using 'profanity'. I fail to see how using a few swear words would up a sentence from detention to suspension.

Mr Clay isn't finished. 'We brought you in here, Stacey, because we're concerned that Laney's absence might … be causing you some distress. We'd like to make an appointment with you to see the counsellor next Thursday.'

They'd tried this one on me and Laney before. The guidance counsellor is a nice guy, but over-worked. He always seems to be rushing somewhere. Probably because he's responsible for visiting all the schools in the district and he only has a day, or sometimes half, in each place.

'Thanks for worryin about me, Sir, and Miss, but Laney'll be back soon so it won't matter.'

Both of them perk up in their seats and I can almost see them mentally dialling the number to the cop shop. Mrs Clay beat her whipped hubby to the punch.

'Oh? Do you know where your sister is then?'

'No, Miss.' *And it's not like I'd tell you anyway.* 'But Laney'd never leave without tellin me.'

The two eye each other, their condescending thoughts practically leaping across the desk. The bell blasts and Mrs Clay and I jump. Mr Clay doesn't move; he's gotten used to it being right outside his window.

'Well, that's lunchtime, go ahead and join your friends, Stacey.'

Again they do the condescending eye-dance thing, and I roll mine as soon as I have my back to them. We all know I have no friends here.

Day 1, Afternoon

Heading up to the port rack, I grab my lunch and some books before we're all chased off the verandah. They don't let us up there during lunches because they say we can't be trusted not to steal from each other. Sitting in the high schoolers' lunch area under the Big Building, I start scoffing the sandwich Mum has thrown together. Normally I ignore lunch in summer – it's too damn hot to eat during the day – but who'd pass up a bacon sandwich? At least it's cooler under here with all the concrete, polished to a shine from epic handball wars. I can see a few of the primary schoolers hanging out in little groups over in their area, but most have already eaten and are off to the playground on the other side of the primary school building. A lot of the older kids have lunch passes so they head home or down to the shops to get their food.

I try not to think about the office. It isn't that I don't have friends or family in the school, but my best friends are all gone now, either to boarding schools or off working somewhere. I get on with most of the others when Cassie isn't around, but I'm not close with anyone except Laney. I have no trust for sheep who blindly follow bullies. Laney and I can go out for lunch too, but in the middle of summer it isn't worth being in the heat for that long.

Lately, though, Laney has been going out to spend them with Troy.

So much for not thinking about it.

I pick up my books and head to the library. Since I've lost all signs of a social life at school I pretty much live down there when I'm not in class. That isn't so bad, but losing my friends also means there's no one to hang out with after school and on the weekends. Laney tried to get me to come out partying for a while, and I'd even gone a few times, usually when I was feeling lonely. But me and Troy couldn't stop baiting each other. It made us sisters fight, so Laney stopped asking.

Settling into the chair that should have my sweaty cheek marks permanently printed on it, I keep working on my English assignment and try not to worry about things I can't change. At least there's air-con here. Life away from this town is the goal; a life of sea and swimming is the dream. The loneliness will be worth it, as long as Laney comes home soon.

What the hell is she even thinking? Some of the property owners around here will take shots at trespassers. Or worse if you're a trespassing black. I push the thought of what that means away. None of it's helping me with my English assignment. I stare down at the piece of paper that lists the requirements. I'm supposed to write some bullshit about what I want from the year. If I'm honest and write 'I want my sister home safe and my nan back from the dead' it will likely get a big fat F. 'I want to get out of this hellhole, filled with tiny, racist minds, especially the teachers', would earn me detention. That last thought blocks up my brain and I wish I could scream it. The blank page of my notebook stares back at me for a long time.

Into that empty space slips Cassie's words.

When did Troy dump Laney?!

I jump out of my chair as the bell rings. Goddammit! Phone calls to parents aren't allowed unless you're sick. Even then the admin ladies will listen in; and anyway, Cassie's probably just shit-stirring. Kicking the heavy wooden desk leg I pack up my books and walk back to class.

The gossip going around at school is pretty much what Mum said, except for the part where the boys in lock-up have been bashed. They reckon the property owners and their workers did it, but the cops are ignoring it. Some bullshit about defending their property, even though none of the boys were armed and they were outnumbered two to one against full-grown men. Laney's right about one thing, this place is fucking racist. Where we differ is Laney responds to it with more hate and I just want to get the hell away, or at least I hope to. There has to be more than this surely? It isn't like we can do anything about the way things are — all the positions of power are held by the property owners, all white, and all with their memories of the days when they owned us, lock, stock and barrel. To use terms like 'slave' you have to be considered human. We've never been that to them.

Hmm, did being bitter count as harbouring hatred? Sometimes I feel infected by this place, as if hate itself breeds here.

Sitting through another two-and-a-half-hours of school is torture. I spend the whole time jiggling, fidgeting and staring at the clock. But it gives me time to think. The moment the last bell rings I force myself to walk to the port rack, pretending to struggle with my books while I keep an eye out. Any of my cousins might know the goss, but I keep my eyes peeled for my cousin Bobbie, she's better than *The Courier Mail* and if you want to piss her off you'd call her Roberta. When I finally spot her she's walking alongside Cassie.

There goes that idea.

I swing my port onto a shoulder and start forwards. There's no point asking now; I might love my cousin but she has shit taste in friends. I underestimate how much Bobbie loves a good gossip; she grabs my arm when I try to brush past her.

'Ere, Tace, any word from Laney yet?'

There's real concern from her so I stop, making sure I can see what Cassie is doing.

'Nuh nuthin, why? Did you hear somethin?'

'Nah, sorry, cuz; they reckon Troy's not talkin.'

My spine goes rigid with shock. I can see Cassie's smug triumph. 'Ay? What do you mean Troy?'

Bobbie's eyes light up; she loves being the first in with any gossip, especially when it's this big.

'Don't you know?' She tries to hide her glee. 'Troy drove back into town late last night. He's dodgin the cops and e's not sayin nuthin bout what appened that night, but Laney isn't with him.'

'Thanks, cuz,' I say, shaking off her hand and turning towards the stairs.

39

'Tace, there's somethin else. They reckon she was out at the Potters' place.'

My face must've gone white because she reaches to grab my elbow.

'You right?'

I shake my head to clear it and focus on the important information. 'Yeah, fine. See ya!' I yell over my shoulder and bolt for it.

'Where ya goin?' Bobbie calls to me. I ignore her.

Home is normally a ten-minute walk but I cut it down to five, even in this heat. Rounding the last corner I push past the burning in my chest and crash through the back door, heart pounding. I have to stop and catch my breath before picking up the phone and dialling the hospital. The woman who answers is one of those stuck-up ones so I do my nice-as-pie thing saying we have a family emergency. I pretend not to hear the other woman dig for information on Laney, just wait till she finally moves her arse to go get Mum.

'Stacey?'

'Mum, didja hear? Troy's back in town but he doesn't have Laney with him!'

There's a pause and a muffled sound, then Mum comes back on, all clipped words and harsh sounds. I hate that ultra-professional voice she puts on sometimes. It means she's burying something.

'Who told ya this?'

'Bobbie told me at school, said he got in last night but he won't say where Laney is.'

'Right, we'll see about that one.' Mum must've covered the phone because all I can hear for a bit is the hum of different voices, then she's back. 'Call Uncle Joe, get him to come pick me up. We're gonna sort this right now.'

'And me too?!' It's a question but for some reason I yell it. There's another pause but this one is shorter.

'All right, get Uncle to swing past on his way. Tell im it's about Laney.'

Click.

I dial Uncle Joe's number and listen to the ring. Uncle Joe is Dad's older brother and he's done all he could for us since Dad died. We'd gone to the cemetery for the ten-year anniversary and he'd been right there. He's our second dad. He answers the phone and Slim Dusty flows down the line. As soon as I say Laney's name the tunes are shut off and I have his full attention.

'I'm gettin in the car now, you be waitin at the street when I pull up, niece, got it?'

'Got it, Unk.'

I hang up and walk to the road, school uniform and all. If I don't want to get left behind then I'd better be where I'm told. I'll be here all bloody night if I have to. I spot Bobbie heading down the road towards me and know that girl is coming to have a dorrie. Luckily Uncle pulls up before she gets close.

Bobbie starts cooeeing and doing a frantic 'pick-me-up-too' wave. I wave back in a friendly 'see-ya-later-cuz' way. Uncle stares straight ahead.

I pretend not to notice how hard Uncle's gripping the steering wheel or the waves of extreme pissed-offness crashing around the car. For once I keep my mouth shut; this really isn't going to end well, hopefully for Troy. Roaring up to the hospital, we pull in to where Mum's waiting. Squeezing between the seats I flop into the back as Mum jumps in the front.

'Where we goin?' Uncle growls.

'Edna's place.' Mum didn't growl back but I know the tight-lipped look that goes with that tone. That's scary enough.

She turns in her seat, eyeballing me.

'Did Bobbie hear anything else?'

'They reckon she was out at the Potters'.' I say it fast, like I'm ripping off a Band-Aid.

Uncle swears a streak and Mum goes pale. There are good and bad property owners around. The Potters aren't the kind of people we'd go anywhere near. Their long-running hatred of anything darker than tan is well known. Nan always said they were a family that bred hate. They'd 'discovered' their bit of land right after the Archer brothers settled on Eidsvold Station, naming it after their home town in Norway. The Potters decided they were going to do one better, calling their property Akershus after some famous castle in Norway. It set off a big rivalry that went on for a while, but where the Archers moved on, the Potters never did. Then again, the Archers ended up with a station renowned for the cattle that came off it, and a whole town established close by and named after their place. Akershus was the poor cousin left to wither somewhere on the back roads between Eidsvold and the next town over, Mundubbera. No one could pronounce the name, let alone spell it, so it just got called the Potters' place. All their grand ideas shrivelled up and they'd blamed the local blacks for it.

No one really knew why exactly, but Nan always said bitter people don't like logic, it doesn't suit their victim mentality.

'That it?' Mum grates.

'Pretty much.'

She faces forwards. Nothing else is said as Uncle burrs up to Edna's. She's Troy's mum and I really have my doubts on whether we'll find him there. If you're hiding from the cops how silly would you be to hang around the place you live? My face drops in disbelief when we pull up to see Troy's car parked at the back, plain as day. Mum twists around again to look at me and forgets her anger long enough to chuckle.

'Some people are beggin to be caught, daughter.' Then she's all business again. 'Now, you stay in this car and do not step a single foot outside, no matter what happens. Is that clear?'

Uncle whips around like he's just remembered I'm sitting there. 'And if you do you'll deal with your mother and then me. Got it?'

My eyes get really big and I nod. Uncle likes to think he's scarier than Mum; me and Laney play along to make him feel better. Mum knows it too. Her lips twitch before they both throw their doors open and march up to the house. A few dogs bark from inside. Rolling down my window, I lean forwards, not wanting to miss a second. While the adults take the stairs of the big old Queenslander, my eyes keep flicking over to Troy's car. I can't shake the image of Laney hiding under it, feeling those hands close over our ankles. Goosebumps flood my body. I look back as Mum starts banging on the screen door.

Edna Dennis comes storming up as if she didn't hear us the second the car pulled into her driveway.

'What do you want?' Our mobs have never liked each other much, but it isn't the inter-generational war we have with the Millers.

'We want to talk to Troy. We just wanna know where Laney is.' Uncle is better at pretending to be calm than Mum.

'My boy doesn't know anything about that girl and he don't wanna know. She's the one who got them into this in the first place!'

'Bullshit!' Mum yells in her face. 'Laney wasn't in any trouble like this before. Now bring the little bastard out here so he can tell me what he's done with my daughter.'

In horrified fascination I watch them square off through the flyscreen.

'That girl's nuthin but a troublemaker—'

'Because your son's so fuckin innocent?'

'Don't you run my son down! Get off my fuckin porch!'

With all that going on I should be transfixed, but my eyes keep sliding back to Troy's car. I could swear there's something moving under it and isn't that spooky as hell? My goosebumps grow worse.

Mum must've hit the screen door because a bang brings my attention snapping back and next minute Uncle has Mum by the shoulders. The four-letter words are flying now.

'Listen ere ya dog, you better get off my fuckin property before—'

'Before what, Edna? Before your sleaze of a man grabs another knife? Come ere and—'

'Eyah! Knock off you two! Al, we didn't come ere for this!' Uncle keeps trying to talk sense, but it has as much effect as Mum telling Laney to go to school.

It's the day for my jaw to flop around unhinged. It isn't so much the foul words that shock me as hearing Mum say them. Laney would've loved this, if only to tease Mum later about rinsing her mouth out with soap.

And still my eyes wander back to that stupid old, banged-up … I do a double-take. There!

I call, 'Uncle! Uncle!' But there's no getting his attention while that's going on right in his ears. Flinging open the door I step from the car, keeping one hand on it like that will stop them from going off at me later. 'Hey Uncle, look ere!'

Uncle Joe swings an irritated look at me, but he stops when he sees me beside the car.

'You get back in that—'

My frantically wiggling eyebrows cut off his growl. I have his attention now, so I tilt my head in the direction of Troy's car. Hesitating for a second he lets go of Mum; she barely notices, going back to banging her palms against the screen while Edna threatens to call the cops. Watching Uncle storm towards me like I am in some serious trouble, I feel a smile creep over my face.

'Stacey Claire Thomson, I told you to stay in that car!'

See, not as scary as when Mum says it, I smirk. Coughing into one hand and doubling over a bit to do it, I slide my other hand down, pointing under Uncle's car, before again tilting my head towards Troy's old bush-basher.

Uncle picks a path that takes him closer to the house. At the last second he veers towards Troy's car. Swerving to the side of it he drops to his knee and grabs a handful of whatever he finds under there. Next minute he's pulling a struggling Troy out, not caring if he gets any scrapes or bruises along the way.

'Get off me!' Troy yips.

Edna must've heard him because she breaks off swearing at Mum and starts screaming to her husband to call the cops. Suddenly switching from banging on the screen to leaning against it with all of her weight, Mum smiles evilly as she watches Uncle handle Troy. She's always fast on the uptake is Mum.

Uncle is a big man, even by today's standards, and years of tordoning and fencing work has left him with a lot of muscle. He gets an arm across Troy's throat pretty easily and has him pinned to the ground in no time. Whatever he's saying to the boy has Troy's struggles slowing then stopping, leaving him looking up at Uncle Joe. Me and Laney might not be scared of our uncle, but any man with half a brain should be, especially if they've harmed his brother's girls. And Troy has done plenty of harm.

I want to run over there so bad it hurts, but the whole thing is over pretty fast. One minute Troy's on the ground and the next Uncle is picking him up and setting him on his feet. Troy isn't a small bloke, just young, and Uncle is good at intimidating without having to harm the young fullas in town. Uncle turns back towards me when two things happen at once.

Edna's man Ray comes barrelling around the side of the house with an axe raised over his head, and the town cop car comes screeching in behind me. I shoot a look at the front door to see Mum step away from the screen like nothing is wrong, while Edna has gone quiet. Troy goes white as a sheet, a neat trick for a blackfulla. Ray does a weird little skid, brings the axe down and throws it under the house. All of the black people in the place throw their hands up. No silly ones here.

I don't know whether to laugh or cry. This is going to take forever, chewing up time we should be using to look for Laney.

'You really expect me to believe that you were "bringing" the axe to Joe because you borrowed it from him?'

Sitting in the cop shop with my head down, I keep pretending to read the ratty magazine I'd found in the waiting area. The whole place smells like stale things and chemicals; probably a mix of the sergeant's illegal inside-smoking and the air freshener he's been trying to hide it with. The cop shop is a brick square, with a tiny waiting area that started out as temporary and at some point became permanent. There are two of those old brown plastic chairs with metal legs and a small side table with magazines from five years ago stacked on it. I'd claimed one when Mum refused to sit down, somehow managing to pace in the miniscule area. Edna sat in the other chair across the table from me.

I shouldn't be able to hear anything the cop is saying, but they only have room for Troy and Uncle Joe in the separate office and single interview room. They'd already questioned me, Mum and Edna 'on the scene', then piled the men into the back of the car. We'd followed them down to the cop shop. After putting Uncle and Troy in the offices, they'd brought Ray to the open area behind the front desk and tackled him first. This had been going on for roughly thirty minutes. At some point the sergeant left to go get some dinner or something, leaving the constable there to 'finish up'. I spent the whole time trying not to laugh, and refusing to look at Mum or Edna; I could feel them not looking at me either.

'Yeah, Officer, he wanted to see Troy about Laney and I figured I'd give it to him at the same time. Save me a trip, see.' Ray is being so respectful, no sarcasm even. Butter wouldn't melt in his mouth.

'Alright, Ray, say I believe that, why did you throw it under the house?'

'If I'd kept hold of it you might've thought I was threatenin you or somethin bad like that. I didn't want you to shoot me! So I chucked it fast.'

The constable is suspicious as hell but it's not like he has anything on them. Right now their biggest worry is Troy, so they finish up with Ray and it's only another hour before they let Uncle Joe go. Edna and Ray give us all dirty looks as we leave; they're waiting to see if Troy will get released or thrown in lock-up. Lock-up wouldn't be a friendly place for him with Clinton and Tyrone already in there. From what the cop said those two are so pissed off they'd dobbed Troy and Laney in for being there that night, too.

Sliding into the car I stay quiet and wait. It doesn't take long for Mum to start. They just have to get enough space between them and the cops first, then she turns to face Uncle.

'Well?'

'Troy says he doesn't know what happened to her. He said they all split up when they got chased. They were supposed to meet up at the car but she never showed.'

'He's lyin!'

My furious shout stops them cold and they both look at me. I could see their worry.

'I mean, he has ta be, right?' How can I tell them I'm so sure because of a stupid nightmare?

Mum shakes herself and nods at Uncle. 'Turn this car around. We're makin a missin persons report.'

Her voice is hollow. It's the voice that I'd only heard two times before: when she told us Dad was never coming home, and the last day she took us up to see Nan at the hospital.

I lean forwards and wrap my arms around Mum's shoulders as tight as our seatbelts will allow.

'It's okay, Mum, we'll find her. We'll make sure she's okay.'

Mum's strong, calloused hands pat my forearm.

'From your lips, baby girl.'

The constable isn't any happier to see us the second time, especially when Mum marches up and declares her sixteen-year-old daughter missing. Edna and Ray shoot her a vicious look while the cop sighs. He looks Mum up and down.

'We've got a warrant out for her arrest, Alana,' he says in a bored voice.

'*Ms Thomson* to you, Cun-stable.' She doesn't wait for him to hear the emphasis on that one, barrelling right across his frown. 'And I want it on record: Laney said she was going to see Troy after school, and Stacey saw her get in his car after school. Troy says he hasn't seen her since last night. So take down the damn report.'

'Well, that's not the story Troy's telling everyone else.'

Mum's eyebrows climb upwards. 'And when did gossip become an official police source? That boy told Joe that Laney never showed up where she was supposed to. I want you out lookin for her.'

'There's a lot of things in this world that we want *Alana*, most of which won't happen for one reason or another.'

Mum looked ready to keep arguing but Uncle grabs her elbow, nods to the cop and drags his sister-in-law with him, whispering in her ear the whole way. Staying put I eye the cop like he's a sample under a microscope. He doesn't seem to like it much.

'What do you want?' he sneers. 'Going to report someone else missing?'

'Yeah actually,' I drawl. 'Your humanity seems to be missin. You might want to do somethin about that.'

Turning on my heel I follow after my family, leaving him with a bright red face. Fully expecting him to race after me and make up some charge, I'm shocked when I make it all the way to the car. Finding Uncle holding a struggling Mum against the car knocks that straight out of my mind.

'Calm down, Al! There's no point dealin with them arseholes, they wouldn't do nuthin anyway. We'll start the search ourselves.'

I can see the tears Mum is fighting behind all that rage and I stare back towards that old building. I can't help wondering how he would've treated us if we were some other shade of brown.

'If it'd been the old constable we'd have been right,' I mumble, more to myself than anyone else.

Uncle grunts. 'Only decent cop this town ever had.'

There isn't much to say after that.

Day 1, Twilight

Walking up the street to Pop's place wasn't my idea of 'helping' the search effort, but I'd finally stepped on Mum's last nerve and been ordered out of the house. After we'd gotten home, Uncle Joe went out to talk to our mob and Mum started ringing everyone and anyone she could think of. It was like watching her shake the limbs of a big ghost gum and getting depressed when nothing fell out. No one had seen Laney. It didn't help that we'd both spring to the phone if it so much as squeaked. Plus I kept staring at her, wondering if I should try to talk to her about my dream. I don't believe but I knew she would. When she went off at me for creeping her out it helped relieve the uncertainty. If she was going to yell, then it probably is a good thing I don't tell her. A nightmare isn't going to help us find Laney. The one upside is that now everyone knows what's happening the biggest mob is turning up. They're all at our place, sitting down, dividing up streets, properties and search areas. And I hate that I'm not there with them.

The feed of barbecue steak, sausages, eggs and tomatoes is still warm on the plate and wrapped in alfoil as I trudge the back roads. There is a big frigging hill this way but a lot fewer houses, and I don't want anyone stopping me to ask how it's going. I focus on keeping the bread from sliding off of the top of the alfoil so I don't have to look up. I know the path to Pop's like the back of my hand; I can walk around blindfolded in this town. Eidsvold is mostly little weatherboards like ours, most I'd been in were small three bedrooms with one bathroom and a kitchen. If you are lucky the toilet is in the house. If you aren't, it means tiptoeing over cane toads to do a dump at night. Even my white mates' places are like that. A bit flasher maybe, not needing anything done, like a bathroom that actually has four complete walls, but still a similar layout. Then again most of them own their places, us blackfullas are all renting from the Aboriginal Housing or private way. There are so few options for us in our town that you take what you can get and are thankful for it.

I can't shake the feeling that all this is useless, that Laney never left that property. The Potters have a reputation with us that goes back generations; there's no way they'd let us out there to look around, no point even asking. Instead, a whole heap of the uncles, aunties and older cousins are going out on the roads around the Potters' place, hoping she made it that far. I try not to imagine my twin walking somewhere out there without food or water. Alone, maybe lost. Others will be out at different places, hoping to get lucky.

Potters' is rare around here, having survived mostly intact through the years. They haven't had to lease out paddocks, or subdivide like others. They have enough sons to run the place and still be able to employ a few jackaroos, none of them black. Then again, not many blackfullas will go out there. On the most western side of the property sits a mountain that none of us will go near. The elders are clear on that one.

I shove those thoughts aside as I hit Pop's driveway. His place is an old weatherboard up on short stilts. The difference is ours is cream and his is white. Most places in town are a shade of white or pink and all of it peeling. His yard is filled with flowers, and out the back is one of the best vegetable gardens in town. Mum said his last job before he retired was as a gardener.

Like always, he's stretched out on the verandah, rollies on the table and one burning away in his hand, watching everything. Men are worse gossips than women, Mum always says, and I believe her.

'Hey Pop.'

'Hurmph.' His grizzled voice grumps and he nods his silver head. I can tell straight away I'm in trouble.

'Bought you up a feed.'

I put it on the table in front of him, drop a quick kiss to his cheek before picking up his gigantic mug and starting into the house.

'Cuppa tea?' I sing out as I walk to the kitchen. I don't even have to ask really. The mug is half full and mostly cold, but it wouldn't matter if it was only five minutes old, he always has a fresh cuppa with his food.

'Bring me the milk and sugar.'

Grinning and shaking my head, I hit the kettle's button and rummage around his kitchen to make us both one. He had to talk to me that time, no choice. We are all under strict orders from Mum to only give him a certain amount of sugar and milk; I can't ignore her but Pop sure does.

'And don't forget the salt and pepper!'

This time I groan.

I cart cutlery and all the fixings out to him, finish the teas and set them on the table before plonking down in one of the mismatched chairs he has strewn about. I watch him pour on the salt and pepper and wince.

'That's yucky, Pop. You're ruinin Mum's cookin doin that.'

'Adds more flavour.' He gives me one of his mischievous eye-twinkles from under his big bushy eyebrows. Then he remembers to be mad at me, frowns and focuses on getting into his feed. The tea is next and it's even worse what he does to that, so I stop looking and watch his hands instead.

Mum says he'd been a giant of a man and you can see it. Into his seventies and he's still taller than all of his sons. His broad shoulders might be skinny now, but they are always straight, his head up and his posture perfect. An upright, big mountain of a man. Those are my earliest memories and how I've always seen him. I love sitting with him like this, even if he's being all sulky with me.

I stare out over the front lawn. Picture perfect as always, Mum is gonna crack. He isn't supposed to be pushing a mower or using a whipper-snipper either. I hide my grin behind my mug because if he thinks I'm laughing at him I'll be in for it. He always says I'm never too old to smack, not that he ever did it, but I wouldn't put it past him.

'Where's your mother?' he growls as he reaches for his mug.

'Callin round to check if anyone's seen Laney.' My grin drops and I lower the mug, looking at him from the corner of my eye. He's too busy looking at his plate.

'She gone?'

'Yep. Didn't Uncle Terrance come tell you?'

'Nobody tells me anythin in this family.'

And there's the reason for his sulk.

'Not! Mum'll go off at Uncle for that, he was sposed to come tell you what was happenin while we started the search.' I am outraged but not surprised. Mum's brother is a known flake, we should've come check he'd done it but we had other things on the go.

'Well *you* shoulda come told me.' The knife gets thrust in my direction to make the point.

'Pop, that's not our fault, Mum was ringin everyone, Uncle Joe went for a drive around to everyone who doesn't have a phone and I was cookin that dinner you eatin. Sides it's not like you never heard about it.'

He waves his hand at me, gumming down his latest mouthful. 'Mmmphmmmphmmph.' See, big gossip, he knows everything that old fulla. He swallows a bit of tea to clear the way and starts again. 'Never mind that now, anyone seen her?'

Accusation delivered, he's straight to the point. Pop never really seems to be that worried about any of us, but Mum says you have to watch close to see it. Once he got into one of his sulks he usually holds onto it for dear life, now he's pushing it aside for news of his granddaughter. I feel my shoulders drop and I curl my body around my mug.

'Nah, nuthin.'

Pop and all the oldies hate tears or any show of sadness so I stare straight into my mug and try not to let them well. I figured they'd been through so much in their time that our lives must seem easy as, and any complaints made us whingers. The silence stretches for a while and I realise he's stopped eating to eye me closely. As soon as I tilt my head towards him he speaks again.

'You been dreamin?'

My eyes go wide with surprise and I look straight at him. He nods and takes another mouthful, motioning with his knife for me to get a move on. Sometimes it's eerie how the old people just know stuff. One day I'll get the courage up to ask how, but Laney reckons there are some things we maybe don't want to know.

'I mighta … I sorta … had this nightmare, but. But it's not real, Pop, it was just a dream!'

He looks at me. No expression, nothing. The focus in his gaze has me squirming till I spill my guts all over the place about the nightmare, which is what he wants.

'So she's under the car, lookin at Troy. Then next minute, something just grabs er.'

He sits there chewing. A swallow, some more tea.

'Didja see what did it?' Another mouthful went in.

'Nuh, but it was like I was her in the dream and she didn't see it neither.'

'Got her from behind.'

'Yeah by the ankles, pulled her from under the … How did you …' I trail off and wait. Questions are the fastest way to shut the old fullas up, either he'll tell me or he won't. My job is to keep my mouth shut and my ears open.

It's my turn to watch him closely as he finally glances down to scrape the last of the bits together and scoop them onto his fork. He doesn't look up as he cleans his plate with the last of the bread. I start to fidget.

'Might be, there was another girl while back, disappeared one night out at that place.'

I suck my breath in, clench my jaw tight and force the breath out through my nose.

'When Mum was little?' There, that sounds calm enough.

'Mm.' He shakes his head and put his plate to the side, takes out one of his millions of hankies and dabs at his mouth before picking up his tea and gulping some down. 'Fore that, when your grandmother was a girl workin out at Eidsvold Station.'

He isn't deliberately teasing me – he has to see and I have to prove that I'm worth it. Knowledge for us isn't like rocking up to school or opening a book and it's all there laid out for you. You have to prove yourself, that you deserve the old people's trust, and even then there are some things they will never tell. I've had those yarns with Nan, but I'm almost an adult now, the rules have changed. I'd never had this kind of talk with Pop. I should be honoured that he was willing at all, especially about Nan. He hasn't said a word about her since the funeral.

I might be ready to jump out of my seat and throw a full-on tanty till he told me what I want, but I won't. It would get me nothing and Mum would pitch a fit if I did something that disrespectful. Worse, Pop wouldn't tell me anything ever again.

'But you would'nt've been ere then, ay?'

He waves his hand in a northerly direction. 'I was up round Rocky then, happened while I was out there. Young woman snatched was all I heard. There was nuthin in the newspapers, not till the end and not about what happened to er.'

It's said to his mug, not me, and I can see he's getting jittery talking about it. Still, this is for Laney. I so desperately want to push, to *know*.

'Do you remember what year, Pop?'

I watch him pull back and look at me, the ends of his eyebrows falling over his dark brown eyes, creating a screen that he watches me from under. There's a second I think for sure he'll clam up.

'Mighta been '47. No, had to be '48, a few years fore I met your nan.'

His gaze goes back to his mug and that moment of sharing vanishes. I could've swum through his sadness, but all he does is take another gulp of tea. Bringing out his tobacco, he starts making his rollies. That's all I am going to get. I feel tears burn my eyes so I grab the plate and mumble something about cleaning up and getting back home. He pushes his mug towards me and says nothing as I take everything inside. Pop leaves me to myself while I scrub away my pain under boiling hot water. Making him up another mug of tea, I place it carefully in front of him. I get the biggest shock when his hand covers mine, patting it softly a few times before pulling back like nothing happened. The tears I've been fighting threaten again. I bend down and give him a peck on the cheek before making a quick retreat. He says nothing, watching me walk off with Mum's plate.

The walk home clears my head a bit, although not as much as that hand pat, and I realise how silly it all sounds. How could a young woman disappearing over fifty years ago have anything to do with Laney? Unless those Potter boys are some kind of *Deliverance* freaks, going around taking black girls every few decades. I want to laugh it off, but what other options are there? I know I'm deliberately shying away from the other possibilities.

Remember daughter, the world is a lot bigger than anyone knows. There are things that science may never explain. Maybe some things that shouldn't be explained.

Mum's voice intrudes. These women are sending me nuts.

Then again, Mum might know the story of the girl, but asking her about it now would be suicide. I see Laney's face and know I have to try. I hope Mum understands.

Day 1, Night

An hour later guilt has raised its ugly head. Not only did I confess to Mum what Pop had told me, it also forced out the story of my nightmare. Mum's complete silence as she stood at the kitchen counter refusing to look at me leaves me with the horrifying feeling that she's crying. I mumble an apology, say something about my English assignment, and go to my room to stare at the ceiling in misery. A soft tap at my open door and I look up to see Uncle Joe's face, glancing nervously around. Another thing men don't do is go into their niece's bedrooms alone. All the family had left before I got back. Uncle stayed so he and Mum can do a few laps around the most obvious places Laney might go.

I sit up, pull my port off my desk chair and wave him onto it. He drops down with a grunt that means his knees are playing up again. Too many years of footy, Mum says.

'I heard what you asked your mother.'

I nod, ducking my head and waiting for the chewing out I know I deserve. When his voice comes again it is much quieter. I look up to see him sneaking glances at the door.

'Your grandfather on your father's side told me a story once, bout a woman that disappeared. Only when she came back she wasn't the same. They reckon she was ...' He looks at me and I swear I see pain there, when normally there's

61

nothing but strength. All of our black men have to be a certain way too.

'I don't think it's the same thing, niece, or I hope it isn't. And knowin this won't help us any. It'll make us worry that much more about er.'

'Please Uncle. Please tell me the story.'

Ordinarily begging doesn't work, but I think his worry over Laney forces him.

'It was May.'

An image flickers through my head and I recoil.

'Mad May Miller?' I whisper violently. Uncle looks at the door again and he makes 'quiet down' motions with his hands. Stuff 'quiet'. There's no way my sister is coming back like that.

'Did it really happen?'

I feel bad saying it, but I've seen this woman talk a blue streak to herself all my life. Her mob try to keep her home but she still gets out, like the other morning. Warngee she might be, but she can still get past them. Sometimes kids will make fun of her but only to each other, no one teases her to her face. I always figure it takes a certain level of cruelty to do that to someone so defenceless, and most people don't have that in them. I'd seen Cassie and her two cousins do it once outside the school gates. I was so full of disgust I went to find Sam Miller at his usual spot in detention. He didn't say anything, just ran out to stare Cassie down before leading May away. I don't think they've liked each other after that. Cassie had looked up to where I was standing and I'd stared straight back. She knew what I'd done.

'It was in the papers and all. Grandfather said that whatever happened it made her that way.' His voice drops even lower and I have to lean in to hear him properly. 'They reckon it was the property owners took her and her father went after them for payback.'

He is so uncomfortable he's shaking both legs uncontrollably, but I hold my tongue this time. My silence encourages him to keep going.

'The newspapers said he was tried and convicted, but they reckon it was an old-fashioned lynchin that day. All those people'd be dead and buried now but.' Uncle must've hit his limit because he suddenly straightens and that stern expression I am so familiar with is aimed fair at me. 'Now you know there's nothing there, leave it at that.'

He pushes up from his chair and goes back to the doorway, having a quick look out to see where Mum is. He pauses for one second to look back at me. 'And don't tell your mother I told you that neither.'

Hurrying out, he vanishes just as Mum comes through the other door, the one that leads to what used to be a verandah and was built in at some point to create another room. She sits on the end of my bed and glares at me. I resist the urge to tuck my knees into my chest and wait her out. She's been swinging violently between crying and fury all afternoon.

'Do you know where your sister is?' Her voice slices off every word.

'No, I swear.'

I know I've stuffed up even before I see her fingers clench the doona.

'And how am I supposed to believe that after all the lyin you been doin?'

I drop my eyes.

'Look at me when I'm talkin to you.'

I force myself to look her dead in the eyes. 'I swear on the Bible, Mum, I don't know where she is.' This is the most solemn oath you can make in my family. We're taught that swearing on the Bible and lying means you go straight to hell. I'm not sure if I believe that so much anymore, but I know that oath is sacrosanct. 'She told me she was goin to hang out with Troy.'

'And how long has that been goin on?'

I want to smack myself on the forehead. Ah well, might as well get it over with. 'Since she got with im.'

'When was that?'

'After school finished last year?' My eyes drop before I can stop them and I curse myself upside and down.

'Are you askin me or tellin me?' Her voice is diamond hard.

'That's what Laney said.' I can't seem to keep still.

'But you know different.'

'She don't tell me everythin!' Anger, the last desperate ploy to divert her. Sometimes it even works. Seeing Mum's nostrils flare is how I imagine a shark scenting blood must look.

'But she tells you the most, and you suspect somethin different. Spit it out right now or so help me, Stacey Thomson, they will write dirges about your fate.' Mum likes reading, a lot. Sometimes I hate that I do too, maybe then I wouldn't know what she was on about.

'Since just after our birthday.'

A horrible silence follows. It is always worse when Mum goes quiet.

'So September? And how many times did she sneak off with Troy?'

'She rings him whenever you're on a late shift.' Mum stewing is like a rumbling super-volcano. You know you're standing too close and no matter what you're going to get caught in the fall out. The difference is that running from a volcano might reduce the damage, whereas running from Mum only guarantees more.

She moves off the bed and faces out the door she came in, putting her back to me. I can see her biceps working as she clenches and unclenches her fists. When she finally turns I think I'm ready.

'"Grounded" is too small a word for what you are.' Her soft tone fills me with dread as she enunciates each word. 'From here on consider yourself imprisoned. This house is your cell block, school is your yard and *I* am your warden. You *will not* go anywhere other than those two places until I say otherwise. Is. That. Clear?'

'But I didn't break curfew!' The injustice of my sentence hits me full tilt. Mum advances towards me, her body held taut. She's vibrating like a tuning fork.

'No. You LIED TO MY FACE for FIVE MONTHS!'

I feel the guilt stab as her accusation hits home. But dammit, I am the boring one who stays home all the time. This is so not fair!

Seeing my mouth open Mum beats me to the punch.

'And if you keep runnin your mouth I'll give you what your sister's gonna get when she finally shows her face. You think you've got it bad? That girl won't be able to *shit* without my say so.'

Clamping my mouth shut because I know full well she'll follow through on her threat, I give her my own angry, tight-lipped glare.

'Your uncle and I are gonna go for a run. Keep close to the phone in case anyone calls.'

I nod and she turns to leave, stopping to look at me. 'Please don't go anywhere.' It is possibly the first time I've ever heard my proud mother beg. She's out the door before it registers.

Someone is crying.

The complete absence of light has my neck hairs lifting. There is water dripping somewhere but that is the only other noise. Muffled sobs bounce around, sounding close. Lifting my head off the dirt floor I smother a groan. My head is killing me!

'Hello?'

The sobs stop on a gasp, there is nothing after that. Talking makes my tongue ache, reminding me that I'd bitten it.

'Who's there?'

A scrape of cloth on hard-packed dirt, a stirring in the air and I can feel the someone moving closer. Panic sends me scrambling backwards, the explosion of pain from my ankles only slows me a little. The someone moves faster, closer; screw the pain!

'Stop it!'

Shoulders hitting a wall, I try to keep crawling through the pain. It takes a moment to realise the someone has stopped moving. I'm happy about that until I realise I don't know how close they got. I can't even tell if they are a few feet back or within touching distance.

Freezing against the rock wall, I strain to hear anything, too scared to call out again. What if that's what they're waiting for, so they can find me in the darkness? I've never understood the phrase 'heart in your throat' until I feel the thing clogging mine up. I have to force every breath past it. The last thing I remember is being dragged from under the car, watching Troy's shocked face get further away. That explains the raw feeling along the front of my body. They must've knocked me out because everything is a blank after that.

Anger comes to my rescue, like it always does. I force my backbone straight. Fear tactics are for bullies and I don't stand down from cowards. The stupid pricks have locked me up somewhere, which is illegal these days no matter your skin colour. They're probably trying to scare me into talking.

Taking deep breaths I think about why we'd come here in the first place. It was just like the first time — a look around for valuables, maybe trash one or two things on the way out. Just us taking back some of the riches they've stolen from our ravaged land. Like we're bloody Robin Hood and his Merry Men. The idea makes me want to scoff now. There wasn't supposed to be that many men out there. I worry about what they'll do to Troy; anything but think about what a lone girl might be vulnerable to in this kind of situation. Okay so maybe I was trespassing, but this is kidnapping, deprivation of liberty or some shit!

Giving myself a proper pep talk calms me down enough so I can speak again. It takes time to wake up my voice and even then it is a shaky thing.

'What do you want?'

Bracing in case I have to move instantly away, I wait. There's only so long you can hold yourself tense. The lack of response slowly, so slowly, has my muscles relaxing. That's when the noise comes from my left. Not a growl or a sigh. More like the rumble of a person thinking something over. It isn't the 'hmmm' that gets me though. It's the fact that the breath of it brushes right over the tip of my ear. Striking out wildly a sharp burning flashes across my knuckles as I connect with flesh that gives way to something sharp. Swinging again I descend into mindless screaming.

Day 1, Midnight

'Mum!'

I jerk awake on the couch and look around wildly. The movie is long over and the blue screen is throwing a weird light over every surface.

'I can see. I can see.'

Whispering it to myself I run to switch on the light. I look over the room again, ignoring the head-to-toe goosebumps and the stabby feeling that has spread from my guts to my chest. My sister is in danger.

My hand on the light switch, I search every nook and cranny of the room as if I expect something to jump out at me, I start to feel stupid. Almost seventeen for God's sake and I'm letting a few nightmares completely mess with my head. Next thing I'll be asking for a babysitter when my mummy is at work. If Laney were here she'd be pissing herself laughing.

Smacking the wall out of frustration, the sharp sting across the back of my hand pulls me up.

Don't look, my mind whispers. *There's nothing there anyway.*

Well, if there's nothing there then why are you scared?

Shut up!

Reason over superstition, big girl.

Turning my head, I scream at the cuts on my knuckles.

The front door bangs like something has hit it and I sprint straight for the toilet. It's just off the sunroom and in full view of the front door. I make it inside as another bang sends the door flying open.

It is all instinct – none of the rooms in the house have any locks, which means I can never keep my nosey twin out of my stuff. But in the toilet I can bar the door by bracing my back against it and kicking my legs up on the opposite wall. Especially handy if you've got a sister out for your blood because you might've tricked her into eating something gross, like off milk. I flip on the light, drop to the floor and assume the position – arms braced outward, body tensed up and waiting, listening to the running footsteps that come straight for the toilet door.

The door handle rattles violently and a weight hits the other side. A noise slips out of my mouth, one I've never made or heard before.

'Tace! Tace, are you alright?'

Rhi's frantic voice comes from the other side and all of the tension whooshes out of me.

'Stacey Thomson, you open this door right now!'

My legs are too shaky to hold me so I do a 180 on my moondee and squeeze up against the opposite wall to let the door swing inward. Rhi near about skins my shins shoving it open. She gives me a quick once over before screaming:

'You scared the absolute shit out of me!'

I open my mouth intent on a sarcastic reply. To our horror I burst into heaving sobs of one-part relief and two-parts fear. She crouches down, wrapping me up in a big hug. It isn't long before those first sobs calm and Rhi leans back to look me in the face. Sweeping tears off my cheeks she offers me a watery smile.

'Come on, cuz, let's get a cuppa.'

Voice gentle and not demanding any kind of explanation, she stands and holds out a hand. After helping me up, she turns her back and I snag some toilet paper, wrapping it around my left hand. We sit at the kitchen table staring at each other, both unsure what to say.

Rhiannon is two years older than us. She'd been in school with Laney and me every year till she quit after year ten. Uncle Billy named her after the Fleetwood Mac song, and Mum said he was cracked because she turned out just like it. Much as I love her you just never know what she is going to do or how she'll react.

'You okay?' she asks.

'Mmm.' I can't quite lie. 'Where you been?'

'Oh man, you wouldn't believe it,' she begins … she always begins. In fifty years' time Laney and I will still expect her to be starting stories like that. 'I met this bloke down at the pub on Tuesday, totally hot and built for it, too. He was headed for Cracow and wanted me to come so I did.'

I ignore her wicked smirk and just shake my head. 'Rhi, seriously? Don't you ever worry one day you'll get in the car with the wrong fulla? What then?'

Her eye roll doesn't impress either of us. She is so beautiful, my cuz, I just wish she'd taken a bit longer to figure that out. Her mother is Aboriginal-Italian and she'd passed on some amazing hazel eyes, long lashes and thick wavy hair to Rhi. No one is sure where the flightiness comes from; her parents blame each other. Whatever the case, she's a walking trouble

71

bundle. Most of the time she comes out of everything with a laugh and a bloody good story, but I worry. No one is lucky forever. Look at Laney.

'Wait, today's Tuesday, so this was, what, last week?' I glare at her.

She shifts in her chair. 'Umm, yeah well, we might've had a fight and I got stuck, but I hitched a lift with a trucker and got in just now. Them fullas down at Keithy's told me what was goin on so I came straight over.'

I shake my head.

'So … why did you scream before?'

I sigh. I'd been hoping to avoid this.

'I've had a couple of nightmares that Laney is in trouble. But they're just dreams … right?'

Rhi quirks an eyebrow. 'I thought you didn't believe in special dreams and all that "stuff" anymore?'

She does the quote marks thing with her fingers and I cringe. I'd lectured them all after Nan died and we'd had the biggest fight. I've been so cocky. Maybe tomorrow once the sun is up I can defend myself, but with the dream so fresh and that rock in my stomach, all I feel is fear for my twin. I drop my head.

'This feels different.'

'What happened?'

Feeling slightly stupid but mostly scared I let the whole thing rush out.

'The first one was last night, Laney was runnin from the property owners. They'd all split up to get away from them fullas. She made it back to Troy's car, but a ghost bird swooped her and she climbed under the car. Troy turned up but something grabbed her by the ankles and dragged her away. That's when I woke up.'

Rhi doesn't say anything, just watches and listens.

'Tonight she was somewhere so dark I couldn't see anything and she's hurt. She can't walk. Someone was cryin but when she called out to them it chased her through the dark. She was so scared.' The last bit came out so soft I doubt Rhi heard me. Taking a deep breath I brace myself for the rest. 'It came right up and whispered in her ear. She tried to punch it and hit something, it felt like a mouth. And maybe … maybe teeth?'

I can't finish. Shifting slowly, I put my left hand on the table between us. I peel back the bloody toilet paper and we both stare at the cuts that gouge my knuckles. Rhi takes my hand, tipping it to the light so she can get a better look. I can't tell what she is thinking, but then I've never seen her dumbfounded before.

'I don't know, cuz. But you said you punched im so why's it on your left hand? You're right-handed.' She looks up with an 'ah-ha' expression.

My hand starts to shake.

'Mirror twins, remember?'

Rhi freezes for a long moment, then shakes herself.

'Well, dream or not let's get that cleaned up.'

A trip to the bathroom, a dose of stinging Betadine and some Band-Aids later, and we are trying not to stare at each other over our joined hands. Neither of us says anything, we are both too busy thinking. It's strange to see my carefree cousin so deep in thought, she's usually all action and no thought to consequences.

Rhi nods like she's come to a decision and in the gentlest voice says, 'Tace, listen. They were some bad nightmares and I know you're worried about Laney. So am I. But I think they're probably just dreams. And maybe when you threw the punch in your dreams you hit the floor or something, and the pain from that is what woke you up.'

Before I'd calmed down I might've fought her on it, but the longer the silence went on the stupider I feel. Pushing aside that increasing weight that has taken up residence down in my guts, I listen to her very reasonable argument. Hell, I want her to be right because that means Laney isn't in that place and maybe she is fine.

'Okay, I'm sorry I scared you.'

She rubs her hand roughly over my head and smiles. 'It's okay, cuz. But … are you okay?'

The blessed sound of Uncle Joe's car rolling up saves me from answering. We rush to pack up the first-aid kit.

I hear Mum come in but she walks straight to her room. Rhi and I stand in silence, looking at each other. The tension is awful. Uncle Joe walks through the kitchen doorway looking like he's aged ten years. His slight head shake is all we need and suddenly no one wants to make eye contact.

'Your mum's got a bad headache, niece, she gone straight to bed. Maybe leave her to it.'

'Mmm. Want a cuppa, Uncle?'

'Nah bub, I need to go get some sleep. All this night drivin really does the old eyes in.'

It was the first time I've heard an uncle admit to ageing. It is kind of frightening, although I'm not sure why.

'Hey Unk, can I get a lift?' Rhi asks.

'Sure thing.' Uncle Joe finally looks at me. 'You be right on your own?'

'Yeah, totally.' My voice is a bit too bright to be real, but we're all pretending things are fine, so they can just give me this one.

Uncle Joe nods. 'Alright then, let's go. Tell your mother I'll see her tomorrow morning, first thing.'

Rhi finally realises I am going to be on my own and hesitates. Uncle isn't a patient man and won't wait for her to make her mind up. He drags Rhi out with him.

'I gotta go let Mum know I'm back, but I'll see you tomorrow, okay?' she calls.

After they leave the panic from the dream creeps back in, leaking from the ceiling and dripping down the walls. I finish cleaning up the first-aid stuff, practising deep breaths all the way, trying to ignore the drips rolling across the floor, heading for my feet.

With no one left to distract me I set the kettle off and run to my steps. The wood is rough under my hands as I lower myself down on the second step. Years of untreated life and exposure to the elements has left the grain exposed and the planks splitting in places. The handrails might've been green at one point, based on the few chips of paint left. I rub my fingers across the deep marks in the step I sit on, grounding myself in it. Tucking my knees into my chest I wrap my arms around them, hugging myself tight. The town is silent. Everyone is probably asleep. I can't even hear the Brown boys' car. It is still hot and sticky so we won't get any cool chill tomorrow. This will be the coldest part of the day. I put it at around 30 degrees.

If Laney were home we'd be fighting over the remote while Mum yelled and forced us to turn the TV off and go to bed.

The panic finds me again, dancing on the edge of my vision. Part of me wants to leap up and keep moving, keep avoiding it for all I am worth. But it isn't helping. If anything it is feeding the panic, making it grow. As hard as it is, I swallow down my defences, dig my fingers into the step and let it come. Just this once while I am alone and can't hurt anyone else with my pain.

Only it doesn't swallow me the way I think it will.

What do you do when it feels like your limb is detached? When a piece of you that's always been there, isn't. Usually that severed chunk of flesh lies there. You can reach out and pick it up. The still-warm skin reminds you of holding some part of another, or maybe your nerves twitch in recognition of their own.

My twin is part of me.

A part of me I've always been able to reach out and touch. An infuriating, sometimes selfish, annoying as hell part of me, but always there even when I don't want it to be. I judge her so harshly sometimes. Guilt mixes with the panic.

I've always seen the golden core of her. The soft melting heart that the hard shell protects. I'm one of the very few who sees it, and only then because she's never had the ability to shut me out. We'd been so close when we were little. If one of us got hurt, the other would bruise. It's been a long time since we've been that connected.

Sitting on those old steps, the night fades into sunlit days filled with laughter, and teasing play. How many times had

76

I sat on these stairs and watched it all? Watched that carefree part of myself that saw no consequences, felt no guilt, but also no deliberate malice? She never means to hurt me.

Even now I know she won't feel remorse for her actions. She'll fight to come home, battle with all she is to return to us. But she'll feel no responsibility, believe herself the victim in all ways and still spare no thought for those left waiting in pain.

I let the panic pull me under, let myself feel the anger with my twin that is bubbling away underneath, the blame that helps no one and only drops me further into shame. She should have stayed home with me. She should never have been out with Troy, and should damn sure have never been on some whitefulla's property, *especially* those whitefullas!

The fury fills me till I think it might burst, shoving back the panic. Then it drains away, so painfully slow, till I am nothing but emptiness.

I open my eyes, stare at the sorrow-filled moon and whisper, 'Come home.'

Day 2, Daylight

I don't sleep. Mostly I listen to the springs in Mum's bed squeaking as she tosses and turns. When the predawn light starts to float in from outside she goes into the kitchen and starts the kettle. Not long after I hop up and go to join her. Mum looks shocked (I am not an early riser), but she also looks shocking. Two days' worth of no sleep is hanging from her eyes and for a black woman she's looking kind of pale. There are already a pile of bags by the back door, from what I can see they are full of water bottles, containers of food and fruit. Everything they'll need for a day out bush.

'Tea's there.'

'Thanks Mum.'

I'm half expecting her to remember yesterday's fury, but she seems calm. That won't make me any less grounded. I get my tea and sit across from Mum. We stare at each other uncomfortably before looking away.

'Daught, I need to know. If Laney calls, you'll tell me right?'

Too shocked to do anything but react I meet her narrowed eyes as she watches me closely.

'Yeah Mum. Straightaway.' I take a second to think about it. 'But if she's been muckin around havin fun this whole time I'll probably go off my head at her first.'

She smiles in relief and anticipation. 'You can warm her up for me then. Since neither of us is gettin any sleep how about a big breakfast to get us started?'

I am this close to telling her that there is no way I can stomach food, but then I see Mum's chewed-up nails, shut my mouth and let the woman cook. According to Alana Thomson, nail biting is a nasty, dirty habit. She probably feels that way because she only ever does it when she's stressed to the max about something.

'Can I help?' I ask.

'Grab out the things from the fridge and start choppin up the mushrooms, ay?'

Thomson women are never ones to wallow granddaughter, gotta keep moving, just keep moving. Ask any black woman, no time to sit and cry about the tough stuff when there's kids to feed. Nan's words echo in my head and, for the first time in a long while, I'm glad.

We work that way for a while, getting everything ready. At some point Uncle Joe drifts in. He doesn't look like he's slept much either.

We eat in silence, each of us thinking about the day ahead. Mum calls in to work and tells them not to expect her for the rest of the week. Uncle Joe calls his boss too, then takes some of the supplies out to his car. While he is gone I realise Mum is staring at me.

'What?'

'Daughter, I want you to go to school today.'

'What?'

Mum winces. 'Don't hit that note, I've got a headache. I'm serious. I want you to go to school.'

'But why? It's not like I'll be able to focus on anythin and I want to help find Laney!'

Again she winces, although I'm not too sure why this time.

'I know, daught, and part of me wants you with us. But a bigger part of me wants you safe where I know, no matter what, at least one of my children is okay.'

Her voice breaks and I feel instant guilt. I stomp on it.

'I need to help, Mum. Please don't get all over-protective on me, not about this!'

When tears start to leak out of her eyes I know I've pushed too hard.

'I know I'm over-protective, but you know why.' She waves a hand at the photos of Dad on the fridge. 'And with Laney ...' Her breath catches and she nearly chokes on the words. 'Please, daughter, please just stay safe for me.'

Uncle Joe walks back in and takes one look at Mum's tears. He turns on me with fury in his eyes.

'What did you do to your mother?'

'Nuthin, she's the one doin shit.'

'Watch ya mouth,' they both bark.

Uncle puts his hands on his hips. 'Tace, you will do as your mother tells you.'

I stare at him in shock, usually Uncle can be trusted to help ease Mum's fears, not back up her crazy.

'But Uncle—'

'But nothing. Go get ready, we'll drop you off before we head out.'

I shoot from my chair and storm out of the room, slamming my bedroom door as hard as I can. Fuming, I abuse my school port, books and uniform while I get ready. I listen to uncles, aunties, cousins roll up and start to divide up the various back roads and places Laney might've gone. Rhi is there with Aunty Mel. She'd stuck her head in the door, taken one look at my face and left me alone, muttering something that sounded like 'she's the one that shoulda been named after her mother'.

Everything ready, I march out of the house and into Uncle's car without uttering a single word to anyone. It takes another fifteen minutes for them to come outside and the whole time I am cursing them all in my head. No one speaks as they get in the car, and no one says anything when they drop me off at school. In my family we do the silent treatment like an Olympic sport.

Computer class is boring as ever but at least the air-con means you don't stick to things. If you pick the right computer Mr Duffy won't move his large bum around enough to see what you're doing. We all pick games that make it look like we're doing the useless typing exercises he usually sets us. Someone needs to tell that man it isn't 1975.

For once I'm following the exercises, too tired and stressed to do anything but tap away mindlessly while I mull things over. It's obvious Mum is going to do everything she can to shut me out of the search for Laney. If I want to get involved I'll have to take things into my own hands. But what?

The year eleven boys are doing their usual stuffing around, and I get hit by a flying spit ball. I turn to glare at them. Ordinarily they'd have laughed into their hands and gotten cheeky with me, but now none of them will meet my eyes.

Not even this is normal since Laney's been missing. My gaze lands on Sam Miller and something clicks. I settle back to the tasks, trying not to be too obvious about staring at Sam. He, more than anyone, spends the most time with his Aunty May and he is the only Miller I can swap two words with that don't involve four letters. Maybe if I want answers, I should go to the source? I open AOL instant messaging, find his sign-in name using his school email and start typing. It takes me forever to come up with something. In the end I have to treat it like a jump from the big bridge into the river. Fast, no thought, just do it. Send.

'Meet me at the back of the toilets after class? I need your help. It's for Laney.'

Sam stops mucking around as his computer lets out a little chime. I watch but can't see a thing because he's angled his body to block the view of his screen from Mr Duffy and the whole room. The next minute my own computer chimes.

'Okay.'

My clandestine meeting with a Miller boy is set. With my heartbeat picking up in fear, I talk myself through my plan again. I need Sam's help and he might not be willing to give it. I'm not sure what it will take, but it doesn't seem like a small thing asking someone to help you get access to their crazy old aunty on the sly.

If it helps me find Laney it'll all be worth it.

There aren't too many places you can hide in school. Hell, if you fart in this town at least two people will hear you and a few hours later the story will be you've shit your pants. Meeting at school isn't smart, but it is also my only option. If I get caught doing this with a Miller boy I'll get grounded; if I get caught meeting one at night on my own, my life is dirt. His too. Only I will be luckier because Mum doesn't believe in bashing your kids. Everyone knows what Sam's mum and dad are like. He's taking the biggest risk, and he could've told me to piss off. I'd been bracing for that.

The toilet block for the big kids sits behind the Big Building, a little white unit like any other with the entrances on the sides and facing towards the rest of the school. The back of the block is a solid wall with two small, high windows. Leaning against said wall, I keep a close eye out. The playground on my left is empty for now, and gives a bit of cover from the road running past the school. The science building, an old demountable connected to the main one by a tin-covered walkway, is to the right. The little verandah that leads into the science block has another set of port racks just for the year eights. In front of me is a little veggie patch along the chain-link fence; the bright idea of some science teacher a few years back. It was supposed to be better than sitting in a classroom learning, but you try digging in rock-hard dirt during one of our summers and tell me it's fun.

Lunch is right after computer class, but I'd waited, pretending to eat my lunch, while the school cleared. Only when I hadn't seen anyone for a good while did I come here. I keep thinking about the time my cousin Kelly was caught sneaking around with a Miller boy. After the screaming slowed, she'd been shipped off to boarding school and he went to the mines in Emerald. Most of the mob stopped talking to Kelly, like she was some kind of traitor. Being cut off from family is a fate worse than death. My thoughts are making my paranoia worse so when Sam walks around the corner, I jump a few centimetres off the ground.

Sam takes one look at me and doubles over, laughing silently. I'm so shame, but I giggle nervously. 'Shut up, it's not funny! If anyone sees us …' I let it hang for a second. 'I know we're not … friends, but I need your help.'

He shakes his head. 'About Laney, you said. What I can't figure is how you think I can help?'

I get all uncomfortable, but this is for Laney.

'I need to talk to Ma … your Aunty May.'

Sam's face stiffens. He knows what I almost said.

'Why?' He could've cut me with the sharpness in his voice. 'You don't think she had anythin to do with—'

'No!' Wincing at my too-loud reply. 'No way, not that, I swear. But I heard … well, that maybe somethin happened to er … like with Laney.'

His expression becomes glacial as Sam stares me down. I can't keep my eyes on his face, and my hands are shaking so hard I have to twist my fingers together.

'I wouldn't bother er, but Laney …'

I take a peek and realise I'm looking at Sam's back. Intense anger and shame fill me. *Hard to know how I could've stuffed that up any more.*

At least no one will wonder why he hates me so much after this. Shaking my head to push away the tears I walk back around the toilet block and come face to face with Bobbie. She swings her eyes from mine to Sam's retreating figure as he heads past the Big Building. By the time her head swings back to me her mouth has dropped open and I watch the shock turn into glee. I am so busted and there is no way she'll keep her mouth shut, but I have to try. Grabbing her by the arm I haul her into the girls' toilets. She is grinning at me as I swing to face her, hands on hips, ready to battle.

'How long's that been goin on?' she asks.

'It's not! And you better not tell anyone or I swear—'

'Get it straight, cuz, either you got nuthin goin or nuthin to hide, which is it?'

She has me there.

'We was just talkin bout Laney. I wanted his help with findin er.'

Bobbie smirks. 'We don't need Millers to help us with anythin. So what's really goin on?'

She's a Thomson too. She's also the biggest mouth in this town.

'Nunya business. Just don't tell anyone or I'll … I'll tell everyone about what appened at Christmas.'

It's Bobbie's turn to freeze. One year younger than me and Laney, I'd caught her out at the reservoir one night when I'd stayed in my favourite thinking spot too late. She'd driven up in the passenger seat of a car that was owned by a local fulla, a very married-up fulla. It's not like I liked it and I warned her about it, but it wasn't any of my business either. Besides, my cousin has my loyalty first and unlike others I know how to keep my mouth shut.

'You wouldn't …' She stares at me, trying to find any weakness.

I look her dead in the eye. 'Try me.' It's a dirty trick and I hate doing it, but I'm desperate.

'But you know his woman is warngee! She'll flog me,' Bobbie hisses at me.

'If you're lucky.' We both know Cinta has done worse. Her man is the biggest slut but she only ever goes after the women he mucks around with. 'Sides, I kept my mouth shut for you, don't see why you can't do the same for me.'

'Fine then!' Bobbie's eyes shift and I know she's coming up with some way around it. I can't risk it. If Mum finds out she'll probably send me off to boarding school with Kelly, final year or not. Reaching out I grab Bobbie by her collar and pull her into my face.

'Do. Not. Fuck. With. Me. Roberta. My secret comes out then so does yours. And since *this* is the only time I've met up with Sam and *you're* the only one who knows, I'll know you opened your mouth. If there's even the smallest rumour about me and Sam I'll know where it came from. Then I'll head straight up to Cinta's place and tell her fuckin everythin. The worst that'll happen to me is gettin grounded; you got a lot more to worry about.'

I watch the shock hit. Bobbie isn't a fighter, but then I'm not much of one either. I'm talking about something much worse than the physical though. She thinks she has more to lose than I do, but I will do whatever I have to for my sister, even fire-bomb my relationship with my little cousin. The thought holds my shame back a bit.

Finally Bobbie nods, wrenching herself out of my hold. Walking out of the toilets she never looks back. I slump back, fighting my emotions. I will find my sister, but knowing Bobbie can't help herself, that threat will only last for so long. I have a week, tops.

Day 2, Afternoon

I power-walk home. It's still way too hot to sprint. I find the house empty and my heart drops to the floor. I do as much thumping around as I can. No one is home to tell me to be quiet. The home phone is on forward to one of the great-aunties who never moves far from her house. The place is so damn silent it starts to feel like someone has died. I fling my port into the corner of my room and take a cold shower to get off the coat of sweat. Only the cold tap is on, and still it's lukewarm from the sun. As soon as I climb out I am covered in sweat again, but it's worth it for that little bit of relief. I pull on a pair of shorts and a tank top, and shove my hair into a cap to try to keep the moisture in as long as possible. I grab my Discman, my favourite CD and storm to the front door.

I am still pissed at all of them and I'm all set for a dramatic exit when guilt hits. Mum will freak if she gets home and I'm not here. I huff my way back into the kitchen. There's always a notepad on top of the fridge for groceries and messages. I pull it down and scribble a quick note.

Gone to reservoir – T. She won't get any love hearts or hugs today.

The entire afternoon has been filled with Sam's and Bobbie's accusing stares. I'm too frustrated to think straight so

I'll go to my thinking spot and try to sort it out. Walking out into the 4pm sun the heat is intense. I plug my headphones in and stride off to the beat of Tupac's *Greatest Hits*. Laney got it for me for Christmas, mostly because she wanted to listen to it. She got the biggest shock when I wouldn't share it with her.

I round the corner onto Reservoir Road just as Tupac is rapping about a poor girl named Brenda. I walked off a lot of anger, sweating it out on the way; that and the song has me feeling wrung out and sad. My shoulders loosen up a little. Laney always gives me shit for coming up here.

'Why would you want to sit at that ugly old place? Isn't it borin?'

'Unlike some people I don't mind my own company.'

'You wouldn't catch me up there; it's creepy!'

'That's why I go.' The last bit is always a loud mumble, followed by a physical assault from my twin. It is such an old argument I almost catch myself responding to her out loud.

Mum says this road didn't always have a name so when they finally gave it one they used what everyone called it. How imaginative. There are a lot of roads around like that. A long dirt road, with deep ruts in it from recent rainfall running down the hill, curves up and out of sight. It isn't steep though and it is mostly shaded. For some reason it always feels cooler on this road. I should ask the science teacher about it, see what would cause it. Probably the tree cover.

This is where the town hits the first hints of bush. Walking this road with Mum is like getting a history and cultural lesson – that is where her uncle used to live, here is where her grandmother lived, and sometimes her family stayed there too.

Every few metres she'll drag us off the road to some bush or tree, showing us the flowers or leaves and talking about the best uses for it. She is our walking connection to this place.

On my own the trip took less than five minutes, with Mum it always takes an hour.

I make it up there fast without looking around, just in case something sparks a memory of Laney. Over the cattle grid and out into an expanse that's been cleared for some forgotten reason. Mum always points out the stumps in the distance where the old hospital used to sit. I shudder, looking instead for the gangs of whiptails that hang out up here. There is usually a joey, and they sit, stock still, hoping you haven't seen them. One small move and off they fly at top speed over the rocky slopes and down into the gullies.

The dirt road ends at the big cement tank squatting on its own raised platform. Like an ugly king on his private little hill. On the edge of the flattened area around the tank is a giant boulder, worn smooth. One of my cousins says our people used the rock to grind food, another one swore it's where women birthed their babies. They aren't much older than me so I don't know whether to believe them, especially that last one; it seems too exposed to me. Whatever its purpose, that rock is comfy.

I find my way to that boulder and fall into my favourite pose, legs crossed, back straight and eyes focusing on the bush. Shutting Tupac off mid-flow I throw myself into the silence. It is so close to the highway here but only the whisper of the odd truck comes through.

Soaking it all in, I sit with my back to the giant pimple of a reservoir that marrs the beauty of this place; its only good deed is the shadow it casts on days like this. I can see rooftops and trees from here, see the hills that surround us. All I can hear is the breeze and the bird calls. The approaching night always forces me home. Being up at the reservoir on twilight can get spooky, especially walking that dirt road. No way do I want to be there. Not because I am scared of spirits or stupid creatures, but a girl walking a darkened road at night has a lot to worry about.

I shut my eyes and try to find some peace.

I pop my headphones back in and switch to Tupac's 'California Love', getting ready to head home, when I hear a car coming up the road. I know it isn't Uncle Joe because of the sound of the engine, but I still feel guilty being up here. Too shame to do much else, I bend over and pretend to be fiddling with my Discman, trying to think what a normal kid might do in this place. It isn't long till an old silver Holden comes bouncing over the grid, growling its way into my sanctuary. Toni Miller's car, Sam's mum. I feel all my muscles tense up. I'm here on my own with most of my mob out searching for Laney and the Millers are heading my way. Not a good place to be. My breath hitches, waiting to see who will get out of the car.

The car bears down on me at a speed that feels unsafe. I see Sam's pissed-off face in the driver's seat just as it skids to a halt. His door flies open and he comes right at me, but I'm watching to see who else might get out. He's leaning over me before I realise no one else is coming.

'Who the FUCK do you think you are?'

Having an enraged seventeen-year-old male standing over them might cow some girls, but not this little black duck. I am on my feet in seconds, forcing him to take a step back, returning the glare.

'Alana Thomson's daughter. Who the FUCK are you?'

The look of shock on his face hits my warped funny bone and I bust out laughing. Sam's lip twitch before he remembers he's pissed off.

'Yeah? Well, that's even more reason to have stayed the fuck away!' Sam's rage has calmed, but he hangs on to it.

'Well excuse me for asking you to help. I won't do it again, dickhead!'

Not really helping, a small voice tries to interject. But fuck him, I won't be talked to like that.

'If I'd wanted to help you I'd ave said so at school. You shoulda taken the hint and left it alone!'

'Since I don't know what the fuck you're talkin bout it's a good thing I did!'

Even I have to admit that last sentence doesn't make much sense, and the confusion is clear on both our faces. I'm not backing down till he does, because if there is one thing guaranteed to piss me off it's being blamed for something I didn't do.

For his part Sam shuts up long enough to try to puzzle that one out. He even takes another step back, which helps me feel less defensive.

'Bullshit. You talked to her.'

'To who? Your mum? My mum? Your imaginary friend?'

His wince stops my smart-arseness and I take a second to register the tightness around his mouth and eyes. It almost looks like he's in pain.

Maybe it's time to shut that big Thomson mouth and open them binangs, girl. Nan loved saying that. *A mouth just like your bloody mother.*

'Look, in case you haven't gotten the hint, I don't know what you're on bout. So tell me what's going on or leave me alone, maybe before someone figures out we're up here?'

'Everyone knows you come up here anyway,' Sam mumbles.

'That just makes it worse then.' It'd be nice to think people don't much care what a sixteen-year-old kid is up to, but in this town they care from embryo to casket. And if they notice me then someone has probably seen Sam. 'Shit, are you tryin to get us in trouble?'

Wind firmly out of both our sails we stand there hangdog for a minute, thinking of our fates. I can't take it anymore so I sit down again.

'Well, you've done it now so you may as well tell me what's goin on.' I will not feel guilty for the flogging Sam has coming. I just won't.

I kind of expect another angry storm off so when he sighs and sits next to me I nearly fall off the boulder. I watch as he tucks his legs in tight to his chest and leans his chin on his knees. He looks out at the landscape. He's brooding. God, teenage boys are such drama queens.

'Aunty May asked to see you,' he whispers.

I feel like I've been stung by a hornet and brace for the rest of the little buggers to come join the party. My body vibrates with the need to shake more out of him. I'm finally starting to learn to hold things in. By the end of this I'll have to find a way to let everything pour out for fear of poisoning myself with all the bad feelings.

'Did she? Why?' My voice is as quiet as Sam's.

'Don't know. Just said it was for you girls to talk about and I wasn't to stick my nose in it. I figured you talked to er.'

'Not me. I don't know why she'd want to see me.'

'I do. She's knows about Laney.' His voice is so quiet I wonder if I've heard him right. 'She found out yesterday, got real upset and had a bad spell. Today after school she woke up good as, askin to see you. I thought you'd told her.' He glances at me from the corner of his eye. 'Sorry,' he mumbles.

'What?' I lean in closer.

'Sorry, okay? I'm sorry for yellin at ya!'

I raise an eyebrow like I learned from Aunty Agnes and he blushes. I can't help but laugh and nudge his shoulder with mine.

'Poor excuse for an apology, but I'll take it.' It's my turn to not look in his direction for a bit, but Laney is never far from my mind. 'So … are you gonna let me see her?'

'She's in the car.' He nods with his head and I whip around so fast I whack him in the back with my elbow. I don't even notice. I'm too busy staring at the grizzled old lady standing by the car. Gone are the nana nighties I am used to seeing her in, replaced with a pair of faded jeans, a massive baggy t-shirt and an even more shapeless flannelette shirt that flaps open. Her frizzy white hair is pulled back in a loose bun.

93

'Ow!' Sam complains.

'Take it like a man ya big sook.' May Miller stands at the back-passenger door giving us a look. 'If you two are done screamin, can me and the girl have a yarn now?'

'Yeah right.' Sam stays put for a bit, but when the silence stretches on he looks at me carefully. 'She made me and that's the *only* reason.' He sighs and stands. I stick my tongue out at his back.

Making his way back to the car, Sam pauses beside May long enough to look her over. 'You sure, Aunt?'

'Get away now, this is just for us women.' She taps him kindly on his arm and walks past him, straight for me. There's something in her eyes that I've never seen before, although it's not like I see her much. She is present and aiming it all at me. It scares the crap out of me. 'And close your mouth, girl, before you catch them flies.'

I snap my jaw shut but I can't stop the stare. She hobbles over to me and then reaches for my shoulder, using it as a brace to leverage herself down. Once she is settled she tucks her own legs under her and faces out to the vista. 'Geez-us, I can't make any move without sound effects now. That's how you know you've gotten old, bub.'

'True?'

'That grandson a mine made me lie down in his back seat, scared he'd be seen takin me to a Thomson.'

Her brown eyes narrow on mine and I have to look away. The circles of blue around her irises just freak me out too much.

'Bet you know why I come though, ay?'

I stay stock still except for a quick shake of my head.

94

'Hmm, ya don't? But my nephew told me you was tryna see me. I guess if you weren't …' She reaches for my shoulder again.

'No, wait! I ah, I … Aunty, I don't know how to ask you this.' My head drops and I feel tears brim. The past is something none of the oldies discuss, not ever. Not unless they want to and you never bring it up first.

'I know, bub, you lost your sister.' With gentle hands she cups my chin and forces me to look at her. I didn't expect to hear kindness from a Miller, especially not this one. She's the one I've always pitied, not the other way around.

'Please just … just say it's not like before.' I can't quite bring myself to say it. I've had a horrible feeling growing inside me. That maybe it's one of those things they whisper about at night, round fires circled only by women, and the ones who tell the stories hadn't been there. Hadn't experienced it. There is always someone who has it worse.

I am desperate for that not to be Laney. The dip of May's mouth doesn't bode well.

'Please!'

'I wish I could bub. Oh, how I wish—'

Pushing her hand away, I stand, shaking. 'You're wrong!' I shout. My voice hits her like a smack and she does what most black women do when attacked – she comes out swinging.

'You the one wanted answers. You the one went to a Miller for them. First Thomson in memory and first ever to name a Miller "Aunt" I bet.' The harsh tones seem too strong to be coming from that frail body. 'You face it now!'

I back away, which only makes her desperate.

'She swimmin in the dark, lost in nuthin and not one person can pull her out. Not one!' Spit flies from her mouth as she shrieks the last two words.

The solid presence of May Miller is fading and her ghost is chasing me backwards. I hit a solid object that sends me staggering. A hood, metal, car.

'But her mirror image might see a way she can't, a way I couldn't.'

The creak of a car door and Sam is there, stepping forwards, making soothing sounds, even while I flee in horrible slow motion.

'They've got her now, girl. Got her good. And no man can pull her out without damage. But what a man can't, a woman does.'

Sam reaches May's side and takes her wildly gesticulating hands in his. I am so shaken I didn't even notice them. He clasps her gently by the wrists.

'Come back now, Ma. You can come back now.'

'No, no! She doesn't have it yet. She's gotta have it fore I can …' Her attention shifts to Sam and for a second reason flickers back to life. 'Potters' place, son, you've got to take her out to Potters'. And she can't go alone.' She grips his face and glares into his eyes, her voice quiet but so intense it carries to me just fine. 'It has to be soon, she's almost out of time!'

Her small body slumps in a dead faint. Sam catches her as she rolls forwards, his horror and fear so like my own. I spin on my heel and take off like the Devil himself is on my tail.

'You could've helped me get er in the car!' Sam yells at my fleeing figure.

Day 2, Twilight

I lie on my back in the old cast-iron bed and stare up at the ceiling. After sprinting home I'd bawled my eyes out for a bit but got over that pretty fast. Tears are weak, they don't fix any of it. All crying does is give me puffy eyes, a worse face and a headache. Mum and them will be home soon anyway. I can't let her see something is up.

I lie there and don't think about May's words.

Flinging myself onto my side, I stare into the open space. The Millers aren't to be trusted. This is probably some cruel joke to get me in trouble. The sheet feels like it has been sitting in the sun and it's sticking to my sweaty skin.

Ah shit. If I'm going to be uncomfortable then I'm going to do some freaking baking.

I hop up and make my way to the kitchen. Mum'd defrosted a cornmeat last night, so I find her big stockpot and set it on the stove to cook. Cutting up the veggies ready to go only distracts me for so long. Thank God the mob did a raid on the snacks this morning, gives me a good excuse to restock.

Baking always relaxes me. Measuring everything precisely, mixing it properly and the results are perfect and predictable. The worse part of the summers here is how little I can bake. Having the oven on in 40 degree heat makes the house feel like a suffocating, wet blanket you can't shrug off. If I try it, Laney or Mum will storm in and go ballistic till I give up.

I pull out the normal ingredients, cookbook and all. I probably know the recipes by heart but I never trust my memory. Reading a recipe also helps block out stray thoughts. I had no peace up at the reservoir, anything but, so this is my last resort.

Potters' place might offer some peace. Or at least some answers.

I shake my head hard – no way am I heading somewhere dangerous on a warngee woman's whim. Especially a warngee Miller. I curl my lip, remembering my family's mistrust and intense dislike.

Besides, everyone knows that place, has been told never to set foot on the south side of that land and it isn't cos the owners are racists with a weapons collection. I'm not too sure why we can't, there's more to it than just warning kids away from racists. We deal with those every day of our lives. It's another one of those rules that the old people fling out there but when questioned get all tight-lipped and glary. All I know for sure is it has something to do with the mountain that sits on the most southern part of the Potters' place. The main house is set up on the north end, an easy drive to the highway. Racists one end, cultural taboo on the other. Did we need much more reason to avoid the entire place? They won't say why the mountain is off limits. I never used to notice how much of our lives included little bits of information, partially offered and never fully explained. But I am getting sick to death of it. If they want to be so bloody mysterious then fine. I should go out there anyway just to see it for myself.

You are NEVER to set foot on that place, Stacey Claire Thomson, you hear me?

Nan rarely forbade anything, but when she did there was no mincing words. If I said what I was thinking to any of the mob I could feel the smack upside my head that would follow. Sure, I'm not clear on where science meets culture and how I'm supposed to navigate it and I don't believe in a lot of it anymore ... but to go against them? To openly defy the elders on something that isn't just a vague warning, but an open 'don't do that!'? Mum will be the first in line to punish me, and she'll let all the aunts and uncles have their say too.

It isn't really that I believe in the warnings, I'm doing as culture dictates – respecting my elders and following their advice.

Yep, that's why I don't want to go out to the Potters' property.

Which begs the question – why was Laney out there with them boys? She believes in this stuff wholeheartedly, she would *never* have defied Nan. Not on her own anyway. Troy must've talked her into it. Probably justifying it by saying only the mountain is taboo. If they were at the house they had no reason to go near that place. I play around with the idea for a bit, throwing flour, sugar, milk and butter in a bowl and stirring on autopilot. Yeah, that must've been it.

For the very first time in my life I don't have enough chores to suit me. After I shove a few batches of patty cakes in the oven I clean the kitchen, do another wash, prep for school tomorrow. Hell, I would have done the toilet and bathroom – my two most hated jobs – if Mum hadn't done them on Sunday. With the cornmeat and veggies prepped all I need to do now is set them cooking at the right time, and it's only just gone 6pm. Every window and door in the house is flung wide open in a desperate and futile bid to attract a breeze or something cooler. The oven is off, but it has lifted the temperature into the torture zone. The heat pushes me outside.

I grab a big bottle of cold water from the fridge and go to the chairs around the fire pit in the backyard. Mum had called in from Mundubbera to let me know what was happening (which was nothing) and also to check I was where she'd told me to be. When I asked to join one of the cars she just hung up, and I felt my blood reaching the same temperature as the house.

May is a no-go so what else can I do?

Nan always said to listen to our special dreams and Pop had all but said the same, but I can't bring myself to see them as anything more than delusions of a worried mind. I'll work this out real logical.

I can't talk to May Miller and hope to get anything useful, but I can read up about what happened. The Eidsvold Historical Society has a huge range of stuff. They might have old newspapers and things I could hunt through. Part of me wants to squirm – it isn't the kind of place our mob go because it isn't exactly our history. Besides, they're only open from 10am to 3pm, so I'll have to cut school to do it. Mum will destroy me if I do that. But she really can only blame herself for shutting me out in the first place.

Decision made, I feel a bit better. Maybe if I can find out what happened to May, I can figure out where Laney is. It's worth a try.

'Anyone home?' The sing-song call from the front is a relief.

'Out the back.'

Rhi comes around the corner of the house, takes one look at me and sighs.

'No one else back yet?'

'Nuh.' I can't look at her. Partly because I don't want to talk about it, partly because I know she'll push it anyway. 'Where's Aunty Mel?'

'Gone to get the kids settled. I'm crashing here with you.'

I finally look at her and smile. I could use the distraction and on a good day Rhi registers in the cyclone category. She drops down into one of the mismatched chairs and kicks off her shoes.

'Didn't see much out there. Uncle Joe's been talking to a lot of the cow-cockies he's worked for before, seein if we can head onto their properties tomorrow for a look. Should be good, ay. Although if that dickhead Troy keeps up his stories, I'm gonna take a detour past is place first.'

'Stories?' I ask casually.

'You memba Clarrie's sister Debbie? The one you met that other Christmas when we was all hangin out?'

I hate these 'you memba' games. For a small town there is way too many people and connections to keep straight. 'Oh my God, no I don't memba, get to the point!'

'Fine then. Friggin ell!' I'd interrupted her story so she has to go back. 'Clarrie's sister Debbie reckons she heard

Edna tellin Mary from the butcher's that Laney took off on Troy with some whitefulla from that property they snuck onto. Reckoned she used Troy so she could meet up with that other man and shoot through without anyone figurin it out.'

Watching the glass bottle shatter against the weatherboard, spraying all of its contents about, is my first hint that I've thrown it. It shocks us both so much no one moves. Usually it is Laney who throws things, who loses control and goes ape-shit. Laney has Mum's temper. Not me. Never me.

From some weird detached place I watch all those emotions I've been bottling up swirl in my chest like a tornado forming. It was so slow at first, almost lazy, but it picks up speed fast and the feeling fascinates me. I'm not even sure I want to stop it.

Rhiannon's hand on my shoulder pulls me out of it.

'Cuz, I … I'm sorry. I didn't mean …'

As much trouble as she can be, Rhi never means to hurt anyone. She isn't a cruel person, just oblivious, and there isn't a mean bone in her body. It makes it hard to stay mad at her. I watch the guilt on her face and feel the swirling stop.

I choke it all down and find my voice, even if I can't look at her. 'You're right. Help me get this clean?'

'Sure thing!' Rhi's glad to have something to do. She sprints inside for the dustpan and I start picking up the glass shards. The water has almost evaporated, at least the heat is good for something. We collect the glass in silence for a bit, but Rhi isn't one for quiet.

'So … are you okay, cuz?'

God, I'm already sick of her asking me that.

102

'Don't tell Mum what you heard, okay?'

Rhi likes being first in with news, but me throwing the bottle, or maybe just seeing me lose it, scares her.

'No worries. But I think it's goin round so you might not ave much time.'

I give her a smile.

'Thanks, cuzzie, you the best.'

'Sides,' she continues, 'Tyrone and Clinton are out of lock-up, they'll tell the truth.'

I snort. 'You reckon? If they're not in Troy's pocket, they're stuck right up his—'

'True, but that was before he dumped em out at the Potters', now they lookin to corner im as much as our mob are.'

I finally stop looking for small slivers of glass and check my hands to see if I've caught any. If the little cousins step on glass Mum will kill me, but I've done the best I can.

Turning to Rhi I put my hands on my hips, considering. 'You reckon they'd talk to us?'

'Course, cuzzie. Me and Tyrone go waaay back. You memba that time I was itchy—'

'God no!' I yelp, bolting up the stairs to get my shoes. The sound of Rhi's laughter follows me.

I know it's wrong. I know Mum will kill me, but I keep telling myself this is what she has driven me to. I'll leave her a note, but that won't save me. The only door I bother to close is the front one. No one worries about locking up around here; anyway, it would mean coming home to an oven that has been roasting all day. Rhi meets me at the front, ready to continue one of her long, gross sex stories. She'll happily shame me out the whole way down to the truck park if I let her so I go on the offensive.

'So whaddya get up to in Cracow?'

That keeps her busy on the walk. We round the corner past the Elders building and cross the road to the little stop with the round cement table and seats. Everyone calls it the truck park because trucks stop there; yep, we're original when we name things in this town. Usually they stop just to run across the road to the only pub in town for a meal and a few beers, but sometimes they stay for a sleep. The local pub does a good counter meal and not much else. They rob people blind with the cost of alcohol and we all know it.

It's a weeknight so the pub will be shutting soon and the truck park is where some hardcores will end up to keep partying. Straight out of lock-up it's a safe bet that the boys will be thirsty. This early, we can sit and watch for them. It never crosses our minds that they'll already be there with a few of their mob around. I wince when I see everyone and look to Rhi for reassurance.

'Isn't Clinton related to the Millers?'

'Yeah, but Tyrone isn't, and he'll talk to me.' She sees my worry and wraps an arm around my shoulders. 'Don't worry, cuz, there ain't no Millers there.'

'Yeah, right now,' I mutter, but allow her to drag me towards them.

'Well if it isn't Run-around Rhi and Stuck-up Stacey,' sneers a voice.

'Shut up, Clinton, don't be bitter cos no one wants your ugly arse.' Rhi cuts him off at the knees and I snort. She stops to pat his arm comfortingly. 'Aww, don't worry. If you grow a nicer personality I'm sure one woman might … umm, you know.'

She waves a hand vaguely around his face, which is sporting an impressive black eye that he still manages to glare with. Clinton slaps her hand away while the people around the table laugh. It's a mix of men and women, most of them related to the boys. A few send me glares and others nod. I never can remember who I am or am not supposed to talk to in any given week, the arguments and make ups move so damn fast. Instead I just wait and see how people treat me and then go with it. Unless they're a Miller; that is the only relationship set in stone as far as the Thomsons are concerned. So I nod to the right ones and ignore the others. Any adult that'll glare at a sixteen-year-old registers as too pathetic for my contempt.

'Fuck you!' Clinton comes back.

Rhi looks at me and we roll our eyes.

'Ty!' Rhi squeals, diving into the only empty seat at the table while I stand back with my hands in my pockets. She wraps him in a big hug and he flinches. Rhi pulls back and makes tutting noises over his busted lip and bruises. 'Ya poor thing! When didja get out?'

'This arvie, cops finally got us all charged and whatever.'

'How come yous are drinkin in the park? Is the publican in a mood again?'

'Clinton's barred until next month so Eddie got us the grog.' Tyrone nods to one of the men.

'That sucks. I heard Troy dumped you out at the Potters' and he's the reason you got caught.'

Subtle, thy name is not Rhi.

'Him and that slut you call a cousin,' Clinton snarls, still trying to make up for his earlier humiliation.

'The fuck you say?' Rhi shoots to her feet, but Tyrone grabs her arm and pulls her back down, holding his hand out to stop me before I move another step.

'That's bullshit, Clinton, and you fuckin know it. He probably dumped her out there just like he did us.' Tyrone turns to me. 'Sorry about your sister.'

I nod, clenching my jaw to fight back tears. 'Thanks.'

Patting Tyrone's hand, Rhi asks, 'When did you last see Laney?'

'After we raided the main house we had to split up because *somebody* knocked over the fuckin woodpile on the way out.' He throws a glare at Clinton, who squirms, dropping his vicious stare at Rhi. 'The whole house came awake and it was on. The last I saw Laney, she was runnin like the rest of us.'

'Troy's sayin she met up with some whitefulla out there and took off,' Rhi says with disgust.

'No way. She was busted just like us. If he's sayin that then he musta left her.' Tyrone sees the look on my face and tries to be nice about it. 'She was faster than all of us. I'm sure those fat bastards couldn't ave caught er. We parked a fair way away too, so they'da had ta keep up all that time, no way they did that.'

I nod again in thanks but can't quite swallow down the waterworks. I might be all ready to go out and get my sister, but I can't even speak. If I could work out a way to slap some sense into myself I would have there and then.

'Where'd yas park then?' Rhi asks.

Tyrone and Clinton share a look. Clinton shakes his head and Tyrone hesitates.

'Come on Ty, we need to know.'

Clinton shakes his head harder, but the guilt on Tyrone's face is clear.

'It could help us find Laney,' Rhi wheedles.

Tyrone caves.

'Out near that mountain,' he mutters.

Everyone in earshot gasps. We all know that place. It's taboo, the elders don't mess around about that one.

'You did what?' Eddie hisses at them. He's the boys' uncle, and his face says they're in deep shit.

'It's a easy road, far enough they won't see or hear the car, and no one goes out there at night.'

'Cos we all got more sense!' Eddie starts swearing a blue streak as Clinton glares at me like Tyrone's big mouth is my fault.

'We didn't go on the mountain! We were just close to it.'

'That's bad enough!'

'Why did yas go out to Potters' anyway?' Rhi butts in. I could kiss that woman, she's so much more than a pretty face, if you pay attention.

'We got some good stuff last week.' He shrugs, making it clear they've been doing this a lot. I want to smack Laney. 'We don't normally go back so soon, but Troy said they had loads of cash ready for the big cattle sales. Can't believe we fell for that bullshit. Wasn't nuthin there but a buncha old shit.' Tyrone rubs his chin, probably trying to show off his tiny stubble to Rhi. 'Ya know, I swear he was lookin for somethin though. Kept mutterin stuff and goin through papers.'

'Yeah, what'd we want with all those old papers?' Clinton's donkey laugh crunches through the space.

'Especially when you can't read, ay, Clinton?' Rhi says in a kind voice that has him hopping up.

'Sit. Down.' Tyrone growls, waiting till Clinton has done as he's told before turning to look at Rhi. 'He was up to somethin and we all got sucked into it. I don't know what it was, and I don't know where Laney is. I swear.' His eyes swing back to me. 'I'm sorry Tace, we shoulda taken better care of er.'

In the face of his sincerity, I find my voice.

'Thanks Ty, but Laney woulda never let you keep an eye on her.' I smile. It's wonky, but I appreciate his honesty.

I always thought he was just Troy's stooge, but maybe I'm wrong. His dark brown eyes are steady and I know truth when it is offered. And honour when it sits in front of me too.

'I promise ya one thing though. If me and Clint catch im e'll be sorry. And we'll get out of im what e did with Laney.'

'I just might hold ya to that.'

'Yeah thanks, Ty. We gotta cruise. Catch ya later.' Rhi drops a kiss on his cheek, gives him a cheeky wink and grabs my hand to pull me away.

We walk in silence, Rhi watching me closely.

'Well, it's somethin I guess,' she tries.

'No it's good, cuz, I'm just tryin to figure out how we tell the mob this without anyone knowin what we did.'

'That's easy,' Rhi declares. 'I'll tell Mum I bailed up Ty. She don't need to know you were there too.'

108

'And if rumours get around we were down at the truck park?'

'Screw em, no one would believe you'd go against your mum, you're the goody-two-shoes in the set.'

I punch her on the arm. 'Gee thanks.'

Rhi laughs and wraps her arm around me. 'It's all good, cuzzie. You gotta love who you are, cos I do.'

I slip my arm over her shoulders and squeeze. 'I love you too.'

Day 2, Night

Working together we get the veggies on the stove and start the oven up again. Thank God the sun has gone down and a little bit of breeze is finally leaking through. I get Rhi to burn my note in the fire pit. Mum is so suspicious right now, I wouldn't put it past her to go digging through the rubbish. The whole thing takes maybe thirty minutes. Not long after, the cars start rolling up outside.

Part of me wants to sprint for the front window, but a more sensible part knows the mob wouldn't be this quiet if they'd found her. Still I look up with hope as the adults come in. Mum's tense face and Uncle's cap, pulled down so low I can't see his eyes, tell me everything. Taking deep breaths to push back sobs while I clear up the table, I focus on stacking the rows of patty cakes ready for icing.

'Dinner'll be ready soon,' I say.

There's a pause and a shuffle as Uncle's boots go for the back door, before thin, warm arms envelope me from behind. A brief kiss to the head and she's gone.

'Thanks, daught. You been cookin up a storm, ay?' Her back is to me as she checks the veggies but she's going for normal.

'Figured we'd have a mob to feed.'

'Good thinkin. Should this pumpkin be on?'

'Yeah, if the oven's ready. The cream needs thickenin for the patty cakes too.'

Mum gets the pumpkin sorted then throws herself into the cream like she's possessed. Whipping it by hand is something she did because no one else is womba enough to want to do it without an electric hand mixer. Of course, you have to own one to use one.

Rhi sits, watching us with concern. We ignore her.

It's so painful in here it's like the air holds daggers that prick and stab depending on how fast you move. Thank God the cousins come pouring in.

'Yum, cuz, did ya do those chocolate ones again?'

Craig grabs for a patty cake and I smack his fingers with the spoon I'm using to mix the icing. 'Oi! Wait for the cream and icing.'

He gives me his best hurt puppy eyes while licking icing off of his hand and I relent. 'Uncle's out the back, you want a cuppa with it?'

That broad grin splits his dark face. 'Yeah, white with three sugars, cuz, you the best.'

He's gone before the others start shouting out their tea orders. The men all head to the back while the women stay in the kitchen. Aunties pull out teacups and all the necessaries, cousins grab plates and cutlery and cart them to the old chipboard table Mum has set up out the back. Cream whipped, cakes covered and placed on plates with biscuits from the cupboard. There's a procession downstairs. I grab a drink and a patty cake and find my usual spot on the stairs, a bit closer to the bottom this time so I can talk to people. Everyone is spread out yarning, but it's quieter than it would normally be with the mob around.

111

The chairs circle Mum's empty fire pit, women take turns bringing more cups of tea and boiling more water. It's still too hot for a fire, but we all need the tea. I sit on my step and take it all in. Trying not to see Laney sitting beside me, making cheeky comments about that uncle or who this cousin was seeing on the sly.

At some point the oven bell goes off and I'm up and checking the veggies. Mum shouts at Uncle Billy to go pick up Pop so he can come have a feed before she follows me in to help. As we're setting up the food on the table, Danny and Fred come walking around the house with a carton. Everyone looks at Mum for her reaction. She frowns, but doesn't say anything so we take it as permission.

Pop rolls up with Uncle Billy, and Aunty Fern gets him settled into a chair with a full plate and his old tin mug filled to the brim with tea. Some of the cousins go to get their kids. I'm glad for them biscuits and cakes then. We can stretch food like nobody's business. Jesus has nothing on my mob.

We settle into old rhythms. Fall into them. The same thing we've done hundreds, maybe thousands of times before at each other's houses. Only it isn't quite right. No games are played, and the kids aren't pestering the older cousins to play with them. Uncle Billy doesn't get his guitar that he always carries in his Ford. Annie doesn't start cracking her dry jokes, and no one puts on the stereo, which means there isn't a war over the volume or the music. Pop would normally finish his meal, sit for a bit and then head home. He's getting tired quick now. But he doesn't go home for a long, long time, and Mum doesn't suggest it.

As many of us as there are, we all notice the missing face around the fire. Nobody says it. Nobody speaks about the day. We stay close, taking comfort in each other and trying not to listen out for an absent voice.

Day 2, Midnight

Opening my eyes on nothing, I grieve to see I have not been dreaming; the same dripping sound of this underground place, the dirt under me, the damp smell. I'm on my side in the foetal position, my knees so close to my chest that my forehead rests on them. Pain radiates through my body and I can't remember the last time I've been aware enough to move position. I force myself to keep still, listening for the breath or the crying. There is nothing but that slow, slow drip.

My mouth is bone dry and my eyes feel gritty. I have no idea how long I've been here. Calling out again doesn't feel like a smart choice, so I carefully move my arm off of my leg. My right arm is tucked under my knees and feels dead, so I start with the easy things first. Left arm slowly reaching over my head, I flex my cheeks. Pins and needles break out everywhere I test, tickling at first but then burning like I've pressed them all into Mum's fire pit. I bite my lips to keep from making a sound and move. I force the pain into my breath and release it through my nose so I won't groan.

Once the worst of the pain is over I force my left leg to unstick from its partner and extend it downward. The pain rages and my breath becomes ragged, but still I keep silent. Moving my right side is going to be so much worse. Rather than risk too much, I shift onto my back, going slowly so I won't clench some muscles before I am ready. The tingles that are already racing over my right side warn me of what is to come.

Using my left hand I clumsily stuff the neck of my shirt into my mouth and bite down. One deep breath in and out and I press my right leg over. I can't quite stop the whimper that escapes, but I let the pain carry me away into its centre. A cramp hits my thigh so hard that I sob quietly through the cotton. Still, I make my foot point, force my leg straight. As soon as the pain is manageable I move my right arm. Focusing only on them, I fight the pain down by promising my body that it will be worth it. That we will make it out of this.

A long time later I lie spent. Sweaty and shivery I take a second to just breathe in relief. I'm not entirely pain free as my left hand still throbs, and my mind shies away from why that is. Instead, I comb through my memories. I'd been with Troy. I know that someone has taken me, but I haven't seen who, and time has no meaning. I feel shaky, weak and so damn hungry it isn't funny so I know it's been a while.

Mum and Stacey would be seriously freaking out. Tace was right, I should've stayed home. Tears threaten before I push them back.

This won't help, and I can make it up to them after I get back safe. First I need to know where I am. It's likely that the Potters have me; Troy probably led them straight to the car, the stupid prick. I try not to worry about where he is right now. I can't help anyone until I help myself. After that I'll do whatever I can to help him.

That promise in mind, I slowly sit up. It takes a lot of courage to stretch out that first hand into nothing. By pure luck I hit wall to my left. I remember hitting a wall when that – not now. I can feel a wall, this must be it. Where there is a wall there has to be a door, all I have to do is follow it. The question is: should I stand or crawl? I try to think it out like Tace would – logic and science. In the end

I can't so I do it my way – on my feet. Getting up takes a bit of doing. The first scrape of sound nearly sends me back to the foetal position until I realise I'm the one that made it. I inch upward, wincing at every noise, till I'm upright, swaying slightly.

Teeth gritted, I keep my left hand on the wall and my right stretched out in front of me. The first time I stumble over a rock I nearly curse, but the echoing noises send my heart pounding. Nothing happens so I push on. This time I extend my foot first, searching and finding firm ground before shifting my weight onto it. It slows things down a lot, but it stops a few stumbles over uneven ground and a few more rocks. My confidence grows and that's when I make the mistake. Trusting it too soon, I think I've tested the ground properly. As I shift forwards the ground crumbles. I slide on my heel, trying to take the step back. No such luck.

I plummet through the dark, tumbling down, down, till I hit belly-first. The wind's knocked out of me. I gasp through it till I can breathe again. I lie face down, cataloguing my bruises and stings, waiting to hear what all that noise would bring.

Nothing.

I count a hundred panting breaths before I finally start to believe I've gotten away with it. Sliding my hands under my shoulders I push up into a crouch and wave my hands around me, trying to find the wall, or something that can explain where I've fallen.

I don't realise there is something worse than the movement in the dark until I realise there is nothing around me. No wall. No feature to guide me. I am crouched in darkness so total I can't see my own hands. I don't know where I am. My sobs rebound from the awful dark.

Bolting upright, I stare around my room in panic. Despite the stifling heat my entire body is shivering. Rhi doesn't move, thank God. I really don't want to hear her ask me if I am okay again. Pulling the old doona up over me I try to return warmth to my bones. The comfort of family had finally helped me get to sleep. Rubbing my arms briskly, I fight the urge to wake Rhi. Somehow telling her more of the dreams doesn't seem like a good idea.

Once I stop shaking I slip out of bed as carefully as I can. Mum must finally be asleep too because the house is in darkness. I tiptoe over the creaking floorboards, my eyes already able to make out the dark shapes. I navigate carefully out of the room, closing the door behind me, before finding my way into the kitchen where I dare to turn on a light.

The brightness burns my eyes and I keep them shut while I steer around the kitchen table, making for the sunroom. Once I feel the blessed darkness close back in, I open my eyes, waiting till the sparkling lights stop dancing in my vision to look outside. Then I just sit, staring, trying not to think.

These nightmares are driving me mad. The thought loops around and around in my head without end.

A scraping noise breaks the loop. I stop. Listening. The air is so heavy I can drink it. I feel it more as a vibration rather than a noise.

There! Near Laney's room.

I'm running before the thought finishes, straight to the room, desperate to see her sneaking back in her window. The door is shut. I hear the sound, rumbling up through my feet. Throwing the door open I look, but see only the empty windows spread wide to catch any stir of coolness in the night air.

Nothing.

Laney's room has four windows across two sides of the house – two look out onto our front yard, through our crappy little fence and onto the street. The streetlight floods the space; she's always complained about that. It shows me how empty her room is.

I sag against the doorjamb and berate myself for imagining things. There is nothing moving out there. Goosebumps race over my entire body, but I can't say why.

I go straight back to bed and try to shrug off the feeling. I don't even bother to turn off the kitchen light, telling myself I need to make sure I can see Rhi in the bed. Tucking the sheet over both of us I reason that it is one way to keep the mozzies off.

I shut my eyes tight, refusing to open them again till morning.

Day 3, Daylight

Morning brings a little more hope. An even bigger mob turns up, driving in from different towns to help. Uncle Joe fires off roads and properties like some kind of drill sergeant, teaming people up, different cars and drivers to different terrains. Some of the local property owners who are friendly with their black workers are happy to let us search their land, especially in the areas where they share a boundary with the Potters' property. We take that to mean even the whitefullas think the Potters have something to do with Laney's disappearance. I spend a lot of time making pots of tea and helping Mum fry up breakfast. Not once do I beg Mum to join, silently helping her cook and clean, before going and setting myself up in the lounge with my notebook and textbooks. She is so busy organising food and supplies that she doesn't notice at first, but as everyone files out she stops and eyes me.

'What are you up to?'

'Mrs Clay hit us with a surprise assignment yesterday and it's due on Monday. She just wants all us kids to have as miserable a life as she does. Bitter old troll.'

Mum chokes on her own laughter. 'Daughter, knock off talkin like that.'

There is no heat in her words; Mum used to go to this school too. She bends over to give me a kiss before heading out the door. Waving them all off is where I go wrong. I know I've overdone it when Mum's eyes narrow. Heading back inside, I finish cleaning up the kitchen and am stuffing things into my port when I feel a presence. I'm not surprised to find Mum in my bedroom doorway.

'What are you doin?' Mum is still eyeing me.

'Gettin ready for school. What are you doin?' I ask, giving my best 'my parent is crazy' face; eyes widening, one brow lifts as if to say, 'And ...?'

A loud beep from outside and Uncle Joe's voice yelling 'Al, move your arse' breaks the staring contest. Mum hesitates. I need her out there looking for Laney, not here watching me.

'Mum, what's wrong? Aren't you gonna go get Laney?'

That's when I notice tears in her eyes and I feel lower than a squashed dog turd. The woman was living her worst nightmare and I'm making things harder. Stepping forwards I grip Mum's hand and stare her dead in the eyes.

'I will be here when you get home, Mum. You can bet your life on that.' It comes out as a whisper from my tear-choked throat. She wraps me in a fierce hug so I know it got through. When she finally lets go we both ignore our face wiping motions. I give her the cheekiest grin I can manage.

'If you got nuthin better to do than hang around the house there's a few chores needs doin.' It's what Mum always said to us when we were younger. She hasn't said it since we hit puberty and she couldn't get us to stay at home. Funny how that works. It's a lame joke but Mum smiles, giving me another quick kiss and heading out.

I get ready for school and even do some work on Mrs Clay's assignment, which is due in four weeks, but still. I put a few extra books in my port and heave it up.

The house is finishing its preheat cycle, which means it isn't quite as hot as outside yet. I do as I said I would and head out. What I haven't told Mum is that Thursday afternoons all the year twelves have free study periods. I will keep my promise, but I'll be doing my own research too.

I stride in, already wishing the hours away.

Rounding the final block that brings school into sight, the last thing I expect to see is Sam Miller sitting on the grass. He lives on the opposite side of town, which means there's no way he is there by chance. He's already seen me and is climbing to his feet. There are people around and this will definitely get back to Mum.

'What the hell?' I hiss.

He brushes his backside off and, pulling his port on, lifts a shoulder.

'I needed to talk to you.' He sounds annoyed, but won't look at me.

'You could've snuck me a note. We're gonna get it for this.'

'It's too late for that. You aren't goin out there, are you?'

'No way!'

Me thinks the girl protests too much. Bloody Mum and her love of misquoting Shakespeare. I didn't even know I was thinking about it, but even as I deny it some part of me knows it's a lie.

His lips twist. 'She's not always like that. She has her good days and I thought she was havin one when I brought her up

121

there. That was my stuff-up. But you can't trust what she said up there. She wasn't … right.'

She'd scared the shit out of me, that's what, and part of me desperately wants to take the excuse he is offering.

'Why do you even care?'

His eyes drop and he fidgets with the strap of his port.

'She used to have more good days than bad, but now it's goin the other way. Since she heard about Laney she's been … better. I thought if I helped you and Laney …' He finally looks at me again and I see concern. 'But I don't want ya ta get into trouble.'

'Thanks. But what I do is my problem.' I try to be stubborn but gentle.

'Come on, Tace. Your mum's already freaked about Laney.'

I try to push past him. He can stick his emotional blackmail. He grabs my shoulder and holds on till I'm forced to face him.

That stubborn jaw gives you away every time, granddaughter. Nan always sighed it, like she wasn't the one who had passed down that jaw.

'Shit,' he explodes. 'Well, if you're goin then I have ta.'

I open my mouth to argue but he gets in first. 'You heard what she said – you can't go alone and I'm the one that's got ta take you.'

We stare each other down, but truthfully, I don't want to go alone either.

Sam grins, seeing me weaken.

I give him my best stare-down. 'It's my choice. You do what I say or you can piss off. I don't play that macho bullshit.'

His grin widens. 'Go to the reservoir after school tomorrow.'

'What about today? We've got them free periods, memba.' I try not to sound desperate, ready to chuck my plans. I am failing.

Sam pulls a face. 'I can't. It's first training of the year, old Krantz won't let us go till dark.'

My face goes pale. Sam is a sports star like Laney, if she were here they'd be training together.

'Yeah, okay.' I can't look at him.

For a brief second his hand squeezes my shoulder. I look up to watch him walk away. There is no point glancing around – we've been seen and the news is going to rip through town. A Thomson and a Miller talked without swear words being exchanged, had even touched. I picture Kelly's tear-shiny face as her parents shipped her off to Rocky. We are in so much trouble. And still my heart lifts. I'll do my research today, tomorrow we'll go out looking.

School is nothing. I'm pretty sure I take in nothing, too. I sleep-walk through the classes, keep my head down and am ignored. Cassie and her crew have spread the word – I'm not to be spoken to or even acknowledged by the other girls in high school, all twelve of them. Bobbie is one of the main ones giving me evil glares. Even the teachers barely look at me. Either they can't handle what I'm going through or they think a missing sibling is contagious.

The bitches are at their best with all the swirling rumours about Laney, but none of them involve Troy. Course not, it's always the woman's fault in this town. It isn't like talking to them would improve my day, but it isn't great feeling like a social pariah. They're going to extremes this time and I'm being ignored in class as well, with no one willing to sit next to me. When I find Laney I am getting out of this shithole and dragging her with me.

Day 3, Afternoon

It's the last class after lunch and I am counting the seconds on the clock. When the bell goes I leap out of my chair and leg it through the door, while the teacher yells about using the free period to actually study. I like Mrs McKenzie, she's my favourite teacher. She actually cares about us, and she is the only person who spoke to me all day, but I'm not sitting still today, not even for her.

I walk like I'm doing what I should be, not wagging school at all. I head straight for the Eidsvold Historical Society. Just off the main highway that runs through town, it's an old log-cabin-looking building filled with photos, paperwork and relics from the town's goldmining days. It has a huge yard filled with ancient train carriages that they manage to keep in not too bad condition. I've never really paid that much attention to it. It's covered in dust and cobwebs, and is wall-to-wall white history.

Everybody knows that some parts of the town are 'white' territory and others are 'black'. Even the pub has a whitefulla side and a blackfulla side. They reckon it's supposed to be all one now, and sure people cross between the two spaces, but it's what everyone calls it. The pub is the centre of activity in the town and it's the best place to see how things work here. The blackfulla side is all concrete, old plastic chairs and the toilets have never worked or been cleaned in anyone's memory. People don't even bother to complain. The whitefulla's side is carpeted, has nice dining tables and chairs and a regularly cleaned toilet that works fine and doesn't smell like open sewage. Mum remembers when there was no door connecting the two sides, but that door is weird territory. Crossing it makes you feel funny, like you don't belong. And anytime someone, black, white or brindle, goes through it, people will turn around to stare. The historical society is like that, a white space where this town was 'discovered' by a pair of Norwegian brothers way back when and no one was here before them. Yeah, right.

Rounding the last corner and seeing that little building set off the squirms way down in my guts. The closer I get to the place the more uncomfortable I feel. Psyching myself up isn't helping at all. I wish Rhi could've come with me as back up, but she was off on the search. I shouldn't really be nervous. Mum always says the old fulla who runs the place is lovely. The problem is you never knew who's volunteering on what days.

My steps get smaller as I walk through the gate and up onto the verandah, feeling a little disappointment when the door swings open under my palm. Maybe a tiny part of me hoped I'd get the times wrong and it'd be shut. I force my feet over the threshold, eyes flicking over the strange territory. The tinkle of the bell above the door isn't the blare of alarms I've been bracing for.

The inside is just like the outside: a big log cabin, with one open area that houses all the treasures, and it is blessedly empty. A couple of doors lead off to one side of the building, probably only big enough for a small office. Wooden beams hold up the tin roof. Sturdy tables line the rest of the walls and the few that are pulled back to back in the centre create two aisles, or a big circuit you can walk around. Stuff is scattered on every surface and on the walls hangs old black and white framed photos. The overall impression is wood, dirt and rust.

My level of discomfort hasn't eased any, but the things on the tables call to me. Weird implements, probably from the mining days, or made to do strange things to cattle, are carefully arranged beside vials of what might be small semi-precious stones. I'd bought something similar for $5 at a market when I was a kid, a chunk of rock with a vein of something pretty running through it. It's probably worth nothing, but I find it fascinating. Deciding to be extra careful, I force myself to read all of the little tags sitting next to each item, along with the name of the person who donated it. I don't know what I am looking for; a familiar last name or property, I have no clue. All I know is I don't want to miss anything.

'Can I help you?'

I jump about a metre and spin to face the lady who spoke. I didn't hear her come in. A quick sweep and I have her pegged as one of the local property owners, but I don't know who. She's doing the same sweep as me. Silver-blonde hair pulled back in a bun, she is the age of a lot of my white mates' mums, around her fifties, wearing a pair of too big Wranglers and a button-down blouse with boots. The only concession to the heat is her thin sleeveless blouse. The office probably has air-con. And she's staring at me like I'm some stray dog that's tumbled in through an open door.

'Umm, I was just … umm, doing a school assignment on the history of Eidsvold, so …'

My silence and stammering response are forgotten as the woman gives me a big grin.

'Well, you've come to the right place! Are you doing a general history or are you focusing on a special time? We've got a lot of things from the mining times.'

'Actually I was interested in when white people first came here.'

'Ah, the Archer brothers, the first to discover this place. You know they set up Eidsvold Station?'

This one seems nice enough so I decide to go for broke and see what happens.

'Well yeah, but I was sort of more interested in how the whitefullas and blackfullas got on and what happened.'

Her enthusiasm drops to the floor along with the smile on her face.

'Oh. Well, I umm … we've got some artefacts …'

'Really? That'd be cool.' I feel kind of bad for her. It isn't like she's being nasty or anything, she just doesn't seem to know what to make of me. Her smile comes straight back up.

'It's all on that table over there if you wanted to take a look.' She takes me to the far right corner and shows me a carefully catalogued group of stones with sharpened edges and petrified wood that looks oddly shaped. I don't know what I'm expecting but it isn't that. Each of the tags list the property where the item was found.

'These have been donated to us over the years by many of the locals. We've had an anthropologist in to have a look and he thought it was a good record of what the local Aborigines were like.'

I have to bite my tongue hard before I ask her what she thinks I am.

'We can only guess what some of it was for. This one here,' she says pointing to a bit of petrified wood that doesn't look like anything but a branch to me, 'might've been used by women to gather food.'

I block out the lecture for a bit. I hate when people talk at me like I'm not black because I didn't grow up in a humpy or run around with my susoos out. Mum grew up on our foods, but Nan said they'd lost access to all that when we got kicked off the stations en masse. It happened right after the government told the property owners they had to start paying their black workers. Funny how that happened.

'... and then they would cook it in the ashes of a fire.'

'Wow. Were there any newspapers that have stuff like this?' She gives me another weird look. 'We're supposed to show we've done research and found old documents and things to back it up.' I give my best innocent smile. 'If I could take photos that'd be great, but my teacher said written records are even better. I think she wants to make sure we actually do some reading.'

The woman chuckles. I'm trying not to shift around from the weight of the lies. I'll probably end up doing an essay on this later just so I won't feel so bad, as soon as I figure out which class I can fit it into.

'Most of our documents are newspaper clippings we've kept in photo frames. The older documents were starting to fall apart so we shipped them off to the state library a few years ago for safekeeping.'

My face falls and she rushes to reassure me. 'There are still a few copies at the local library and I've heard you can get electronic copies from the state library. The staff over at the council offices could probably help if you asked.'

'Oh. I guess I was just hoping to see something real, hold a bit of history, you know?'

I don't need her insulted look to know I've said the wrong thing. 'Well, if you picked up any of the items here you'll find they're as "real" as any old newspaper.'

'Oh yeah, totally. I just meant more from the words of someone who was alive back then … you know?' Hell, I don't know what I mean at this point, but she tries to be nice about it.

'So … umm, what exactly were you hoping to learn?'

'I don't know. Maybe if anything exciting ever happened here?' I make sure enough of my sarcastic, know-it-all-teen is in that sentence as possible. I swear she stifles a sigh.

'Well, aside from the discovery of gold, which brought in loads of people and change, we've got a few clippings from the bigger events in the town.'

She waves me to follow and steps towards that mysterious little office. All over the walls to one side are framed newspaper clippings that I'd looked right past before. They're the plain black type with dusty glass on the front. The woman is frowning at the state of them but points to a couple.

'That's the first time gold was found, and here are some of the local men setting up the first hospital.' I shudder. Everyone knew that place. It's this old demountable that has been broken up and turned into houses spread across the town. My cousin used to live in one of them but she moved out pretty quick. I never liked to go visit her after dark. The house would feel fine all day long, but the moment the sun went down you knew you weren't alone. The only time I'd ever slept over I kept the doona over my head and refused to look, no matter how close the giggling and scratching sounds got to my bed. Later, Nan told me that house used to be the old children's ward. I never slept over again. Even now, when I don't believe in that stuff anymore, I know what I heard that night. As much as I want to believe in logic, I'm not sure if I'd be game to test it.

'This was the first time the town was flooded back in the late 1800s. It was national news back then.' Maybe for them. My Uncle Mack grumbled to me once that if idiots wanted to build houses where water levels rose, they got what they deserved. 'But this is probably the earliest clipping we have. Look, see, there are some Aborigines ... but those aren't the Archer brothers I'm sure.'

No, the town heroes would never have clapped chains on men's necks, wrists and ankles. I stiffen as something hurts deep inside while she brushes past. I have to wonder if any of those men are my family. Does Laney know how they felt right now? I try to pull my mind from that while the lady keeps talking, showing 'this' being built or 'that' being burnt down.

'And this is an old-fashioned bush trial that happened right here.'

A spread of men stand in their old-fashioned finery, bleached out facial features staring out at us. I'd ignored it,

131

thinking it was some other all-white event, like most stories in this town. But now that I look close I can see the one man in chains sitting at their feet, like a prized dog. The old blackfulla's hands are chained in front; his long white beard flows in a way that they'd banned long ago. That old blackfulla doesn't look cowed, with his chin tipped up, staring down the lens like he's daring the photographer to say something.

'The man in chains went on a killing spree, one of the worst in the state. He was the first serial killer in Queensland. He murdered a group of stockmen that trusted him, one by one, and got about eight before they finally caught him. Important men came from Brisbane and even Sydney to keep the whole thing fair. It was felt a normal trial would've been too biased as many of the men were local.'

Her words leave a bitter taste in my mouth. If killing black people actually counted as murder, there'd be a lot more serial killers than that, stretching back 200 years.

I do a double take as the words 'Oscar Miller' leap out from the faded print. My stomach does a motion sickness dance and I have to fight to sound normal.

'Did they say why he did it?'

'Oh that's not too clear, something about a dispute over property. They found him guilty the same day this was taken.' I almost snort. 'There is a newspaper article or two on this; they would probably give you more detail.'

I force myself back into the present. 'So is that all there is then?'

I can almost touch her sarcasm. 'As I said, you could always try the state library and see what they have.'

132

I pretend to think it over. 'Nah, that's cool. Could I take these up to the council and get them photocopied so I can make up my mind later?'

She shakes her head. 'Sorry, they have to stay here. But I can take some copies and email them to you if you like? I can get the frames cleaned up at the same time.'

'Yeah cool, thanks.' I smile, more genuinely this time.

'Write your email address down here and which ones you want, and I'll get it to you later this week.'

I scribble the information down and carefully list the articles she's shown me. Shrugging my port on a bit tighter I nod in the woman's direction, eyes on the ground. 'Well, umm, thanks for that … I'd better, ummm, get back to school.'

'My pleasure. Make sure you ask your teacher if we can see what your class comes up with for their assignments.' Her encouraging smile is all I wait on before I'm out the door, the guilt is back and I'm panicking a bit about her going to one of the teachers.

I shrug it off. Hopefully she forgets about it. So what if she asks? I'll tell them I was thinking of doing it but decided not to. Right now I have two choices. I can head in to what passed for a library in this town – a small room in the council office that is filled with mostly terrible romances about the wild, empty and untamed Australian outback and all the white people who lived there (vomit!). It's also the only thing that passes as a bank. If I go anywhere near it I'm guaranteed to get noticed, ensuring Mum knows about it all that much quicker. Or I can take a breather and make my way to my favourite place.

First, I'll go drop a note at home letting Mum know where I am going, just in case. I can pick up a new CD at the same time. Today I need something a bit less angry.

Britney Spears keeps me company at the reservoir. She's my secret shame. In a town divided by country and western, rap and R&B, I'm one of the few who'd sneak in some pop music and the odd alternative rock band. Laney would use my love of Britney and the Backstreet Boys as a threat.

Loan me your dress or I'm telling people you know the dance to 'Baby One More Time'.

A grin slips across my lips as the sound of a car engine leaks through my headphones. A weird sense of déjà vu creeps over my skin as I watch the silver Holden come across the cattle grid. I get a double shock when I see who's in the passenger seat. Part of me is still terrified, but the steel determination at my centre that I built up on the back streets last night won't let me do anything but wait. The old girl might be scary damaged, but she might also be right.

Sam gets out, looks at my shocked face and shrugs. I glare back – this was so not over. Running around to the passenger door he helps the fragile lady out, walking with her over to me, bracing her so she can lower herself down. Neither of them looks at me. Sam goes to sit next to May and her head whips around to glare at him.

'What you think you doin, boy?' The stern growl would've sent me running but Sam sets his jaw and stares down the barrel.

'If I'm gonna get a hidin for it I deserve to know why.'

May eyes him for a bit longer but when he refuses to look away she finally nods.

'Fair enough, son.' Then she swings those freaky eyes to me. 'So you decided to take my advice. Know what you gettin into, do ya?'

I stay quiet, not too sure what to expect from Mad May.

'You gotta know what them boys are capable of. What their fathers, grandfathers and family done to blackfullas in this town. Especially the women.' Her rheumy eyes watch me intently while she hits on all my fears. 'We're meat, girl. Meat to be used like any other native animal.' She spits the words at me and I can't help the flinch. 'Bah. How can someone so weak face that?'

I look at her straight and say the only thing that matters: 'Cos I need to find Laney.'

My voice shakes. It is my worst nightmare but I know the possibilities. We all do.

'Mmm, then maybe you'll find her, ay?' She reaches out a frail hand and rests it under my chin, thumb pressing just under my lip. 'Don't fret, girl, wherever your sister is, your connection can bring her back. Our women been lived through worse. I did.'

I don't realise tears are flowing down my face till she gently brushes them away. Her paper-thin skin feels like dry leaves.

'How did you survive?' I whisper.

'Not well, bub. Not too well. But I lost my strength, them bastards ripped him from me doling out white justice.

You gotta make sure to be that strength for her when you find her.' She smiles at me and for some reason the sadness in it hurts. 'You gotta make sure you end up back here with her or you may as well never have pulled her out. At least there she can believe in you, here, living.'

'Do you remember where you was?'

'You know where.' I can see pity in her face.

'They were parked on the other side of the property from the house.' The old girl looks at me, lets me say it myself: 'Near that mountain.'

A single nod of encouragement is all she gives me.

'But Aunty, we're not sposed to go there. Nan said so. All the old fullas say so, and Laney always listens to em.'

Another nod. 'And maybe she did this time too. Maybe she got taken there, against her will.'

Goosebumps race everywhere reminding me of last night's dream.

'Aunty,' I pause, not really sure I want to ask this, but I push the words out, 'I thought I heard somethin outside the house. Do you know what it is?'

The old girl's hand drops so fast my head falls forwards. Only then do I realise I've been leaning into her.

'No. No! Not that. No, no, not again!'

And just like that she's gone. Only this time I've seen the real person under that trauma. I am still scared but I don't run this time. Grabbing her flailing hands I grip them tight, forcing her eyes back to mine.

'No, it's not. Me and Sam'll make sure of it.' I say it firmly with utter belief. There is no other option.

She reverses her hands and grasps mine just as tightly.

'Check your house, girl, rip it apart. If they're there, it must be close. Do it soon, almost out of time!'

Sam's hands appear over ours. Honestly I'd forgotten about him in that strange little tableau she'd caught me in. He mutters soothing words and phrases, which seem to help. When we can't get her hands to release mine, we work together to stand us all up and manoeuvre her into the car. A few more minutes of soothing, she slowly releases her grip and settles back in the seat. Sam closes the door as gently as he can and turns to me.

I try to be subtle at wiping the tears from my face, but he's seen it all.

'Well, thanks for stickin around to help this time.'

'You weren't even supposed to be here today.' I make it an accusation and he looks a bit guilty.

'Yeah well, she was waitin in the car for me when I got ome. She told me where she needed to go.' He drifts off but I hear what he doesn't say. He's scared he won't have her like that for much longer, so all of them were precious. I don't say it because he won't thank me for it. Besides, when an elder tells you to do something, you do it. No questions. It's my turn to shrug.

'Thanks then. She seemed to know what was goin on.'

'Yeah, her clear days. She's a real cluey old girl, most people forget that though.' He won't look at me.

'Well, she knew about Potters before anyone else,' I say, getting defensive for some reason.

He smiles at me then. It's kind of nice.

'It's too late to go there now?' I can't hide my disappointment and he looks a bit guilty.

'Yeah, sorry. Takes bout a hour to get there. And if I rush I can get to the end of practice. Sides, goin there in the day is bad enough, I don't wanna be there at night.'

'Yeah ay.' Nice to know I'm not the only one shitting themselves. 'We're still goin from school tomorrow though, ay?'

'Course.' Sam smiles again.

I nod and what I'm really thinking slips out. 'We're so gonna get busted.'

My words rip the smile from his face and I feel terrible.

'I'll see you tomorrow,' I say, before turning to walk down the track while he goes back around the car. I wave at Aunty May as I go past, but it looks like she's going to town talking to herself.

'Tace,' Sam calls.

I stop and look back, watching this weird little foot shuffle he does. 'Umm, did you want a lift?'

I laugh. 'No thanks, I like my life.'

He grins at me and shakes his head. 'Had to ask or Aunty would never let me hear the end of it.'

I laugh, raise a hand in farewell and keep walking. Everything is getting so complicated.

Day 3, Twilight

The front door to the house is wide open so I stride in and stop. Mum is sat on the sunroom couch glaring. The silence stretches while my eyebrows climb higher on my face. Option one is to just ask her what's wrong, but that seems like a bad idea. She hates it when I don't know what I've done. Telling her sarcastically that I'm not a mind reader always gets me in bigger trouble but, really, adults can be so freaking stupid.

It doesn't help that I've broken so many rules the past twenty-four hours that I have no idea which one she's angry about.

Option two is to walk right past her and into the house, but that's a bit like edging past a king brown curled up in a corner. You're never sure if it's sleeping or not, and it might lash out at you for getting close. And the slow edge past is also extremely undignified.

Option three is to walk back out the door. That one is seriously tempting and before I've even finished the thought my body steps backwards.

'Freeze,' Mum growls.

I am getting sick of this game. 'Don't you need music to play statues?'

I want to sigh at myself. When will I learn to keep my big mouth shut?

'Knock off the smart-arse comments and tell me where ya were.'

Panic snatches at my stomach and throttles me with it.

'Do you have any idea how worried I was?' Her voice breaks and I realise it isn't about any rumours or bad behaviour. I have to fight to keep the relief off my face. But now I have an emotional Mum on my hands and no idea how to deal with it.

I swallow it all back and find my most gentle voice. 'Mum, I left a note for you on the kitchen table. I needed to go up to the reservoir for a bit to … think.'

It's lame but the best I can come up with. I watch her physically choke her pain down and now glass shards join the roiling in my stomach. Slowly I settle beside her on the couch, taking her hand in mine, rubbing it. She doesn't like people to see her upset any more than I do, so I keep my eyes on our linked hands.

'I'm sorry, Mum. I thought the note would be enough. I won't do it again.'

She grips my hands with both of hers.

'It's okay, I panicked.' Through my hair I can see her staring at our hands too. 'I only just got home and when you weren't ere …'

'I know.'

The quiet stretches again, but this time it's filled with pain, fear and understanding.

'I want to lock you in the house and throw away the key, but I know that's not fair.'

I snort. 'And I wouldn't much like it. I'm your daughter, don't forget, and Nan always said she couldn't keep you put short of hogtying.'

We make eye contact and laugh. It isn't funny but we need that laugh. It's something we've always used, us mob, to give relief and make the hard things more bearable. Not less heavy, only help it sit more comfortably on our hearts. After we stop laughing we're both calmer.

Squeezing her hands I hesitate a long while. She sits with me in silence, seeming to know that I need to ask her something. I don't want Mum involved, but there's no way I can rip the house apart without her noticing, even if I put everything back. The woman has the sharpest eyes out of all of us. She never misses anything.

'What are you doin ere anyway?' I hedge.

'Your uncle's car blew a tyre and his spare was bally, so we drove in. He's over at the RACQ fulla's place gettin two new ones. We'll get back out then.'

'Could we ...' I force the words out. 'Could we search the house again? Together? To see if ... you know, there's anything?'

It's probably the shittiest sentence I've ever said, but I feel her hands squeeze back. Mum ripped Laney's room apart right after that first attempt to report her missing went so wrong. But May's words are still bouncing around in my head.

'Homework first, then we'll search. Just to be sure.'

Fighting my rising anxiety I let go of her hands and hop up.

'Great. Want a cuppa?'

'Yeah please, daught.'

I head in and set off the kettle before retrieving my port from my room. I have my books spread out on half the table and the tea brewing before Mum joins me. I ignore her and focus on the maths textbook I pull out first. I hate maths with a passion, but I know if I invest that into the work I can churn through it fast. Not necessarily right though.

As Mum walks past her hand brushes my hair and I feel tears threaten.

While she gets our drinks ready I fight the tears down with everything I have, burying my face in the book. A mug appears to the side and Mum goes out the back to sit. She's the reason I hate being confined. Mum says you can't keep a good Murri out of the open air. Four walls eventually suffocate us.

Staring at the pages I don't see a word, focusing instead on what I need to do tonight and tomorrow.

We sit at the kitchen table, both freshly showered to get off all the dirt and dust we picked up climbing through everything. The two of us ripped through the house, even outside in the laundry and garage. Laney is the person you ask to hide presents and things, we can't leave out anything – she's seriously crafty. Other than a drum of dirt and cobwebs, we found diddly squat. Sitting at the kitchen table afterwards we look completely defeated. Uncle Joe walks in and goes off his head at both of us. It's the only way he knows how to deal with our sadness. It's how a lot of our mob are. At least it gets us up and cooking the sausages and cutting up the salad. Once everything is ready we cover up the food to protect it from the unending flies.

'Get us some tea there, daughter,' Uncle calls from the back.

Mum gets some of the leftover patty cakes while I finish up the cups and take them out back. I'm a bit shocked they don't leave straight away – there'd be time before the sun goes down. It's weird not to have Laney there. Our family is broken and we keep right on moving. Like a car that's lost one of its tyres, we're riding the rim and wearing it down. Eventually we won't be able to do that either.

Only after I sit down do I realise something's wrong. Uncle and Mum won't look at me. They've come to a decision. It has something to do with me and they want to talk before the mob turn up. They're expecting a fight. Adults are so stupid. I keep my disapproval in and wait for the shoe to drop, already fuming.

'Tace, we need ta talk ta you bout somethin.'

Uncle Joe is more impatient than me. If it'd just been Mum she'd take most of the day to get there, probably wait until we're brushing our teeth.

I gulp down some Ovaltine to stop up my sarcastic mouth.

'Mmm?'

'Yeah, I umm, we think we'd like to start lookin for Laney at night. Maybe, you know, after dinner.'

I nod and refuse to help.

'But we don't want to leave you home alone.'

I try not to show my excitement as I swallow. It can't be this easy, surely?

'Why not? I do it all the time when Mum's got a late shift.' More shifting and glancing while I fight not to roll my eyes. 'Finding Laney is more important than someone staying home to babysit me.'

'Your mother and I need to know that someone is with you. We can't go running after your twin without knowin you're okay too.' Uncle Joe said the words but I heard Mum's fear in them. I took another mouthful of hot chocolate and thought about it. I didn't realise Uncle Joe hadn't finished. 'We were thinkin you could go stay with your Aunty Fern.'

I nearly spit Ovaltine everywhere. Luckily most of it goes back in the mug.

'Aunty Fern? The one with a hundred kids? Where would I sleep, the dog kennel?' I'm not even being funny. That woman needs another kid under her roof like I need a hole in the head.

'Now daught—'

'No way Mum. I have homework and assignments, and I'd never get a second's peace.' I can see her wavering, her need to ensure we get a good education trumps most things. 'I'd end up babysittin, and not gettin paid for it neither.' Her eyebrow quirks and I'm on the wrong track. 'I'll be so smothered in kids all the time I won't be able to do any of my school work!'

Her eyebrow lowers slightly and she eyes Uncle Joe. His frustration is clear.

'What are we sposed to do, Tace, one of us stay home to look after you while the others go off lookin for Laney?'

'Who said I need one of youse? I've been home alone most times anyway.' And sprinting past that comment, 'I don't run around town. I'm the borin one who stays home and studies. Since when do I need a babysitter?'

I can see them teetering on the edge but I don't know what else to say. I've done a pretty bad job so far and am

144

shocked Mum isn't booting me up to Aunty Fern's after so many reminders of what Laney and I did that started all of this.

'Mum, you need to be out there. For Laney.'

Maybe it's my sincerity that finally tips the balance. Uncle Joe is converted – he's eyeing Mum the same as me: a little pleading, kinda hopeful.

'Fine!' Mum sputters in disgust. 'But I need ya ta do somethin for me, daughter.' She looks at me dead in the eye and I know I'm not going to like the next thing out of her mouth. 'I want ya ta look me in the eye and promise ya won't leave the house while we're out.'

My mob joke around a lot. We talk shit to each other all the time and practical jokes are normal. There are a couple of ways to be sure if someone is having a joke at your expense. Two signals that you must never ever violate or we firmly believe you'll damn your soul to hell. One of those is looking someone in the eye when promising something, the other is to swear on the Bible.

I look square in my mother's eyes and lie.

'I swear to you I will not leave the house while you and Uncle are out at night.'

I'm going to burn for eternity. But if it means finding Laney it will be worth it. Still, I am bitter. She screws up and I get screwed, it's so typical. The bitch better appreciate this.

Day 3, Night

'Anyone home?' Aunty Mel calls.

'Out the back,' Mum yells.

The searchers start arriving in dribs and drabs, grabbing their food and drinks and joining us in the backyard. It's even quieter this time and it's killing all of us. Rhi went and got Pop and he's perched on the comfiest chair. Everyone keeps eyeing the empty fire pit as if it will reveal Laney's location to them.

'You know what I been thinkin?' I say to the air. 'That Troy, he's been tellin the biggest load of bull …' I stutter seeing my mother's face, 'since he got back.'

'Yeah,' Rhi says. 'And Tyrone reckons he was out there lookin for somethin but he wouldn't tell em what. You know, before he dumped them all out there to get a hidin.'

'That boy said she never showed,' Uncle Joe says, but more like he is thinking it over.

'That's not what Ty told me, Uncle, he thinks Troy took off on all of em.'

'Maybe we need to go ask im again,' Mum adds.

I grin evilly and look around the group to see a few frowns, a few smiles and one searching pair of eyes staring straight into mine. Pop has been trying to get me to sit with him all night, but I can't do it. I don't want to tell him I've met with a Miller, and definitely don't want to repeat what she said. I look away, feeling his soft scoff of disappointment.

'Come on, we're goin to Edna's place.'

I stand up with them all, following close around the house and head for Uncle's car. Mum opens a door and turns to look at me.

'Where do ya think you're goin?'

'With you!' I set my jaw and get ready for it.

'No you're not — you're stayin and cleanin up after dinner.'

'What!' My tone hits sky level and Mum's eyebrows drop.

'Do. As. You. Are. Told.'

Mum's clipped tone and carefully enunciated words are usually enough to send me running, but not this time. I step forwards, getting right in her face, when a hand snatches my arm and pulls me back.

'Okay, Aunt, I'll stay and help,' Rhi says, taking hold of my other arm and dragging me backwards.

I feel tears of frustration beating at me and, for the first time in my life, I want to take a swing at my mother. Pain rises up inside, demanding I hit something, even the much-loved cousin-sister saving me from certain doom.

Rhi's mouth is at my ear whispering. The buzz in my brain makes it hard to hear, but she keeps repeating the same phrase so eventually I catch it. 'Not this way, cuz. Pick ya battles.'

I relax back into her and she wraps her arms around me, holding tight. It doesn't stop the evil glare I give my mother, but the woman unwisely ignores it and gets into the car. Pop is already settled in the front seat, eyeing us with suspicion.

Mum is so used to me being the good one, the one she doesn't have to worry about, that she never even questions my sudden calm.

All the mob drive past casting me sorry looks and I stay put, making sure they all see me and know how unfair she's being.

The silence in the house is even more depressing somehow. Mum has been back hours. She walked in and went straight to bed, letting me know how successful the trip had been. Everyone else gave us a full run-down of what happened, then went off to their places or where they're crashing for the night. Aunty Mel went to take care of her other kids, leaving Rhi and me sitting at the back, staring at the sky. The moon is weak and the stars are out. It seems wrong that they're so beautiful when everything else feels so dark.

'I got a idea,' Rhi offers.

'Oh no,' I moan.

'You don't even know what it is yet.'

'Yeah, but I'm not gonna like it or you'd have said it before.'

Rhi giggles. 'Yer ay.'

'Gorn then, out with it.'

She takes a deep breath. 'Troy knows somethin, but he's not sayin.'

'Yeah and?'

'Maybe if he's lookin straight at his guilt he'll admit what he's done.'

148

'What the fuck does that mean? Just spit it out already.'

'God, you're a cranky bitch! Fine. I think if we dress you up like Laney, sneak you into his room and tell a few lies, he'll squeal.'

The stars lose my interest as I look at her, tilting my head and frowning hard.

'What?' she demands.

'Just tryin ta figure out if you're a genius or mad as a cut snake.'

Rhi grins. 'Definitely a genius.'

'What if he realises? We're not exactly the same, memba?'

'Pfft, he's a man. If it's not boobs or a bum he's not lookin that hard.'

'Nice, real nice.'

'Plus, he was already tipsy when Aunty went over there before. What's the bet he's drunk now?' She leans forwards in her chair, willing me to listen. 'Come on, Tace, we can do this.'

Maybe I'm going a little mad myself because the more I think about it the better Rhi's idea looks. Laney and I dress differently, wear our hair differently. But with a bit of darkness as cover and a whole lot of make-up, there's a decent chance someone will mix us up.

'Alright. It's worth a try.'

Rhi whoops before she remembers to be quiet. I hold a finger up to warn her. 'But if he tries to touch me I'mma start swingin.'

'Fair enough.' She grins back.

Day 3, Midnight

'How do you talk me into these things?' I mumble to Rhi.

She'd gotten me kitted up in Laney's hip-hop clothing and massive hoop earrings, slapped some make-up on to cover the freckles and wrapped a bandana around my hair to hide the fringe I had but Laney didn't. I looked into the mirror and burst into tears. Rhi let me go for a bit, then quietly fixed everything up. No car tonight so it's a long trek, which is the only reason I am in my Nikes and not in Laney's high-platformed strappy sandals that Rhi tried to force me into. The need for speed and silence won that argument for me.

We keep to the sides of the roads, cutting across paddocks and through places we know can't be seen easily in the dark. When we have no choice but to use roads we walk like we aren't sneaking around. Rhi says that's the key. If someone looks out a window and you're running or sneaking, then they'll look harder. If they see two people walking they'll look to see who it is, but that's all. Rhi is the queen at this stuff so I do as I am told.

Rounding a corner I spot Troy's place and baulk. Rhi is frigging psychic because her hand is already on my elbow, dragging me forwards. I feel bile rise in my throat.

'I can't do this.'

'Yes. You can. And you will.' Rhi spins me around and brings us nose to nose. 'Because we need to know what the fucker did with our sister.'

It's the most serious I've ever seen her and the steel in her body slips through to my spine.

'It's all about breath, Tace, follow mine.'

She talks me through some deep, calming breaths. I have no idea how long we stand on the corner like that. My shoulders drop and my heart slows. When I feel like I'm not going to vomit, I nod. As Rhi pulls away, the only thing I can think about is how grateful I am there aren't any streetlights down this side of town.

'Whenever you're ready,' she whispers.

'Grow some patience.'

'Can't grow somethin outta nuthin.'

We look at each other and laugh softly. If our chuckles are a bit high-pitched neither of us says anything. We talked about this bit before we left. I am on my own from here, but Rhi will stay close in case I get into trouble.

Turning towards the house I walk off, keeping my head up, making myself walk calmly, calling up all the times I wished for my twin's confidence, and fake the hell out of it. I know exactly where I am going – Laney told me how she'd climb up onto the chair that Troy had put under his window. After I faked a dry retch I asked if the chair was there before or after they started seeing each other. Then I ran from the mad cow.

Forcing my breath to calm I step into their yard and drop the confidence. Sneaking to the back of the house I almost fall over the chair as I round the corner. Taking a second to

151

test it for strength and any sound, I step up. All the windows are wide open and these ones are sliders so there's no window pane to duck or manoeuvre around. The moon has gone dark and only the light of the Milky Way guides me. I can see a plain bedroom with a dresser and a bed. Nothing else but the shape lying in it and the fan going full force, pointing at the bed.

One leg goes over before I have time to think. I reach for a firm grip with my slippery hands. I nearly yelp when my foot finds carpet. Pulling myself up and into the room I stand for a long moment, not breathing. When no one screams I release my breath. Turning, I walk as lightly as I can to the bed and stand over it. Staring down.

The idea is to be creepy and scare the crap out of him, but first he has to wake up. I'm contemplating how I am going to do that without actually touching the prick when he jerks awake and stares up at me. His wide open eyes glow in the starlight and I wait.

'La … Laney?'

I tilt my head to the side so he can see the outline of my face and he gasps.

'You … you're okay?'

Shaking my head slowly I lean down to him. He flinches towards the wall at his back and I smile, hoping he can see my teeth.

'Why?' I whisper.

'I'm sorry. Oh God, I'm so sorry, please forgive me,' he begs.

That pisses me off so I reach out with a hand and he squeaks before I even make contact.

'Please. It wasn't my fault! Mum told me ta do it!'

My hand stops about halfway to its target, hovering between us.

'You left me.' I don't have to fake the accusation in my voice.

'They had you, Lane. There's no comin back after that. Oh God, what are you?'

I have no more words. He's just confirmed that he left my big sister and I want to kill him. I'm also deliberately not thinking too hard about it or it'll distract me from my goal. I can't ask too many questions or he'll twig it isn't Laney asking, but I can scare the shit out of him. I stretch my hand closer and he presses back into the wall, trying to climb through it. I trail one finger down his cheek and he whimpers.

'It was the necklace. It did something and they came after me, Lane. I couldn't get rid of em. Mum said I had to pass it on or they'd get me too.'

'Coward,' I snarl.

I don't recognise myself in that moment, I just want to hurt him. I ease my hand down and around his neck, wrapping it softly there. A tangy smell rises from the bed and I take satisfaction in his humiliation.

'Confess.'

'I will. I will, I swear I will. First thing, tomorrow I'll go straight to the cops.'

Tightening my grip a little I growl.

'Your mum too,' he squeaks even higher. 'I'll go to your mum and tell her where I left you. What I did.'

I lean as close to him as I can and stare at the holes where his eyes should be. His face is turned away from me, refusing to look. My other hand is already reaching for his sheet and I'm praying it doesn't touch anything wet.

'You better.'

I let go at the same time I throw his sheet up and over his head. I'm all set to throw myself out the window like Rhi and I practised, but he beats me to it. Sheet wrapped around his head, he leaps sideways, arms and legs flailing in a mad scramble away from me. He clears the door and the last I see is him stumbling over that raggedy sheet, and nearly knocking himself out as he goes round a corner. I almost bust out laughing, but when I hear Ray yelp and Edna scream 'What the fuck?', fear wins. I bolt out the window, skinning my shins as I go. Every noise I make is like a car backfiring in my ears, but I can't force myself to slow down.

I'm almost out of the yard when lights start coming on in the house. They would see me if they look out the window. I give Laney a run for her money on speed then.

Sprinting past the corner, Rhi appears at my right, our arms and legs pumping hard. The breath is already burning in my chest, but fear and fury push me past it. Neither of us speak as we race each other till we hit the first open paddock, and dive into the dirt and grass. We spread ourselves flat, waiting for a car, running feet, anything. Staring into Rhi's face I can see her wide grin.

That girl is so cracked.

The exit is the weak part of our plan. Having to run and make noise would break the spooky spell so we'd planned a run and hide sprint. Rhi knew about this spot with the perfect little ditch in this field that hid a body laying flat. I'd rolled my eyes at her and didn't ask, even though she wanted me to.

We lie that way for a long while, looking into each other's faces. Nothing happens.

'Where are they?' I swear Rhi sounds like she's pouting.

'Dunno,' I whisper back. 'Think it's been long enough?'

Rhi pokes her head up, scanning around before dropping back.

'Don't see anythin.'

As if on cue, we both stand, dusting ourselves off.

'He must not ave twigged it was you.'

'He's probably too busy cleaning his sheets.'

'Ay?'

'Pretty sure he pissed imself.' Does it make me an evil person that I say it with a grin?

Rhi doubles over, stuffing a hand in her mouth to hold back her laughter. I slap her on the back, hard.

'Come on, that thing between his ears might start workin soon. Let's get home.'

Rhi camps in my bed and we spend the night arguing over what Troy meant with the weird things he'd whispered. Neither of us expects him to have the balls to turn up and confess in the broad light of day. But that's okay, we'd only been on a fact-finding mission.

The people after him must somehow have known he'd palmed this necklace off to Laney. Hell, he probably told them. Rhi and I don't agree on exactly who has Laney, but I ignore Rhi's arguments and point to the Potters and their neo-Nazi ways as enough bad guys to be facing without having to make up boogie men. Eventually she gives up. We do agree that Rhi is going to talk to Tyrone again, this time alone, to see if he knows more. I ignore her eyebrow wiggle. While she sorts that, I'm going to school to pretend things are as normal as they can be right now. I try to fight her on that one but she won't budge.

Eventually she falls asleep. I lie awake. Listening.

Day 4, Daylight

I hear Mum moving around in the pre-dawn but don't get up. Uncle Joe's and Aunty Mel's cars pull up at the front and I listen to the murmurs from the kitchen. It is so familiar, and so wrong. I try to keep my mind blank. The lack of sleep is helping.

Mum ducks her head in and blows me a kiss. Aunty Mel looks in at her wayward daughter, shaking her head with a smile and waving before heading off by herself. No one bothers asking why I am awake. The bags under my eyes are almost as bad as theirs. The only upside to not sleeping is no nightmares.

Rhi doesn't even twitch when I hop up and get ready for school. I walk out the door to the sound of her snoring.

I ignore my churning guts. I am early again and alone, and it is all wrong.

School is filled with attempts to catch Sam's eye and trying to figure out how the hell I am going to talk to him without anyone seeing. It might've been his normal way of operating, it's not like we spent much time staring at each other before this week, but there isn't even a casual glance.

I'm brimming with anxiety, almost dancing in my chair with it. Why won't Sam look at me? Is he feeling guilty about something? Has he changed his mind? Oh my God, what if he has? What am I going to do? I don't want to go out to the Potters' on my own.

My frustration with Sam gets so bad that by the last class I've had enough. It's my free period for distance education study in the library, while all the others have manual arts across the oval.

I'd watched Sam down two bottles of Coke over lunch and I know where he'll go before making the trek across the oval to manual arts. I crouch at the back of the science building, getting a good view of the toilets. Sam waves at his mates as he makes a beeline for the toilets. I hold my breath to see if any of the boys will follow, but they all go on ahead.

I give him one minute. I time it. Then I break cover and follow him, walking casually.

'Please be finished and washing your hands,' I whisper under my breath as I make a last minute detour from the girls' entrance into the boys'.

'Oops. Timed it wrong!'

'Jesus Christ!' Sam flinches and does a double-take. 'Get out!'

Since he's facing away from me, pulling up his shorts and stuffing things back down them, I decide to stay put. I suppose I could turn away, but I'm enjoying his horror way too much.

'Not until ya tell me what the fuck is goin on.' I fold my arms and stare at him, pretending I am trying to drill holes in his skull. 'Why ave ya been dodgin me?'

'I'm not. Ya havin a paranoid girl delusion, now get out!' He yells at the wall.

I lean back against the corrugated iron behind me and cross my ankles. I move around a lot to make sure he can hear me.

'What are ya doin?'

'Gettin comfortable. There's only one way out've ere so ya may as well just face me.'

'I. Can't.' It's angry but I can deal with angry.

'Why not?' Came my best 'butter wouldn't melt in my mouth' reply. 'I thought we were a team. Why the change of heart?'

Maybe some of my hurt unintentionally slipped through. Whatever the reason he lets out a big sigh and finally turns.

'Don't forget to wash—' My triumphant crowing cuts off. I'm too busy staring at Sam's massive black eye. My wide-open trap doesn't seem to impress him as he marches to the sink to do a quick rinse and then tries to push past me. As he draws parallel I grab his shoulder and pull him around to look at me. 'Sam?'

I can't find the words. As much as I consider myself tough, no one has ever hurt me like this, nor would they if they valued their life. My sister, mother, uncle and large extended family would never allow it. Those shards of glass stuck inside my gut dig deeper and I can't stop the tears from forming. I would never understand an adult hurting their kid, any kid, this way. It is so wrong. But I know who hurt him without even asking and I have a horrible sinking feeling as to why.

159

'Sam, please, tell me,' I plead. His avoidance now makes complete sense.

'They found out. Someone saw me drive up to the reservoir and you comin down. It's all bullshit anyway, Tace, don't worry bout it.' He tries to push past me again but I hold firm.

'How can I not worry? I'm the reason ya got hurt.'

'No.' He stops trying to push my hand away and turns so he can look me in the eyes. 'I'm doing this for May. And in some part for you and Laney, but mostly for her. I'm sorry, Tace, but she's the one I care about.'

I flinch and finally let go. 'Thanks for the honesty.' My ego could've done without it. 'Still, if ya hadn't met me at the reservoir ya wouldn'tve got hurt. Does this mean ya can't come with me taday?' I kind of hate myself for how weak and small my voice sounds.

'No way, I'm comin!' Sam spits the words and the violent rejection isn't aimed at me. I could practically taste the rebellion. 'I promised Aunty that I'd take ya. Do ya think ya can get away?'

'No problem. They don't get back from searching till about seven so we got heaps of time.'

'We can head straight from school. They can't do much worse.'

I fight another flinch. Sam would hate it if he thought I pitied him.

'Yeah but no point flauntin it. And besides, just cos your mob know don't mean mine ...' My voice trails off. If the Millers know it won't be long till others do too and then someone will tell Mum. Instead of putting me off it urges me

160

to move faster. 'It has to be today then. I'll walk around the corner up past the fire station; we'll have to make it quick.'

He gives me a little salute. 'Is it okay if I head to class now, Miss?'

I glare and nod.

'Good. Think you could leave the boys' toilets then?'

His cheeky grin makes me flush with embarrassment. Damn, I forgot where we are.

'You go first. If it's safe for me to come out, tap the wall once softly.'

He walks out with another salute. Not long after the thumping boom of a fist on corrugated iron sends me squealing from the toilet. I slap him on the arm as I bolt past; he's too busy laughing to notice.

Day 4, Afternoon

I feel stupid sitting in the gutter. I could've tried hiding behind one of the scrawny gumtrees along the footpath but don't see much point. Besides, suspicious behaviour would draw attention a lot faster than just standing here would, so spoke Rhi the queen of sneaky. This way I could jump in the car and Sam could take off as fast as possible. Still, a few people go past having a good look. Fuck this town is full of dorries. I conveniently ignore my own past dorrie-ing behaviour.

I keep second-guessing this whole thing. From where I said to meet down to the whole misadventure. My mind keeps circling back to my twin and getting stuck. I have to find Laney.

'Waaaa!' Someone screams right in my ear and fingers dig into my sides sending me up about two metres. I spin and swing, straight at Rhi's stupid face. I pull the punch just in time and get her on the susoo instead.

'Argh, ya bitch!' She doubles over clutching her chest. 'That hurt.'

'Well, it wasn't meant to tickle. Don't sneak up on a black one or you'll get what's comin to ya.'

'Bloody hell. I just came ta tell ya I talked to Ty.' She eyes me resentfully, rubbing her hurt susoo.

'Well, come on then.'

As the last words leave my mouth a beat-up Holden pulls up beside us.

'Ah fuck!'

Rhi is staring open-mouthed at Toni Miller's car. Too late. I grab her by the arm and dig my fingernails in. No one realises I have long, hard fingernails because I never really use them or paint them. They also tend to forget that I have my mother's height and my father's build, which means height, weight and strength, enough to handle her anyway.

'Ow, ow, fuckin ow!'

Only Rhi could express pain, anger and get in some swearing in just four words. I fling open the back door and push her straight in. I keep shoving till she slips across giving me space to jump in. I slam the door behind me and look at a shocked Sam.

'Drive!'

Grabbing Rhi's head, and a whole lot of unnecessary hair, I yank us both down low. Sam takes the hint and hits the gas. Rhi's shock only lasts till the end of Mount Rose Street and she starts struggling. Even without looking I know where we are because Sam hasn't turned once.

'Up to the aerodrome, Sam,' I gasp while holding my slippery cousin down. Things escalate fast to swearing, elbowing and hair pulling. The car stops and I release her, leaping out and ripping my hands through my hair in frustration. I hear two car doors open and feet come storming up behind me.

Pulling my hands free I spin on the nearest target. 'What the fuck, Sam?'

'Don't even – this is your problem! I thought you asked her to come!'

'You're the dopey …' I choke the words back as his face turns mutinous. Boys' egos are too fragile for a serious truth-telling. Laney is the main focus, nothing else. I turn on Rhi who's fixing her hair while glaring at me, standing only a few steps behind Sam.

'What the fuck, Tace?' Rhi's sarcastic question makes me flush hot for a second. I want to tell her 'nunya' and leave her up here to walk home, but knowing her she'd run straight for her mother and then a call would go to Mum and everything was just plain—

'Fuck!' I do a rage dance, stamping my feet and flailing my arms around. 'Just once, can't things go the right friggin way?'

I stop my dance, take a deep breath and let it all go. Turning to find two gawking teenagers staring at me, I lift my chin and do my best Alana impersonation.

'We're out of time. You …' my finger goes to Sam, 'get in the car and take us to Potters'. You,' same finger, different person, 'get in the car and shut the fuck up. I'll explain as we go. Or you stay right here and if you say one goddamn word to anyone I will cut you.' My hand slices the air and Rhi's mouth turns stubborn. 'I'll cut you from my life so fast it'll be like you never existed. We'll be done, finished! Because if you fuck this up and I lose my sister you'll be dead to me.'

Rhi freezes. Mutinous mouth turning to tight-lipped fury. But she isn't my sister-cousin for nothing. It's my turn to be shocked when she spins on her heel and gets into the back seat. She slams the door shut. Guess I'm riding shotgun.

Sam hasn't followed orders, but the look we exchange is enough. Striding to the car we climb in and ignore the sullen silence from the back.

My breath rushes out.

Into that awful angry space I can't help but say what's driving me. Something I'm not even sure of has been pressing harder and harder, the surety of it is grinding its way into my skull. I whisper into the window I am hunching against, so close that the glass fogs with my breath. Tangible evidence of a feeling I've been too terrified to give voice to until now.

'We're running out of time.'

I tell her everything. And my super-mouthy cousin says not one word in response. Guilt for how I spoke to her tries to fill the quiet, but I won't let it. My reasons are important. We drive that way for a good bit until I realise a fatal flaw in my plan – I have no idea where the Potters' place is other than a general sort of direction. I feel like a total idiot asking but there's nothing else to be done.

'Umm, Sam? Do you know where we're goin?'

Rhi's snort of disgust gets ignored. Sam flicks a glance at me and there might've been a slight lip twitch.

'Dad goes out tordonin near there sometimes, but Mum won't let me. Says she doesn't want me out there at night. But we've been out to drop stuff off and that for im so I know the way. But are you sure …'

I know what he's asking. If we really want to go not just to Potters' but out to the worst part of it. I nod and turn to stare out the window again. Silence descends again as we turn off the paved road and onto dirt.

The land is like most others around here – calf-high grass that's so brown it probably will poke through all your clothes and scratch you ten ways to Sunday. The cleared paddocks are mostly empty, just a few groups of cattle here and there, not looking that healthy. Whatever trees there are stand silent and alone, tiny remnants of what once would've been pure bush. It didn't used to be this bare. They cleared it for the cattle, sure, but not like this. Ever since the government said property owners had to stop chopping down trees, then gave them a few years to get used to the idea, the property owners have been going insane. Poisoning whole areas for no other reason than they could before that new law came in. You could drive anywhere around here and see the mass graves of gums and ironbarks, their bodies stretched out into neat piles to be torched later.

Something inside me hurts every time I see those plumes of smoke rise above the town or drive through a haze on the road. Mum and Dad grew up on separate stations around here and they both talked about the magic of the scrub. The food, the creatures, the hunting. I can picture the little animals that call the scrub home, their bodies lying unmourned and forgotten among all that flame and inside I cry. For them and what we are losing. Every time.

It makes no sense, this mass slaughter. The scientist in me is equally appalled. I'm only sixteen and I know about soil erosion and habitat loss. White people are supposed to be better educated. So why do they keep doing this?

I feel the tears building. Shaking my head I pull myself back into the car. I should've been freaking out. I don't know this place and I sure as hell don't know where I am. A Miller is driving me to God knows where. Instead of looking for escape routes I'm just staring out the window trying not to think of Laney.

We bump up to a gate. Jumping out I run over and swing it open for the car, pulling it shut and taking extra care to latch it tight. The Potters might be pricks but I'm not, and no decent country kid would leave a gate to swing open. I get back in the car and we continue on, finding our way onto a road that's a couple of ruts through long grass. I grab the panic handle and hold on tight to keep myself from bouncing around too much. This 'road' and the gate is how you know you've passed from council land onto private property. Once upon a time the shire had been filled to the brim with rich property owners that would've paid for their own roadwork, but that was back in Nan and Pop's day when it was all dirt anyway. When the money they didn't have to pay their slaves went in their back pockets.

Like most places around here this one is hilly. You can't see much but those open graveyards where trees should stand. We're headed straight for the base of a mountain. I've never seen it before but I don't need to ask which one it is. At least here the trees aren't totally decimated, rising up around us like sentries. I'm not sure whether they're there to protect or to warn, but the closer we get to that hill, the more freaked out I'm feeling. The track comes to a little open area where you can see people have done U-turns. The end of the line for us too, because from here and beyond the trees, the mountain towers before us. Sam pulls over and stops.

With the engine off the silence feels oppressive.

'I've never been out here without Mum and Dad before,' Sam murmurs.

'I think this is close to where Ty said they parked,' Rhi's tiny voice comes over the back seat.

A sense of dread is building. I have to escape it.

Stepping out of the car, I fight the urge to hug myself. The foreboding is rolling down from the hills. Part of me wants nothing to do with this, just back out now, cry foul and be the little kid trusting the adults to deal with it. My strong conviction is deserting me. That annoying inner voice keeps asking – what do we even hope to achieve out here? We've driven out to a place we've been warned never to go on the whim of a woman who's so psychologically damaged she regularly loses touch with reality. Plus two thieves, who were so bad at it they got caught. And to do what? Stand by a car and look around?

I hear Sam's door open and close. Rhi hasn't moved, other than to wind down her window. All the doubts and questions inside me are diving over her face. The urge to get back in the car is intense.

'Tace.' Sam's voice comes from across the top of the car. He's looking at me with a steady faith. 'Aunty said we had to be here. So just be here.'

I used to have that kind of faith in Nan. Unshakeable. Having that disappear had destroyed the bedrock of confidence I'd had inside, the core of who I was went out the window and I had to find something to replace it. Science is logical. If I can hypothesise it, prove its existence through experiments, it is true. My logical mind is telling me clearly that I've been operating on instinct and I need to stop this headlong rush forwards and *think*.

'What if she's wrong?' I blurt out.

'If ya didn't believe her, then what are we doin ere?' I thought he'd be angry, but he just seems confused. I don't blame him, I am too. I'd pushed to be here. But now there's no one to fight with, I have to listen to my own doubts.

'Tace,' Rhi asks through the window. 'Let's just leave, ay? This place don't feel right.'

I take a breath and shove it down where the things I can't deal with go.

'We're ere now, might as well look around.'

'Tace.' I hear the fear in her voice and smile reassuringly. I've been such a bitch to her and Rhi doesn't deserve it. Not really … not most of the time … not this time anyway.

'You don't have to come, Rhi. We won't be long.'

Looking at Sam I raise an eyebrow. 'Which way you reckon?'

'Homestead's that way.' He points east. 'From what Dad says it should be a fair ways.'

'So they'd ave cut that way?' The mountain leers at us from my left as I face the way he's pointing. I can feel the relief pouring off me at just the idea of not walking closer to it.

He shakes his head. 'She's your twin. You tell me.'

God I wish he hadn't said that.

My head wants me to walk towards the house, search the ground, anything but what my gut was saying. Somehow even facing the Potters seems less scary.

I snort at myself in disgust. Science says there isn't anything out here scarier than a dingo, or emus with chicks … maybe a scrubber if it felt like being a mongrel. Gut feelings don't count for anything. I need to think this through.

If I let childhood fears dictate my choices, then I'm being irrational. Possibly to the point of endangering my sister. My feet point towards the hill and I take a step forwards.

'Why that way?' Sam's voice has gone up a bit and I smile.

'Not sure, come on.'

The crunching of my feet through dirt is the only sound until I reach the first tree. All the breath I'm holding rushes out when I hear Sam's footsteps crunching behind me.

'Wait!'

A car door opens, slamming as a panicked Rhi rushes up to my side. She really moves. I can see shame all over her face as she blushes.

'Ya not leavin me ere alone!'

I nod and start walking again. I'm too busy fighting my own nameless dread to make fun of hers.

'We've only got a couple-a hours till sundown, better get a move on.' Sam's reluctance is clear, but still he turns to that mountain. I'm grateful. I don't think I can force myself forwards alone.

Reaching the tree line we all hesitate. The shadows stretch out over us. Trees are comforting and feel like home, except for here. Right now they feel menacing, concealing horrible secrets. I push through. The temperature cools under those trees. A thick canopy branches out above us, one of the only untouched places I've seen recently, blocking out the light and making it feel almost twilight. Through the gloom, the conical shape of the mountain sits. Waiting. All the colours are muted, even the bird calls are absent. There's a stillness that doesn't feel right. Goosebumps race over me and I remind myself of the science, that the lack of sun will make the temperature drop – nothing else.

Rhi's arm finds its way through mine; her whole body presses against me as we walk. I pretend it's only her doing the holding. We might've been tiptoeing for all the noise we make. The world and us – we hold our breaths.

Two hours later and I am still creeped out by the place, but we haven't come across anything but more trees and a lot of rocks. At some point you adjust to your fear. I mean, there's only so long you can hold your breath, right? Climbing uphill for that long leaves me hot and sweaty, and that chill that was so bone-deep before isn't even on my radar now. I am damn uncomfortable, frustrated and annoyed with everyone.

Rhi let me go at some point and we've even stopped walking so close, spreading out and looking around, but always staying within eyesight. The climb was rough, with jagged rocks scattering the slope, making it impossible to walk normally. We hold on to sharp edges, lever ourselves onto boulders, drag each other over the top sometimes. We see nothing but trees, stone and dirt.

It's a difficult climb with dim light, but when the sunlight weakens further, Sam points us back to the car. He takes us around and down a separate slope though. No point covering the same ground twice.

My heart keeps squeezing, like a bratty kid that wants you to keep 'playing'. No way am I staying here when it gets dark, so I sure as shit am not spending the night either. I move along in silence. I'm not even trying to look around anymore. Our pace picks up as the sunlight fades faster.

We finally make it back to where we parked. Stepping out of the tree line, Sam puts on the brakes and Rhi gasps. My head jerks up. There is something to be afraid of alright, and not the illogical, nameless thing I've been battling in my imagination. There's a massive Dodge parked beside us, and Sam's car now sports three men lounging over it. This is real and far scarier.

All of us freeze, like we've spotted a big Brahman bull between us and the car. Maybe if we're still it won't charge. But it's already too late and we know it.

None of us are strangers in this odd little tableau. We know each other by name and reputation, one of them has even been at school with my cousins. They said Eric wasn't a bad bloke back then, most of the girls were after him because he was hot, but instead of leaving town after school he stayed. Maybe he spent too long out here with the others because now he's a raging racist too. The silence beats at us.

'Now what would a bunch of Abos be doin' out here on *our* land?' Dan Potter snarls from his perch on the roof of the Holden. Nobody says anything good about Eric's older brother. He's the type who'll take shots at black kids with slug guns, although the cops always says there's no 'proof' of that. Never mind we can identify all the local cars in town by the sound of their engines, let alone the make and model. The statement of a bunch of blackfullas isn't ever proof enough.

'Maybe they're tryin' to find a place to sneak around?' Eric laughs. 'He's a Miller and those two are Thomsons; they're all

172

fuckin' dead.' He's sprawled across Sam's hood looking bored. The others' eyes drill into us, but Eric barely seems to be paying attention.

'Or maybe they're tryin' to find a way to claim this place for themselves?' Mick Franks straightens from his spot against the passenger side door.

He's old enough to be my father, has the brains of a fifteen-year-old during puberty and is one of the workers out here. Rumour is he's doing some cattle duffing for them to help pay the bills too.

If I wasn't so scared I would scoff at his words. All the property owners are paranoid we're out to get their land. I feel a sick thrill at the idea of them living in panic that someone could roll in and take it out from under them. Karma.

Sam steps forwards, drawing all eyes to him. 'We were just goin for a walk.'

'Bullshit!' Dan's face twists and I see something ugly. He isn't just pissed we're trespassing, he's enjoying himself.

'You're right.' I stand shoulder to shoulder with Sam. 'We came out to find my sister.'

Mick laughs. 'Why? That little slut's hitched a ride on someone out of town so she wouldn't have to face trespassin' charges.'

I swallow my fury at their words. We're trespassing too, and I'd seen for myself the beating that Tyrone and Clinton had copped. We aren't safe and I've put us right in the middle of it.

'There's way too many boongs out here lately.' Mick glances over his shoulder at Dan and I hear the smile before I see it. 'Maybe another example would stop more comin' here in their dirty bombs?'

173

Dan grins and jumps off the roof. The sound it makes as he hops down makes me wince. 'Yeah, maybe a worse one to put 'em off for good?' Both men move forwards, relishing the violence.

Sam shifts subtly in front of me. Rhi slides up to my side and grabs my hand, squeezing it tight. We all know not to run from predators. My eyes flick to the ground searching for a stick or rock, but away from the trees there isn't much around. I don't want to turn my back to go looking and leave Sam and Rhi alone.

Sam's family are fighters from way back when the boxing tents would come through. They drew all the mob in, not just for the prize money. It was the only time our men could stand toe to toe with the whitefullas and not go to gaol for it. The Millers were legends under those tents (although I'll never admit that out loud), but there's no way Sam can take on two full-grown men alone. We all know they won't fight fair. They'll double or triple-bank him and then turn on us girls.

My breath's coming fast, but I force it to calm. Fear won't help and it will only encourage them. Mum always meets hate and violence with anger. I've seen her use it like a shield and a battery to fuel herself. Fear can't help me, but fury might.

'Wow, what heroes,' I scoff, leaning around Sam's shoulders to look at them. 'Two big hairy arses against one high school boy and two little girls, bet you feel like real men.' I curl my lip with disdain, doing my best impression of Mum when she's forced to interact with someone she considers scum, like the cops.

Rhi's hand tightens so much I have to force my expression to stay in place. Sam sends me a frown. Neither of them are happy with me, but I can't see another way out. Running isn't an option; all they'd have to do is sit on the car and wait us out. My words have stopped their forward motion. They look like hunting dogs facing prey that has suddenly turned and attacked.

'Is this how you rednecks get your kicks, goin after teenagers? What's wrong, boys, can't take on our uncles and cousins without gettin flogged?' I move around Sam, chest up, mocking face in place. Rhi won't let go of my hand so she's forced to come with me. Sam doesn't move, just keeps staring hard at me like he's trying to mentally shut my mouth.

'Isn't it sad? A bunch of grown-arse men stoopin to this level. No wonder yas can't get a woman between yas.'

Dan jerks. 'Fuck you, what would a little gin like you know?'

I give my best bitchy grin. 'Guess I hit a nerve. You know it's not too late to stop being a prick. Maybe then you could keep a woman.'

It's a low blow. Dan's fiancée ran off with a Hogarth fulla last year. The fact he was black hadn't helped anything, and Dan knew everyone was laughing at him, especially his own mates.

'I'll kill you!' He steps menacingly forwards.

I use my shoulder to keep Sam at bay and push Rhi back so hard she goes over onto her bum.

'Go on then, hit me you coward! No real man would raise his hand to a woman, let alone a little girl.' Masculine pride wars on his face. He can't decide if he wants to hit me more than he wants to prove his maleness and disdain. I almost have him, till Mick ruins it.

'You gonna let some little Abo whore tell you what makes a man? Or you gonna show her like that last one?' Dan starts forwards again and I have to scuffle with Sam to keep him back. I get jack of it and turn on him.

'Stop it!' we shout. I don't really know what I'm doing, but I'm not going to hide behind anyone and let them take the consequences for my plan. Sam's fear for me is eroding my bravery, letting my own fear leak back in. I have to shore it up and hold it all in. Fight till the last.

'Tace!' Rhi's scream has me turning and I feel the knuckles brush my cheekbone. Dan's massive fist doesn't land. I'd turned in time. It's enough to send me staggering back. Sam swings at Dan. This one lands and Dan wobbles backwards as Mick runs up. He comes in hard. Sam's already under his fist and landing a gut punch. I can see Dan straightening, ready to join the fight.

Spinning on my heel I sprint to the tree line. I saw something back here, something big. Solid. Fuelled by anger I run to where I remember seeing it. I was looking so hard at the ground I can't have been wrong!

More whacking sounds as fists met flesh. I have wings on my feet and my heart in my throat as I spot the massive tree limb that's been brought down by a lightning strike. The tree looks dead but it's recent enough that the shattered limbs are still whole and strong. Using my entire weight, I wrench a thick limb off. I blink and am back in the clearing. Sam's on the ground, the two men laying into him with their massive boots. Rhi is screaming. Eric spots what I'm carrying and jumps off the car. Too late. I race up behind Mick, lining him up like a softball, and swinging for home. There's a sickening sound like a watermelon hitting cement and he drops.

Dan is on me, tackling me to the ground. I cop a mouthful of gravel and land on top of the branch. He tries to rip it away, grabbing my hair and wrenching it. I jerk my head back, cracking his nose with my skull. He lets go of the branch and raises his clenched fist. I brace as Rhi comes screaming in. I feel her hit Dan, see her hand grab his arm and hold on. I let go of the branch and land an elbow to his gut. His breath rushes out and he rolls further over, holding me with his full weight while he tries to deal with Rhi. I can't see what she's doing but it must hurt because he's swearing a blue streak.

Dan's weight lifts and I immediately flip over onto my back, legs raised and ready, searching for Rhi. Sam has her wrapped in his arms, while Eric holds Dan back. I can't look at Mick's still form.

Dan wrestles with his brother, still swearing, although not much of it makes sense. I find my feet but stay crouched, waiting. Sam gives me a look that says to stay down, but fuck that. I am a Thomson woman. I pull the branch to my side and grip it double-handed, ready to swing.

'Fuckin' hell, Dan, we gotta get Mick to the hospital!'

Eric's shout finally reaches Dan and he stops fighting to get to me. We all look over at their stockman. Dan turns back to me, and I'm grateful for Eric. 'You little bitch! You wait.'

'Wait for what?' I stand, ignoring the pain and how I wobble a bit on my feet. 'You attacked a bunch of underage kids ya silly fuckin moron. Not even the cops could help you on this one.'

It was a blatant lie. The cops can and had ignored a lot of bad shit. Dan isn't exactly smart, but he'd figure it out if I give him time.

'But it's not the cops you wanna worry about. It's our mobs.' I nod at Sam. We're the two biggest families in town, everyone knows it. 'Word gets out you did this and it won't matter what the cops say, you won't be able to step foot off your place again. Who knows, maybe revenge on you will be what ends the war between the Millers and the Thomsons.'

And there it is. The fear of us, of what we can do as a people when we put our minds to it. Community politics and infighting aside, we back each other.

'Dan, she's right! She's the fucking golden girl of the Thomson mob; you'll have 'em all out for us. And Toni's fucking psychotic about her boys.'

Sam smirks with pride at that one. 'Don't forget my brothers and father.' That they mentioned the mother first tells you how unhinged that woman can be.

'Fine!' Dan yells. He shrugs out of Eric's loosening arms and gives me the evil eye. Eric goes straight for Mick and checks him over. I hold back my concern as they lift him up and drag him to the Dodge. He's a massive man, and they struggle to get him in the back seat. Rhi, Sam and I stay frozen in place, watching.

They pile into the car, Eric behind the wheel, and chuck a U-turn. As they drive past Dan's eyes never leave mine.

We watch the Dodge bounce along that excuse for a track. As it crests a rise and disappears, a sigh goes around the clearing. Then we're sprinting as one for the car, jumping in and taking off.

'Slow down, Sam, we don't want to catch up to em.'

He eases off the accelerator. We stay tense and watchful. There are a few tracks along here that they could've veered onto, a few places they could be waiting. We bounce and watch. Sam's knuckles stand out bright white against his brown skin.

Only after the tyres hit pavement, only after we find our way onto the highway again, does it hit. Rhi's quiet sobs from the back cut me. Sam squeezes the wheel harder, like he's trying to crush it. My hands start shaking, the tremors spread up my arms and through my whole body. I double over my knees and force myself to take slow even breaths.

'You okay?' Sam's question comes out through clenched teeth.

I nod my head with no clue if he saw it. 'You?'

'Yeah.'

I snort. *And the award for biggest liar goes to …*

I take a final deep breath and count it out before forcing myself to sit up.

'We need to get cleaned up. Head to the river.' He nods and I turn to check on Rhi. Her sobs have stopped but she's still shaking. 'You okay, cuz?' Her tear-bright eyes look at me blankly. Her teeth are chattering.

'I thought you'd left me,' she whispers. I reach over the back and grab her hand in mine, looking her dead in the eye.

'Never! You hear me Rhiannon Louise Thomson, not ever!' My answer is absolute and unshakeable. She sobs again but a laugh is mixed in with it. She squeezes my hand and lets go. We head to the safest place any of us could think of – our river.

Day 4, Twilight

I start cataloguing my injuries as Sam drives. My cheek is aching, I have gravel rash around my mouth and I've bitten my tongue. There are scrapes along my hands and arms where I landed, and my scalp is hurting from the hair-pulling. Everything is stinging, but there's nothing too drastic. My clothes fared better, they're dirty but no rips or holes that I can find yet. There are a lot of marks that will need to be explained. The man-sized problem that's probably at the hospital by now is a worry for later.

— *I did what I had to.*

We make it to the river with no further assaults.

The spot Sam picks isn't one I've been to before, but I'm glad. It'll mean less chance of running into anyone out doing some fishing or swimming. The sun is setting in full red glory as we pile out. I go straight to Rhi and look her over.

'Did he hurt you?' My question starts her sobbing again. I cuddle her close and watch Sam move carefully over to the riverbank.

'Sam?' He finds a spot he seems happy with and lowers himself down. 'Sam, you're startin to freak me out.'

'I might need help gettin this shirt off,' he mumbles.

Cupping Rhi's chin I pull back and peer into her face. 'Ya right, cuz?'

She nods between hiccups, but I still do another once over. A few scrapes and dirty clothes is all I see, thank God. But there are fresh bruises forming that make me want to cry. I go to the car and pull out my port. I'd dropped it there just a few hours ago, but it feels like a month. I pull out the little pack of tissues I keep around for my hay fever, and my water bottle. Stepping up to Sam, I look him over. His face is a mess and I can see bruises and marks on all of his exposed skin. His eyes look a bit glazed. He's in pain. My guilt ramps even higher.

Crouching in front of him, I wet down a few tissues and start wiping at the blood and dirt I can see. 'Where's it hurt worst?'

Grabbing my wrist he stops my gentle wiping and looks me in the eye. 'Are you really okay?'

I manage a smile. 'I think Mick got the worst of it.' My voice breaks a bit but I cough it back and we pretend I have a scratch in my throat. Sam stares at me for a while longer, before letting go and looking down at his hands.

'I managed to protect my head, it's probably just bruising.'

I nod. 'Let's take a look anyway. Lift your arms.'

Taking hold of the bottom of his shirt, I lift it off him as gently as I can. Looking down at his chest I can't help the sympathetic wince. His dark skin is covered in rapidly rising bruises, new ones forming fast over yellowed older ones. I stand and circle around to his back. It's even more mottled here where he hadn't been able to protect himself. He's right about there being no cuts but there is plenty enough. I place a careful hand on the least bruised area on his shoulder.

'I'm so sorry, Sam.'

He covers my hand with his own and squeezes. 'It's not, you know.' He glances at me over his shoulder and smiles at my confusion. 'It's not your fault.' Then he seems to get uncomfortable and turns back around, dropping his hand. 'Can I get some of them tissues, Tace?'

I set him up with a heap before heading to the water's edge. I squat down to splash water over my face. The stinging gets a lot worse, but I make sure to get everything. The river water isn't as pure these days; Pop says it's all the weirs and dams they keep building upstream. But it will do till I get home and find some disinfectant.

I splash over my hands and arms as well, getting as much of the dirt off as I can. Sam joins me. At some point Rhi's sobs dry up. I hear her stand and come up behind me, figuring she needs a wash too.

Hands on my back shove me headfirst into the water. It's deep enough I go all the way in and come up spluttering and coughing. Rhi stands, hands on hips, laughing her susoos off. She should've known to run. I grab her around the ankles, yanking her in before she can scream. I hold her head under for a bit as punishment.

'Oi!' She splashes at me once I finally let her up.

'Don't dish it out if you can't take it, cuz,' I mock.

Sam is laughing and groaning in pain. Rhi and I share a look, before grabbing one leg each and dragging him in.

We end up wrestling for a bit like that, splashing and carrying on. Laughing out our relief at having made it through. There's something so normal about it, playing in the river. We might not have done it together before, but it's what every mob does. Sam's too sore to do much, so it's only a short play. We stay in a bit longer to rub ourselves clean and get the mud out of our shoes.

Semi-presentable we climb out, squeezing out as much water as we can. My energy is draining fast and the last of the light is fading. The mob will be home soon. How're we gonna explain this?

If the sun had been out in force we'd have been dry in minutes. As it is, the humidity will keep us damp for a while yet. Sam says it's cool for us to get in the car still damp so we climb back in.

Bruises have begun to bloom brightly on all of us. We'll all have pretty body art tomorrow.

'So what's the story?' Rhi sits forwards between our seats and checks our faces.

I chew on my lip. 'You and me were swimming all afternoon. I guess we all … got in … a fight?'

Rhi giggles. 'Do ya really wanna send our mob after Sam? They'd kill im!'

'Not if I started it!'

Sam opens his mouth to protest but Rhi lifts a finger and shushes him. 'You're such a goody-goody, no one would believe you started a fight so it'd end up all Sam's fault. This is why you suck at lying – we need something close to the truth. Why can't we just say that the Potters started it?'

Sam shakes his head. 'The only way they'll keep their mouths shut is if we do. If we let it out that they did this, they'll have Tace charged with assault, and you know whose side the cops'll take.'

We go silent for a bit.

'Okay, Plan B,' Rhi crows. 'Sam, you were out lookin to go for a swim. Tace, you and me were off doin our thing when we got charged by a bull. We got marked up trying to get away from it.'

We're that desperate I think her idea sounds decent.

'I guess … if we maybe had to crawl through barbed wire. And if I fell face first. But what about Sam's face and bruises?'

'Most of those are on his back and that right?'

'And his arms.'

'Right, so if he doesn't go swimming or take his shirt off, then we only have to explain the bruises we can see. Sorry Sam.' Rhi gives his shoulder a sympathetic pat. Not swimming in this weather is pure torture.

He shakes his head at us. 'You don't need to worry about me.'

'What do you mean?' Rhi asks.

'It won't matter if I show up like this.' He says it like it's nothing, but he won't look at us.

Rhi's eyes go wide. She opens her mouth and I am terrified about what's going to come out.

'Alright Sam, if you're sure?' I beat her to it, but I still feel bad. It's like we're only worrying about ourselves when he's the one that has taken the worst of it.

'I'll tell Mum I got into a fight after school, and no one at school will ask.' His voice gets all tight, so I sit back and shut my mouth. It's true too. No one at school even mentioned his black eye. Rhi hasn't asked either, and I can see her thinking about it now. Guilt tightens her jaw. I turn to stare out the window until we come to the edge of town.

'Both of you better duck down,' Sam says. 'I'll take you to the back of the town hall and drop you there. I'd drop you closer to your place, but …'

'No worries, thanks Sam,' Rhi assures him.

We make it without any problems and Rhi gets out of the car. I stop with my hand on the door, before turning back.

'Sam.' I can't think of what to say. 'Thanks.'

He nods and I follow Rhi out. There aren't any words that'd do it anyway.

As he drives off I turn to face Rhi. She's smirking at me.

'What?' I know I sound defensive.

'Stacey and Sammy sittin in the tree, K-I-S-S-I-N-G.' She finishes with a squeal as I go to grab her. She dances out of reach. 'First comes love, then comes marriage.'

'Then comes the floggin from the Millers and the Thomsons.' My sarcasm gets through where my horrible rhyming doesn't.

'Yeah true,' Rhi muses.

That's all I need. Rhi is an eternal romantic, falling in love as fast as she falls out of it and never regretting anything. She's always after me to open myself up to 'possibilities'. I usually say something about keeping away from the 'possibilities' of getting an STD or 'possibly' getting with someone who turns out to be related to me. I can wait till I'm out of this town to get a man, there are just too many relatives and racists here.

'Come on, Mum and them will be home soon. You can get into some of my clothes.'

We head up the street and into the house. As always it's unlocked with all the windows wide open to let the heat of the day out. What shocks me is the note on the table.

185

Babe, we stopped off to get food. Gone back out. Left some chicken and salad in the fridge for you. Stay safe and INSIDE. Love you xox

'Holy shit, you are one lucky cow.'

'Ya mean "we"? I wouldn't be the only one in trouble ya know.'

Rhi gives me her trademark cheeky grin and I pretend not to notice it's still a bit wonky.

'You get in the shower first, I'll get us some clothes.'

When she's finished I toss her a fresh towel and my most comfortable pyjamas. My cousin has gone above and beyond for me today, and the guilt is catching up. I pull out dinner while she dresses. As expected, there's heaps. My throat closes and I blink back tears while I divide up the food and set the kettle off. Thankfully Rhi is quick so we dive in.

'Want to stay over tonight?' I ask between mouthfuls.

'Yeah cool.'

After we clean up the kitchen I go for my shower. Despite the heat, I turn the water to hot. I need to beat some of the aches out of me.

Still, I never linger in the shower. I can hear Nan going off about water wastage even now. I dry off, dress and call out to Rhi to help me with the Savlon. While I wait I stare at the bruises and scrapes all over me. Mum is going to kill me.

Rhi busts in and takes over. She does the clucking thing a lot better than me, so I let her fuss. It feels nice. She checks that each cut is clean before pasting me up. I can't help but wonder who's helping Sam with his cuts.

'Ya could always go help im,' Rhi says sweetly. 'I'm sure he'd love that.'

I roll my eyes and damn myself for saying my thoughts out loud. 'You're a dickhead.'

She laughs at me but lets it go.

As soon as she's happy we go to my bedroom, crawl into my double bed and lie on our sides, whispering to each other like we used to.

'Were you scared?' she asks.

'Yeah. You?'

'Yeah, but ya didn't seem scared.' She hesitates. 'I … I'm not a coward normally.'

My heart softens. 'I know that and ya still aren't.'

'But—'

'But nuthin. Ya jumped on Dan Potter's back for me, nough said. What'd ya do to him anyway?'

Rhi blushes and my eyes go wide. Rhi never blushes.

'I … I um, I poked im in the ring.' There's a long pause.

'What?'

She cringes. 'I poked my finger up his ring.'

Laughter rocks the bed as I lose my mind. Tears stream down my face and I roll around, clutching my stomach. Rhi whacks me on the side in offence, but it isn't long before she joins in. We laugh long and hard till our sides and throats ache.

'It hurts, it hurts,' Rhi groans through her guffaws.

'You're a mad bitch,' I gasp. 'You wanna go wash your finger with Dettol.'

'Nah, I already found Aunty's bleach.'

That sends us off again.

I fall asleep with my cousin, both of us chuckling, sometimes sending us off into more laughter. I can't wait to tell Laney.

Day 4, Midnight

Foul tasting, squirming things fill my mouth. I want to spit them out but someone clamps their hands around my jaw, digging their nails in as I put up a token resistance. Their fingers pinch my nose and I am forced to swallow. When they finally let go I gag, my body fighting to expel what I've only just gotten down. I feel something brush my lips and recoil, but the hands are insistent, returning to dig in again and force my mouth open.

Ice-cold water hits my tongue and I forget about everything else. I gulp it down as much as the hands allow, but far sooner than I am ready the water vanishes. I moan.

I remember falling. I remember needing to get out, to go home. But the need to explore is gone now, broken under the weight of hunger and thirst. I've never felt like this.

None of this makes sense. I haven't seen a single Potter. No one talks to me, or asks any questions. It's left me too much time to think. To worry about what was happening. To question why I'd done it to begin with. Troy made it sound so adventurous – a midnight raid, a run on country that should have been ours. I never even got to wear the present he gave me before our trip out to the Potters'. All of it sits on my chest and suffocates me.

I force my eyelids open. As soon as I do I regret the impulse. The darkness holds me still.

The hands are the first sign I'm not alone, other than when I'd made contact with my fist, which I am not going to think about, especially now. Since the fall and the frantic search for some identifying feature, which turned up nothing but a few rocks to stumble over, I eventually came to a stop.

There is no night or day here, just dark. I don't know where I am, and I'm too scared to call out. It occurs to me that maybe something is wrong with my eyes, and it isn't pitch black at all. If that is true I don't know what else to do. At some point I gave up searching. I shed tears that I can't afford and continued to wait in the dark. Only the soft sounds of this person moving about tells me I'm not deaf. They never speak. Maybe they can't? I'm desperate to hear another voice, to hear anything other than my own fears.

'Who ...' My voice emerges, crackling like a dead leaf dropped and stepped all over. 'Who ...'

It is all I can manage, and the frustration leaves me in the form of more precious liquid running over my cheeks. The hands reach out to brush them away, scraping claws where fingers should be. I flinch. Fingers press on my jaw and this time I voluntarily open my mouth. The water returns. Cold bliss flows over my tongue and I gulp it down. It vanishes again far too quickly, but now I can speak.

'Who ... are ... you?' A creaking groan, matching the tacky feeling of my lips and tongue. I wait in the silence. Wait and hope.

The hands return to brush my face, a harsh texture to them, like a wolfhound's rough fur, but all over. The hands rub over my cheeks, stopping on my chin, pinching slightly at the tip and angling my head upwards. A slow, reverberating growl begins and at first I think the world is shaking. Two bright red pinpricks of light appear and I rejoice. Is my sight returning?

My eyes slowly adjust, taking so long to focus it almost hurts, I realise what I am looking at just as the soft pinch of my chin turns to a bite and claws spike into my skin. I open my mouth and scream and scream and scream.

The red eyes watch and the world shakes from its growl.

I feel my self rip backwards, away from her. I'm not Laney now, but Tace. I fly through the blackness, exploding out into light. I have seconds to see the cave, the mountain. I know this place.

I jerk awake. Rhi is lying there snoring with her mouth wide open. The room is claustrophobic as the heat presses in. I pull myself up, careful not to wake her and tiptoe into the kitchen. I am so stiff and sore I move like an eighty-year-old with a hunchback. I know it's hot but I feel ice cold.

Tea in hand I head to my steps. I sit on that spot and let go of all my mind is telling me, staring up at the waning moon. I open myself up to the certainty that my twin is alive and waiting for me. I ignore the voice that says I am imagining it, if only for tonight. I know she's out there, I know I have to find her.

It's like watching a horror movie and the black chick heads into the house. Everyone is screaming 'No! Turn back!' but the silly cow goes in anyway. Hopefully the ending will be better for me, but regardless, I have to go find Laney.

The old man in the moon stares down at me with concern.

I whisper into the night air, 'Nan, I need your help.'

I have to go out to Potters' again and I need her with me. It might be easier if I can find whatever is in this house.

That little reminder flicks an unknown switch. Goose-bumps race and suddenly I don't feel safe in *my* spot. A soft rustle in the trees over the garage, a gentle scrape over by the tank stand. Once it would've been okay, but something tells me these aren't normal night sounds.

A silver shape glides through the night air.

My heart stops as the tawny frogmouth lands on the tank. It sits and stares. Its low thrumming call vibrates through my chest and every hair on my body stands on end. Tears fill my eyes, but I don't move. Not yet.

Never run, granddaughter. Sing if you're scared. Nan's words give me strength and TLC's 'Waterfalls' flows out of my mouth without thought. Slowly, so slowly, I stand. I take a step backwards. Up the stairs. Over the doorjamb. One hand creeps around the door and I swing it closed. My hand shakes as I lock it. I feel safe enough to stop singing.

I stand there staring at the door. Listening.

A soft scrape on concrete.

A creak from the bottom step.

My breath churns. I take a step back.

Another.

The steps creak in time with my movements.

Something is pacing me.

A smell hits me. Something musty, damp.

I make it into the kitchen. Drop my cup on the table.

Whatever it is stands on the top step.

The doorknob twitches.

Twists.

I stifle a scream but a whimper slips out.

A low hissing chuckle.

The knob rattles violently.

A huge bang on the door sends me bolting for my room. Throwing on the bedroom light I vault into the bed. Gripping the sheet, I pull it over our heads and stare into Rhi's wide open eyes.

I hold my finger to my lips. We stay like that for ages. Listening.

There's only so long your heart can pump that fast before you start to calm down. The longer we go without hearing anything, the more we relax. It is stifling hot but neither of us lowers the sheet.

Somehow, hours and years later, we fall asleep.

Day 5, Daylight

'Stacey Claire Thomson!'

Mum's scream jerks me up in bed, half asleep and confused. 'Uh?'

My eyes feel like they're filled with chewing gum, all icky and stuck together. I'm sore all over, but worse is the grit in my eyes that says I've had maybe a few hours sleep.

'Why the fuck do ya look like ya been fightin?'

I blush to my roots as a groggy Rhi pokes her head out of the sheets.

'Hey Aunty.' She blinks.

Mum's outraged gasp has me turning to look and I wince. Rhi hasn't gotten off as easy as we hoped. Her big black eye is like an accusation. And if that's what she looks like, I don't want to look in a mirror. Somehow the bull story is looking more and more like … bull. Rhi goes from staring in horror at my face, to looking innocently into my mother's.

'Well, Aunty, see it's like this, we were out at the river dryin off when this bloody big bull come along and chased us. We tried to run but ended up fallin down that steep hill out there, and, well …' She waves at my face, not realising her own isn't great either.

Mum's eyes move to mine and I know that story isn't going to fly. I hold my breath and wait. Her lips twist.

'Ya got five minutes to get ya arses in the kitchen. I'm gonna need a coffee to deal with this one.' She turns and marches out of the room, pausing to duck her head back in the door. 'And before you think about tellin me that shit again the two of ya better stop and look in the mirror.' Then she's gone.

Rhi and I exchange a look. 'Well, at least we tried.' Hell hath no fury like a Thomson mother disobeyed, and we both know it.

The mirror is way worse than I expected. My eye and cheek are more bruised than Rhi's, with some artful cuts and gravel rash thrown in. She presses up against the glass touching her eye mumbling, 'He must've got a shot in. I didn't even feel it.'

'That's what adrenalin'll do. We look like we got roughed up by our pimp.'

'How're we gonna go outside like this?!' Rhi wails.

'At least it's the weekend and I don't ave ta go ta school like this.' I touch my eye gingerly. I don't want people seeing me like this either, but I'm more worried about the reaction of the woman in the kitchen. 'Time to face the music.'

I wash my face, wishing I could wipe away the evidence as easily, and head out. I give Rhi her due, she stays right there with me.

We trudge into the kitchen; it's now a firing squad.

'Aunty, I gotta get home, Mum needs me to—'

I glare at Rhi. She's already edging her way towards the door when Mum speaks.

'Stop. Right. There.' She casts the evil eye over both of us. 'Sit.'

We drop into chairs and I stare at my hands.

'Speak!'

'I'm not a bloody dog,' I mumble.

'No, but ya act with about as much sense. And if ya don't start talkin I'mma treat ya like one.'

I don't see a way out of this so I pick at my nails and start, hoping something ingenious will occur to me. 'Well, we went out yesterday, in the afternoon.'

'No shit, Sherlock.' Mum folds her lips together. It isn't hard to see where Laney and I get our mouths from. 'Where did you go?'

I hesitate, not quite able to spit it out, but nothing but the truth is pushing forwards. 'Potters' place,' I whisper and duck.

It's like expecting a volcano to explode and getting nothing. Silence. I peek through my fringe and immediately regret it. It's hard to say what colour Mum's face is. Her brown skin is normally this lovely shade that reminds me of Nan's. Right now it looks more like the burnt umber I used in art class last year.

'It was my idea, Aunty, I wanted to—' Rhi tries to deflect what's coming but I shake my head at her.

'I made Rhi come. I wanted to go lookin for Laney. It's, it's those dreams, Mum. It feels like they're pointin me somewhere.'

'Ya went to Potters' place? At night?'

'Not night—'

She cuts me off with a slice of her hand. 'Ya went to Potters' place at ALL.'

I wince.

'And ya went even after I asked ya not to go out. After I *begged* ya to stay *safe*.' Her voice breaks and I realise there are worse things than my mother's fury. Her pain and betrayal reach across the table and suffocate me. She takes a moment to breathe. 'Keep goin.'

'We headed to where they reckon Laney and them parked that night, just to see if we could find anythin. Nuthin happened Mum, I swear, nuthin! And we got out of there before sundown.' I rush to explain myself, to somehow make her understand that I am being safe.

'So the trees come up and bashed ya then?'

My eyes drop.

'Would this have anything to do with Mick Franks lyin up in the hospital with a concussion?'

I look at her again. 'Is he … is he okay?'

'For now.' Her reply isn't supposed to comfort me, but it does. I don't like the man but I didn't want to hurt anyone. I'd only wanted to protect Sam.

'He jumped us when we were walkin back. I … I picked up a branch and whacked im with it.'

Mum's eyes turn brutal. 'Good. Did he hurt you?'

She's looking at both of us now. I know what she's really asking so I look her dead in the eye. 'Not more than you see, Mum, I swear.'

She lets out another big breath. Not a sigh but that moment when you're holding it in anticipation or fear. The answer you've been dreading comes and the worst doesn't happen, so the breath rushes to escape you.

'At least ya listened to *some* things.'

There are rules around fighting in our town. Rules that you have to play by if you want respect, and one of the firmest ones is to never, ever pick up anything in a fight.

It's fists or nothing. And at the end of the fight it's supposed to be done, finished. I'm not sure when people stopped living by them, but now they do all kinds of dirty things in fights – double-banking, holding grudges, men fighting women. It's disgusting. The lowest dog act, Uncle Joe calls it. Mum made us promise that if anyone's looking to fight us and it isn't fair, we will pick something up for them. Since I was facing three men I hadn't even thought about it. Without a weapon I might as well have rolled over and taken what was coming.

Mum isn't finished. 'They shoulda stitched the dingo up without anaesthetic. Just wait till your Uncle hears about this!'

'Mum, you can't!' I gasp, my head flying up. 'If it gets out he'll have me charged with assault.'

The silence stretches. Mum knows the score better than us. Her thirst for revenge turns to exasperation. 'Where did ya even go? Don't you know how dangerous that place is?'

'Umm … to one hill there,' I mutter it, but she leans closer.

'What hill?'

'Some big one Aunty, how're we sposed to know what whitefullas call it.' Rhi waves a dismissive hand.

Mum's hand slams down on the table and we jump.

'Please tell me,' she says in a calm, reasonable voice, 'that you did not go to *that* mountain on the Potter property?'

Rhi and I share a look. Mum lets out a quiet scream, which is quite possibly the weirdest sound I've ever heard her make, before jumping to her feet to pace. She's taking deep, audible breaths.

'Do you think your grandparents warned ya away from there for fun?' She finally looks at us and the rage is real.

'No Mum, and I wouldn't ave. But ... Laney.' I lift my hands and shrug, feeling helpless.

'Oh ya better believe *that* little excuse isn't gonna save ya.' She eyes Rhi. 'Either of ya. How'd ya even get out there?'

'We walked.'

'We rode.'

We look at each other in horror.

'Out with it! If I find out ya lied about any of this, Stacey Thomson, ya dead.' The casual way she says it disturbs me. Ordinarily a threat will be delivered with fury, this is just stated as fact.

'Mum ... I ... please don't be upset. He helped us and protected us. If he hadn't been there who knows what those cow-cockies woulda done!'

'Stacey ...' The warning growl is all I'll get. My head goes down.

'Sam Miller drove us out,' I mumble so quietly that I think for a second she hasn't heard me.

She stares down at me. I can feel her gaze drilling into my head.

'You've been talkin to a Miller? Ya got in a car with Toni Miller's son?!' Her voice rises in volume and pitch with each question.

'It was my fault, Aunty, I got a crush on im.'

The horror on my face is only outdone by Mum's as we both stare at my cousin, our jaws flapping.

'I ... I like him. He's nice. And he protected us yesterday.' She stops talking, a blush running over her cheeks.

'You kids. Ya want to send me mad.' Mum is talking to herself. 'Every taboo we have, almost every single one, ya violated. I don't even know if there's a punishment strong enough.' She dropped back into her chair and puts her head in her hands. 'I suppose we could get out the nullah nullahs, do it the old way, but ya've already been hit around pretty good. Mum woulda known what to do.'

I'm not sure how I feel about Rhi's sudden declaration, but I can't help feeling amused at Mum's reaction. Rhi has well and truly taken the wind out of her sails. A grin twitches at my lips just as Mum's hands open and she gets a good look at my face.

'Think this is funny, ay? You leadin your cousin to Potters', to danger, getting flogged up and all with a Miller boy in tow. One your cousin is after!' It's not entirely clear which of those things is worse to her.

'No, Mum, it's not funny, I'm sorry.' Her glare doesn't let up and I can feel the wheels turning.

'Sam Miller ... That's the one lookin after May all the time. This is to do with what your grandfather told ya, isn't it?'

All the funny walks out of the room and I go back to fidgeting. Laney would've cursed me for being such a bad liar. There's a long pause while Mum thinks it through some more. She isn't silly, dammit.

'I'm still furious with both of you. I will be talkin to your mother, Rhiannon Louise. She's got a better imagination than me anyway, and we'll be workin out a punishment to fit the monumental stupidity of what you done. Something worthy of just how much you've betrayed our trust.' I wince and am sure Rhi does too. Decree made, Mum sits back in her chair and sighs. 'I can see ya won't let this go, Tace, and now you've gone and drug your cousin into it.'

'Mum please. What would you do if Aunty Mel went missing? Or Uncle Joe, Aunty Fern, any of them?' Tears in my eyes, I beg her to understand. Her lips twist.

'And that's the problem, isn't it. Cos I'd be out lookin for my sister too.'

I feel like I've won a huge victory, for about two seconds. 'But I wouldn't be doin any of this! You're runnin around half-cocked with no idea what you're riskin.'

'Then tell me! Since when have we kept secrets in this family?'

'Since forever, little girl, and you'd do well to remember that.' Her stern voice backs me up in my chair. 'There are things the old fullas will never tell you, things whispered about. And you aren't old enough or mature enough to learn any of it. At the rate you're goin ya might never be ready.'

That hurts my pride a little … or maybe a lot. Everyone says I'm the most mature of my generation.

'You're learnin too well the whitefulla's way, my babe. Knowledge isn't free and given whenever you want it, ya gotta earn it.' Her hard stare pricks me.

'You the one said to get a education!'

'Yeah and maybe that was my mistake. Maybe I was so focused on whitefulla education I forgot to educate you proper way.' She shakes her head. 'Rhi, you better head home to your mother. We'll finish this another night; I got some thinkin to do. Tace, you can take this food up to your grandfather.'

She motions to a plate over on the stove.

Horror fills me. 'You expect me to go out? Like *this*?'

She grins. 'Maybe I found a good punishment after all, ay?'

Walking up to Pop's place I'm freshly showered and dressed in shorts and a hoodie. I'm sweating my ring off, but the hood covers most of my face, and I keep my eyes on the ground. Rhi borrowed the same type of outfit from me before going back to her mother's. We'd taken off as fast as we could before the mob rolled in and saw our faces. I didn't have time to think about what happened last night or what needed to be done. First I have to face Pop with my technicolour skin and no hope of hiding it.

Making it through his front gate I see him in his usual spot, out on the verandah in the shade.

'Hey Pop.' I keep my head low but still give the usual kiss to his cheek. I won't look him in the face. 'Want some tea?'

He grunts at me in a way that means 'yes', so I go about the routine of prepping it. I get the food all in front of him, make us both a cuppa and tuck myself in the chair near his with the least amount of sun on it.

'It's hot, ay.' It's lame but it's all I can think of.

'Hrmm,' he agrees without touching his steak.

I can feel his eyes on me.

'Look your grandfather in the eye, girl,' comes his gruff command.

With a deep sigh I lift my face.

'Holy bloody hell! What appened to you?'

I sigh. If I lie to him Mum will kill me.

'Rhi and me got jumped by Mick Franks and the Potter boys.'

His big bushy brows drop down over his eyes.

'WHAT? What is your uncle and mother doin bout this?'

His deep voice makes the words carry and I could've sworn it bounced around the hills surrounding the town. I sit upright in my chair, hands together, begging.

'Pop, please, ya can't say nuthin! I whacked im with a big stick and he's up at the hospital. If word gets out e'll ave me charged.'

I've never seen my grandfather furious before. He is the most calm, stable person I know. I watch him swallow that fury back down. It's amazing to watch and makes me sad to think about how many other emotions he's had to push down like that before. I sit and wait for his response.

'Ya hit im good?'

'He's got a concussion.'

'He hurt either of you more than that?'

Again, that question that isn't.

'No, Pop, I promise.'

He nods. When he picks up his knife and fork and starts eating his steak, I settle back in my chair with a sigh. The danger has passed, for now. At some point he'll find out we've been out at the Potters' property, and then I'll be in for it. My life is turning into one round of trouble after another.

We sit quietly after that. It isn't just habit, it's communication. Pop doesn't need words sometimes, and neither do most of us. Besides, just being here makes me feel safe; maybe that's why Mum sent me up.

'Need to sleep, granddaughter?'

'Mmm.' I watch him out of the corner of my eye.

'Want to sleep out ere? You'll be right.'

Tears threaten. He can see my tiredness, probably more than that. I tuck my knees into my chest and put my head down onto them.

'Can't,' I mumble.

'It's right, I'm ere,' he promises.

Turning back to his food the silence returns. He'd given his order and considered it done. I'd never disobeyed my grandfather, but I am so terrified to sleep.

'What if I see …' I choke on the words.

'It's right,' he repeats. 'You sleep.'

I close my eyes and rub the wetness on my cheeks with my knees. I am so tired.

As I drift off I feel a hand on my head. Comfort pours from it and I know I am safe. For now.

Day 5, Afternoon

'Granddaughter, time to get up.'

'It's too early,' I murmur, half asleep.

'Work won't wait and you got lots to do.'

'Aww, Nan,' I whine.

My eyes open and for a second she's there, waking me to start my mornings in the garden with her. Then memory returns and crushes me all over again. I sit up, looking around, dazed.

The long shadows stretching across the ground tell me I've slept most of the day away. I wasted an entire day, but I desperately needed that sleep. I can't bring myself to be too angry about it. Rubbing dinghee out of my eyes, I look up to see Pop in his spot. He's reading a newspaper and has a fresh cuppa beside him.

'Sorry, Pop,' I say around a yawn and a stretch.

'Ya needed it. Them dreams keepin ya wake?' He stares at me from under his bushy eyebrows and I can't meet his gaze.

'Yeah. They gettin worse.' I don't want to tell him what was around the house. For the same reason me and Rhi hadn't talked about it this morning. If we talk about it, it makes it all real somehow.

'Well, have ya listened to any of em?' He sounds exasperated, like I've done something stupid.

'Whaddya mean?'

'Your grandmother taught ya better than that,' he spat. 'She be rollin in her grave.'

He snatches up his paper and storms into the house. Still groggy, I watch him in shock. He never talks about Nan like that. I must've really pissed him off. But how the hell am I supposed to listen to nightmares that only left me terrified? Sure, I'd decided to accept they meant something, but it's not like they came with a bloody map!

Half annoyed and half bemused I stand up and stretch out the kinks from sleeping in an upright position. Pop has left his now clean plate on the table, so I pick it up and walk away.

Old people are weird.

If my head wasn't swirling with Laney, I might've been paying more attention to the engine rolling up behind me. A sudden acceleration has my head popping up and I stare at the dark blue commodore bearing down on me. I can see Troy's face over the wheel and, for a blackfulla, he looks pretty red. Rage and fear hit me hard, and I get twisted up in the need to take a swing and run all at the same time. Anger wins, as it always does, and I turn to face him as he pulls up beside me. I curl my lip at him as he bounds out of his car and gets in my face.

'What the fuck do you want?'

'I know it was you,' he spits, moving closer to intimidate me.

All that planning and neither Rhi nor I had thought about what we'd do if he came after me like this.

'Who? The one you left all on her own at Potters'? That would be my twin.'

'Admit it!'

'You first!'

We're yelling into each other's faces and neither of us is backing down. I can see the need to hit me climb into his eyes. I stay high on my anger and thrust my chin up.

'Gorn then. Do it. It'll be the last thing you ever do.'

'Gonna run to ya mob?'

'I won't ave ta.' I drop my voice and lean in. 'Somethin been creepin round your place, Troy?'

His face loses all colour and he stops dead. I'm not even thinking, just hitting the sore points he'd shown me the other night.

'Somethin's been creepin round our place. Like it's lookin for somethin?'

He takes a step back and I follow. I want to chuck the plate I hold at his head, and I would've if it wasn't one of Nan's.

'Whaddya do?' I demand. 'Whaddya drag my sister into?'

'It wasn't supposed to be anything. It's not supposed to be real.'

'But it is and ya got my sister mixed up in it. How could ya do that?'

He flinches like I've hit him and I see a sheen in his eyes that shocks me.

'It was a accident.' His eyes focus on mine and I see the deepest terror coiling inside him. 'Mum said if it was out of the house it'd be better. I didn't mean for them to go after her. I thought if I gave it to Laney they'd leave me alone long enough to go back to Potters' and figure out what ta do. I just wanted em to leave me alone.'

My anger flies away like burnt paper and I see Troy for

the first time. Not as Edna's boy or Laney's man or even one of his mob, but a scared boy. I recognise that fear, I'd felt it. He'd given her something, and it clicked with the dream last night.

'The present you gave to er? What was it? Where'd she put it?'

Looking like I'd pulled a weapon, he sprints back around to the driver's seat and I see my last rational chance of finding Laney run with him.

'Where is my sister?' I scream as he takes off at high speed. He leaves me crying on the side of the road. Begging.

I hold the fear and pain back, swallow it down like Pop had done.

Rational be damned. I'll try anything to find Laney now. Troy might be useless but he'd confirmed giving Laney something. Mad May said I had to search the house and I am starting to think I need to be looking for a necklace of some kind. I don't want to think about what I'll do if I find it.

I get home and found a note on the table waiting for me.

DO NOT LEAVE THIS HOUSE STACEY THOMSON!

I get straight into another round of searching, going back over everything. But it's so hot inside I feel like my skin is going to melt off. In the end I'm forced to admit defeat and temporarily retreat. I'll try again when the heat has backed off.

I have another shower, change my clothes to something breathable and go out to the back to sit where the shade makes things a few degrees cooler. This time I avoid the steps, choosing a chair by the fire instead. I'm there for a while, staring into my tea, wondering what else I can do.

Rhi comes whizzing along in Aunty Mel's car, roaring up the driveway to where she can see me. She hops out and joins me on the chairs.

'Fuck it's hot!'

'Why you got the car?'

'Mum let me have it, she's drivin with Aunty Al.'

'After ya told her what we did?' I'm shocked.

'She's more pissed at Mick, Dan and Eric. Had to do some fast talkin to stop her from stormin up ta the hospital.'

'Gee you're good. What a con job.'

She smirks at me. 'Don't be jealous, cuzzie, we can't all be smooth.'

I laugh and go back to staring into my mug like it holds the answers to all my problems.

'Let's go for a swim out the river,' I declare.

She looks at me strangely. 'Didn't Aunt say ya had to stay put? Or are ya just in the mood for more punishment?'

'Shut up, it's hot and I need to cool down. I can't think!'

She snorts. 'Your problem is you need to think *less*.'

But she hops up and we both get into the car. Rhi is a pretty reliable taxi service when she's in town. I've never been able to get my driver's licence. Laney has hers but getting my opens seems to be the one test I was born to fail.

'Should you leave a note at least?'

I send her a dirty look and she raises both hands. 'Fine, it's your funeral.'

'Is Aunty Mel really not pissed at you?'

Rhi scrunches up her face. 'I didn't say that. We are most definitely in the shit.'

'Well, I guess they can only kill us once.'

'Now you're startin to sound like me.' Rhi laughs. Still, we both know whatever those evil women come up with we'll be hurting for a while.

'What about the Sam thing?' I ask.

'What about it?' She raises her eyebrows but keeps her eyes on the road.

'Didja tell her that it wasn't true?'

'No, why would I?'

My mouth drops open.

'Didja see the six-pack under all those bruises? And those arms … yum!' She gives a little wiggle in her seat. I can't decide what I hate more, that Rhi likes a Miller or that she likes Sam. Which only freaks me out more.

'Are you going to go off about that whole Miller–Thomson thing too?' Rhi asks. 'This isn't Romeo and Juliet. At some point we gotta get over this shit. Maybe us gettin married up would do it.'

I point an accusing finger. 'Now I know ya fuckin with me, ya hate the idea of gettin married up.'

'Not long term, but no harm in some fun, ay? Never keep a man round long, cuz, otherwise they get this idea they can tell ya what to do.' She winks at me and I bite my tongue. It's still sore from yesterday and it hurts enough to distract me from the feelings rolling through me. This is just too confusing for words.

I turn to face out the windshield. 'You got a death wish, cuz.'

209

Rhi is a force of nature. Trying to change her mind is like screaming at the wind to stop. Once she gets something into her head you just have to let it play out, no matter what you think. I've been around to help pick up after a lot of those already and we're only sixteen. Laney is usually the one who tries to talk her out of this stuff, not that it ever works.

I shake my head. If the Thomsons and the Millers don't end up killing each other after this it will be a miracle. But who am I to judge? I'm the one that engineered everything. Rhi has stuck around like the loyal cousin she is, but she's going to cop an epic load of shit for it.

I ignore the little voice inside me that says I'm upset about something else. 'Okay. If that's what ya want. But I'm tellin ya right now this is not a good idea.'

Rhi looks at me in surprise, then pouts. 'Damn, I guess ya really don't like him. What a waste, he's freakin lovely. And I'd finally stop bein the drama-causin cousin.'

Frowning hard at her it finally clicks. 'You troll.' Laughing, I smack her on the shoulder. I'll never admit she hit closer to home than she realises. This is going to the grave with me.

'Come on, lil cuzzie, let's go get wet.' She wiggles both her eyebrows at me.

'You're disgustin.'

Only after we're stretched out in the water do I start to feel settled. It's not just the cool of the water, the trees stirring around us, the baby perch nibbling at our toes. It's all of it. There are some places that just make me feel clear, like the water around me I can see straight to the bottom of any problem. The riverbed will stare back at me and I can focus. Magpies are calling somewhere and the stinking hot day is held back by the arms of the gums.

Something inside me that has been tight and painful loosens. Stretching back in the water I extend my arms out and let myself float. I fill my eyes with the blue sky, white clouds and gum trees that bend over from the riverbanks. Limbs reaching towards each other but never quite meeting.

If the reservoir is where I go for space, the river is where I go for peace. I let the flow take me, doing its best to lift me away from my troubles. I've been doing this since I was a kid. Uncle Joe says if they didn't give me time alone in the river as a little kid, I'd freak out.

Slipping below the surface I roll around and stand. Massive smile in place I look for Rhi. She's sat cross-legged on the bank, lounging in the shade. I'd floated out into the middle and downstream a bit. A few vigorous kicks and I am back in the shallow bit where we started.

'That's really creepy, ya know?'

'What?'

'The way you do that. You get lost.'

I bust out laughing. 'Get lost in our river, yeah, that's bad. What kinda blackfulla are ya?'

She flips me the finger. 'It's good to see ya feelin better.'

'Thanks for bringin me out ere, cuzzie, I needed it.'

She side-steps my sincerity. 'No problem. This is easier than taggin along on a trip with a Miller to forbidden territory.'

I sigh. 'Yeah, about that. I'm sorry I said all that stuff.'

For once she goes serious. 'I know. And ya don't ave to be

211

sorry. I'm worried about Laney too.'

We both go quiet.

'How's your face feelin?' I ask.

'It looks worse than it feels. You?'

I grimace. 'Feels about as good as it looks.'

I sink backwards till the river catches me and stare up at that sky again. The blue is starting to darken from that bright day colour, the first hint that the sun is thinking about dipping to the horizon. I talk a big game but I don't want to risk Mum getting home and finding me gone. Based on yesterday who knew when that would be.

'We should probably head back.' I groan.

'Mmm.'

I smile up at the trees. She's so full of it, I know she feels the peace here. Connection. It flows as calm as the river.

'So, are you sure you don't want to poke Sam somewhere?'

I go under and come up choking, coughing out all the water I swallowed. Rhi learns from yesterday and is already up the bank losing her shit.

'You're a dirty bitch!' I yell, racing out of the water after her.

She runs screaming ahead of me to the car. I stop at the towels and dry off.

The giggles from the car have me shaking my head. Womba thing.

Rhi drops me home and stays long enough to see I'm alone, before taking off to go check on her siblings. I don't want to shower off the chill from the river, but Mum will take one look at me and know I've been swimming. I take a super-fast one to keep Nan's lecturing voice at bay. Stashing my dirty clothes at the bottom of the laundry, I walk to Laney's room.

Pushing the door open I think about the last time I'd seen her here, forcing her to get up. Between then and now, Mum and I have searched together and separately, and it didn't look right anymore. There are no clothes on the floor and not a single shoe to throw. Laney's bedside table is neatly stacked with her books and different things she usually leaves around the house, like her lip glosses, nail polish, hairbands and whatever else. Mum must've been bringing them in here bits at a time. It's so stupid that it hurts to think of her presence leaving the rest of the house and coming to settle only in here. The bed is made, and everything is ready for when Laney comes home.

Sitting on her mattress I let it sink in. This space that she'd filled is now blank and empty. We are both pretty private, even being twins we don't trespass in each other's rooms. Being in here without her feels like a betrayal. When we find her I didn't know how we were going to explain this to her. I pick up the black nail polish she loves so much and turn it around in my hands. There's only so long I can put this off.

Swallowing my guilt, I reach for the top drawer of her bedside table. Inside everything is stacked as neatly as the outside and I frown. Of course Mum has been back here too. I flip through everything, and other than some defaced notebooks that Mum will shout about later, there isn't anything that sticks out.

My motivation lasts through most of the room but it's all like that first drawer. Mum has been through it all with a fine-tooth comb. Finding the yarndi pipe tucked inside Laney's track shoes makes me wince. When she got home she'd have a little grace period, but it wouldn't last. She'd be hauled over the coals for all of this. Thomson women hold grudges like it's a competitive sport. Maybe I should petition the Sydney organisers to add it to next year's Olympics.

I flop back on Laney's bed, discouraged and confused. I stare up at all the posters she has lining the walls and ceiling. She collects all the teen magazines and reads them from cover to cover, but the posters are her favourite bits. I teased her constantly about all the shirtless actors and musicians she had up there, till she caught me watching *Days of Our Lives* just so I could perv on Jensen Ackles.

The memory makes me smile as I skim my eyes over Laney's gallery. She swaps them out regularly with each new heart-throb, all except for the Tupac one on her cupboard door, and the LL Cool J one on the ceiling, right above where her head lies. His trademark bucket hat and sexy grin are the only things he has on, giving a full view of that lovely chest. I trace my eyes over it, drawn to something in one corner. One pec is popping out in a weird way, making him look lopsided. I snort a laugh, Laney will be so pissed if her precious poster is damaged.

Still, it does look strange and I can't resist standing on the bed and reaching up. I trace around the pec, feeling like a pervert, until I feel something shift. Frowning, I prod each of his nipples, and nothing moves except for that first one. My heart skips a beat as I work to loosen the Blu Tack on one corner. I do not want to be the one that damages it or Laney will damage me. Once it's free, I peel back the top corner and jump back with a yelp as something drops, hitting me on the head and brushing down my body. I see a furry black thing fly past. Huntsman! I leap a metre in the air and off the bed, brushing frantically everywhere the thing touched.

Only once I calm down, do I look again. The small black thing is still there. A velvet bag?

Picking it up, I realise it's a jeweller's bag. Pulling open the drawstring, I push the bottom up until I see a glint of gold. I drop the thin gold chain into my palm. The pendant is a sweet little rock that has streaks of different colours in it. There are heaps of different rocks and things like this just lying around the hills. No one bothers with them because they aren't valuable, but they're pretty. Still, none of us would turn something like this into a necklace for fear it might be one of 'those' rocks. The ones Nan and all the aunties and uncles warn us about, that you only ever find in the caves around here. Not that I believe in those things anymore, but Laney sure as hell does, so why did she have this?

The last time I saw her played out in my mind's eye, letting her brush by me, watching her run off to Troy's car. The feeling in the house that afternoon, like something wasn't right. She has always been more trusting than me. The present from the dream? If he'd given it to her and told her he got it from a shop? The black velvet bag even made it look official. Laney would buy that. Besides, only the old people could tell which rocks were normal and which were taboo.

Everyone knew the story of the anthropologist who'd come to town way back when my great-grandmother was a girl. He'd gone up into the hills and come back with a rock from a cave, talking about how beautiful it was and showing it all around the pub. The old people warned him, told him straight to take the rock back and do it fast. He scoffed at them and did what he wanted, as whitefullas will do. He got sick that night and was rushed to the hospital. When they couldn't find anything wrong with him, he got scared and asked the old people to take it back. They told him it wouldn't do any good – he had to be the one to take the rock back and put it exactly where he'd got it from or he'd die. They reckoned that man crawled up them hills he was that sick. Later that night he came walking down like nothing was wrong. The anthropologist left town after that and no one saw him again.

A cold shiver runs down my back as I sit with that pretty rock in my hand. I might not believe it myself, but I don't want to test it out either, not after last night. Besides, it's almost dark, I'm alone and just because I'm being logical doesn't mean I'm not shitting myself just thinking about it. I shove it back in the bag, tightening the string like I can tie it off in my mind.

The big question is, do I tell Mum? I think about all the other stuff I've seen. The notebooks with the swear words and hate speech that Laney had written on it, and that pipe sitting in her shoe. Maybe this is one thing that could stay as mine and Laney's secret. Besides, the person who needs to see this is May. It probably isn't even one of those special stones, and she'll laugh at me for having it.

Decision made, I hop up on the bed and tuck it back into its hiding spot. I am grudgingly impressed with the spot, and it gets me thinking about all the places Laney could've stashed other things. She's crafty, and I'd have to start thinking like her if I was going to get anywhere. Pressing the poster firmly onto the Blu Tack I feel better for having found one piece of the puzzle, and want to ensure it stays safe in its well hidden spot. Maybe I also put it back because I don't want to look at or touch that necklace all that much.

Hopping down I eye everything in the room with new purpose and think about all the spy movies we'd ever seen. There is no telling if this is the 'present'; I have to be sure. I am going to do this again and this time I'll do it properly.

Half an hour later I'm just getting started feeling up Laney's mattress when I hear Uncle's car out front. I stay where I am. Laney's room is at the front of the house, so I can hear them talking as they climb out and come inside. It's clear they've had another useless day of searching. I swallow my disappointment and go back to the mattress.

'Tace?' Mum calls from the lounge.

'In here.'

She walks into the room, watching for a bit.

'Daughter, what are ya doin?'

'Laney's crafty like a fox so I'm not takin anythin for granted.'

She looks at me like I've lost my mind. 'Ya really think Laney hid something in her mattress?'

'Never underestimate a Thomson girl up to no good. Nan said you were the worst one for it when you were a teen.'

Mum actually blushes, and I try to not to laugh.

'Right. Well, come and ave a feed now, ay? Ya can keep lookin after.'

I drop the mattress and follow her out, trying not to stare at the ceiling.

Day 5, Twilight

Listening to Mum and Uncle Joe rave on over dinner isn't what I expect. They've been sending cousins out looking in every direction and Mum has a map she's drawn up. Sitting over it they mark up the places Uncle and some of the cousins have covered today. It's the weekend so more family have joined in the search. I am so proud of my mob it makes my chest feel a bit lighter.

Uncle won't look at me. Mum gives me a few hand gestures behind his back to say leave it be for now. He doesn't say anything about my face so I guess she told him what happened. The guilt weighs down in my guts again, but I force myself to pick at the fish and chips they brought home.

I sit through their strategy meeting twirling my cutlery, trying not to think about how bored I am. Everything seems so much more dramatic when I'm sneaking around behind their backs. I should probably feel bad about that.

Every now and then I cast an eye at the map, noticing the markings Mum has made, following them with my eyes. I take my plate into the kitchen and get another pot on the go. I'm bored but I don't want to be left out when I've made such a big deal about being included, so I walk back to the table. Before I sit down I take a better look at the page. It is a couple of A3 sheets Mum has stuck together and sketched from her's and Uncle's memories. There are a few glaring open spaces where property owners haven't allowed us to search, not unexpectedly. But they've found a lot who will help, and they've been searching along the boundaries of where they can't go. There's one place that has multiple lines criss-crossing around the edges and none inside it.

'What about the Potters'?'

Both heads swing around to me and Uncle's anger hits me full force. I'm shocked — he's usually a pretty laid-back kind of man. His look promises a private talk later that I will not enjoy.

'Youse ave been everywhere except there, but we saw some of it,' I try again.

'We go where we have permission. Most of us aren't silly enough to cross white people with guns,' Uncle growls. Still, I can see it's playing on his mind because he points at the surrounding properties. 'We've gotten as close as we can. Most of the owners out that way don't like the Potters much either.'

'I know they won't let us look, Uncle, but maybe it's time we just did what we had to? Isn't that where Laney went in the first place?' His face darkens as I remind him of all the reasons he is furious with me.

Mum intervenes. 'Not accordin to Troy.' She pulls the map closer and points at a different property. I can't remember the name of this one but it shares the Potter's western border. 'This is where he told the cops they parked, then they walked over onto the Potters' place. We've been all over there but.'

'That's not what Tyrone told Rhi.' I frown. 'He told her they were near the m—' I look up into Uncle's face and change tack. 'Place we shouldn't go. But Dan Potter and

219

Mick Franks said something … about too many blackfullas out there lately?'

I can't look at Uncle but I swear he's snarling under his breath.

'Daughter, if we're gonna go near *that* place, you need to be sure.' Mum doesn't have to spell out the danger.

I try to remember but the specifics just won't come. 'I'd have to ask Rhi to be sure.'

'Give her a ring, quick.'

I bolt to the house phone that's stashed in a corner of the dining room and call Aunty Mel's number. The hectic sound of kids going mad floods my ears.

'Oi, what's up?' Rhi's voice throws me right off.

'That's how you answer the phone?'

'We got caller ID now, cuzzie.' Rhi laughs. 'So what's up? Quick, I'm in the middle of feedin the kids.'

Aunty Mel has a fair few of them and Rhi is the oldest so she's always busy round this time.

'Do ya memba what Mick said bout blackfullas being out there?'

'Something about settin a example to stop more blacks goin there?'

My memory jolts. 'Boongs and their bombs! Thanks, cuz!'

I hang up as she shouts something.

'Rhi said Mick went on about too many blackfullas bein out there and how they needed to set another example to stop them comin out in their bombs. Why would they talk about the car if Troy and his mob hadn't been there?' Folding my arms I dare them to tell me I'm wrong. I can see their hesitation.

Mum puts her head in her hands. 'Why there of all places?'

'We can't go out there, Al.' Uncle is tense and I see something I never thought I'd see. Uncle Joe is scared, really scared.

'Not us, but the cops could.' Mum's head comes back up. 'We're goin to Mundubbera, Joe, right now.'

'How do we get them to look in the right place?' He isn't trying to poke holes, I can see that, but he is pissing Mum off.

'We'll report her missin first, because that arsehole won't ave done it. Then we convince em that we need to search the Potters' place. We've got a thirty-minute drive to think about how we do it. The important thing is to get em involved, even if we ave to force the bastards.'

Declaration made, Mum is up and moving. I've seen her like this only once before. The night we lost Nan she'd been this grim and almost as determined. God help the Mundubbera cops. Uncle knows it too. He drags along in her wake, looking worried.

I walk with them to the door, wishing I could go but I know she won't let me. 'Mum, is there anything I can be doin?'

She turns on me and growls. 'Stay. Here!'

I nod like my head is going to bob right off.

Grabbing her purse, she marches out. Uncle gives me one last dirty look. 'Do as you're told, Stacey Thomson.'

Once he's out the door I roll my eyes. So not as scary as Mum.

I go to the kitchen and clean everything up while I listen for any doubling back by my paranoid parent. Not that I can really blame her. I am definitely up to no good. I keep a close eye on the clock while I clean. An hour to get there and back, probably a fair bit of paperwork. Lots of shouting from Mum to get the cops to listen, although they're usually better than the Eidsvold fullas – they will at least listen. Maybe two hours max.

With a shiny kitchen and no sign of Mum, I go to the phone and call information.

'Number for Toni Miller in Eidsvold please.'

I don't need a pen. The first five digits are always the same.

I hang up and dial. I haven't given myself much time to think, I decide to just bullshit my way through and hope like hell the Millers don't have caller ID.

'Hello?'

The air rushes out of me.

'Sam, it's me. Don't hang up!'

There's a brief silence when a woman's voice in the background yells out.

'Bloody telemarketers,' Sam calls back.

'I'm sorry! But I found somethin and I need to show it to May.'

'Look, this is a really shit time. I'm about to head out fishin.'

'Great! Where? I'll come to you.'

'No, there's no good time, don't fuckin call back,' he snarls and hangs up.

I look at the phone in shock.

What the hell?

I shake it off fast. I need to get in touch with Rhi. We're meeting with May, fuck Sam Miller and his opinions. I try Aunty Mel's place but get no answer. The clock is ticking in time with my heart. My window is narrowing.

Their place is only a five-minute walk. I can do it in less.

I take a quick detour to grab the necklace, stuffing it into my back pocket before I head out. I get a block away when Toni Miller's car pulls up beside me in full view of every man and his dog. The driver hops out and comes around the front, right at me.

'What are ya doin?' I hiss.

'I could ask you the same thing. What, ya want me to get a third floggin for your sake?' Sam stops in front of me, his lip curls like he smells something bad.

My conscience rears up and bites me. 'Shit, Sam I'm sorry, I—'

'Save it. The only reason I'm ere is cos Aunty wants to see ya.'

'You told er I called?'

'I didn't tell er nuthin. She told me to take er fishin, then said we had to come into town and pick somethin up. What she meant was come tell you.' His bitterness hurts in a way I don't have time to think about.

'Sam, I said I was sorry.'

'Whatever, Thomson. I'm doing this for her, not you. She says if ya don't meet us tonight you'll lose ya sister to the dark, whatever that means. I'm takin her fishin at Tolderodden, at that spot I took youse both. Ya know, after I got flogged up for ya the *second* time. If ya aren't there that's your own fuckin fault.'

Spinning on his heel he leaves me on the sidewalk with my mouth open and my chest hurting. I really managed to screw that up.

No time! I bolt for Rhi's house and hope the tears won't fall.

Day 5, Night

'What are we doin, Tace?'

Rhi's words hit me as I slink into her car, keeping my eyes peeled for any movements in the dark surrounds of the house. We haven't been punished for our dirty deeds yet so she still has a car and I have a bit of freedom. Laney has them all distracted for the time being. This waiting time is weird. I feel like I'm a mouse tempting fate by gnawing at a bit of cheese that may or may not be attached to something that will swing down and crush me. The mouse analogy works for right now too, as I hunch down in Rhi's front seat not looking at her.

'What? I wanted to get out?'

'Mmm hmm,' is her response. Great cousin that she is, she puts the car in gear and takes off.

'So we're goin fishin?'

'Yep, but I thought we'd try a new spot this time.'

'And Aunty Al knows about it?'

'Ahuh,' I mutter. 'Didja, umm, tell Aunty about it?'

'Nah, she's down the pub tonight. Matt's watchin the kids,' Rhi states oh so casually, like she trusts her doughy younger brother with their siblings all the time. 'So … if we're goin fishin, where's the gear?'

I freeze. God, I am an idiot sometimes. I turn to look at her and she shakes her head at me.

'I don't know what I'm more disgusted with, that you're gettin me into more trouble or how shit you are at lyin. I should take ya straight back ome.'

'Come on, cuz, I need to get out there tonight,' I plead. 'Mum and Uncle Joe are in Dubbs, but we've only got …' I check the car clock, 'one and a half hours tops, before they get back.'

She turns the car towards the aerodrome road and takes us up to the seating area there. Stopping the car, she turns to look me in the eye.

'All of it, now.'

I sigh. 'I found something Laney was hidin so I called the Miller's place but Sam got pissed and hung up on me. I thought I was screwed. But then he came and found me.'

She fist-pumps. 'I knew it!'

I look at her strangely. 'He told me May needs to see me and it's tonight or never.'

Her jaw drops. 'Is that it? No secret tryst, no forbidden romance? We're going out to meet a hot boy out in the middle of nowhere so you can talk to his ancient crone of an aunty?!'

Slumping back, she bangs her head repeatedly against the headrest.

'Ah, cuz, now I'm even more disappointed in ya.'

I'm starting to get pissed off. 'Will ya stop it with this me and Sam shit? I need to focus on my sister, you know, the one who's been missing for almost a week? The one I'm havin nightmares about? The one who needs me and I'm not there?'

It's my turn to spin away from her. This scene has gotten a little bit more hysterical than I wanted. A tentative hand touches my shoulder.

'I'm sorry, cuzzie, it's just … you've always been the good girl. It's been nice seein ya break a few rules and not worryin so much what the mob thinks.'

I snort. 'I'm not doin this for fun, Rhi.'

Her hand squeezes. 'I know. I'll stop, okay?'

I face her again. 'Rhiannon Thomson givin up. I'll believe it when I see it.'

She laughs and hugs me. 'Am I forgiven?'

'Only if you forgive me for lyin about what we're doin.'

'Done!' She leans back and we do a pinky promise. Rhi might be as mad as a cut snake, but she's a solid-gold cuzzie.

'But, Rhi, are you sure? We might actually get disowned for this.'

Her face crinkles in thought, but she soon tosses her worry aside. 'It is what it is, cuz, and you gotta trust your gut, just like Nan always said. They can't be too pissed at us for doin what we were told.'

It's Rhi logic so I'm not too sure it's sound, but I need the comfort.

'Right now my gut says we ave to stop off and leave a note for your mum.'

'Rhi—'

She cuts me off. 'Non-negotiable, cuzzie. The gut says we leave a note.'

I sit in silence and sulk while she drives back to our house.

Going fishing with Rhi at Tolderodden. Should be back before you get home.

I stare at it for a second and my guilt makes me add: *Sorry. T xo*

I slip back into Rhi's car and try not to look at her.

'We'll be back before them, right?'

She ignores my question and puts the car in gear.

'Let's away, to your clandestine meeting with an octogenarian where absolutely no romance is allowed with er hot nephew.'

'Got a new word-of-the-day calendar, cuz?'

'Shut up bitch, I'm expandin my vocabulary.'

I bust out laughing.

Bumping our way across open ground we follow the tracks. The headlights show only thigh-high grass all around us with distant shapes of trees. Good thing Rhi remembers the way because I've forgotten. I have zero sense of direction. She mumbles something like 'good blackfulla you' when I confess this and then drives us straight there. Or I hope it's 'there'. I have no idea.

Seeing a bank of trees ahead is the first hint we're closing in on the river. We come across a steep drop down towards the water. Below, a fire winks at us through gaps in the scrub and I relax. There's someone here. It has to be them.

Coming into an open space our lights fall on the Miller's car first. Beyond that the fire beckons through the trees. I can make out two figures further back, spread out along the banks of the river, probably with fishing lines in hand. As we roll up I see Sam set up his line around a branch shoved into the ground, before going and helping May do the same.

Sam gives me the dirtiest look while helping May hobble to the fire.

'Wow, you weren't kiddin, he is pissed. Did he say why?' Rhi whispers.

'Cos I called his house. He said I wanted im to get another floggin.' I blush.

'Well, that's a bit fucked up.'

She breezes past me and eventually I remember to follow. Shoving my hands in my pockets I walk up, keeping my eyes on May as Sam lowers her into a camp chair he's set up. Once she's comfortable he busies himself getting a billy on the go. It's kind of awkward and words stick in my throat; never a problem with Rhi.

'Hey, you mob, anythin bitin?'

May smiles. 'Not on the fishin line; although somethin's bitin him on the arse.' She tips her chin at Sam.

'Yeah, this one too.' Rhi copies the tip, aiming it in my direction.

My finger goes up before I think about it, then I blush as the old aunty looks at me. She stares till I drop my eyes.

'Hrmm, so ya came then. Nephew said ya wouldn't, but I know ya been seein her still, ay?'

I wrap my arms around my middle and move closer to the fire, despite the heat. I nod. 'Bad nightmares, real bad.'

Rhi shoots me a concerned look and settles down by the fire. We know how to listen, us mob.

May nods again and stares into the flames. 'They won't let er go, not easy way. Ya find her soon and make them or they'll keep er.'

I gulp past my heart. 'Who's got er?'

'No good to name that ere, girl.'

'Then how'm I sposed to find her?' My frustration flies

out of me and I feel Sam's glare amp up. *Right, don't yell around the crazy lady.*

The old lady gives me a long look. The light flickers in her cataracts, reminding me eerily of a cat's. 'Don't be stupid, girl. Ya grandmother taught ya better, I know she did.'

I've had about enough of this.

'Look, either ya know who's got er or ya don't, but ya gotta stop the vague warnings. I need to be out there lookin for my sister!'

Those old eyes watch me in disgust. 'Forgot it all, didja? She's not been gone that long. Poor old thing.'

Rhi's head tilts to the side. 'You knew Nan?'

'We were best friends once, me and her. Don't they teach you kids nuthin?'

'But ... you're a Miller.' Rhi's confusion mirrors mine, even Sam's.

'Ahh, that old bullshit. It never bothered us none, but she was there when they took me, hid like I told er to. Then my dear old dad ...' She seems to gasp past that point, like I've seen Pop do when forced to talk about Nan. 'She got blamed cos I got grabbed and she didn't. Cos she was alive and whole, and me and Dad weren't. People do and say stupid things when they're grievin and I was too lost in darkness to help er.'

I watch, fascinated, as tears leak out and over her cheeks. She doesn't even seem to notice. A Miller crying for a Thomson, and they call her the crazy one.

'Never got a chance to help er then, so I'll help er granddaughters now, cos she'd ave helped me if she could.' May eyes Rhi. 'Spittin image ya are, girl, hurts and heals to look atcha.'

Rhi's face crumples and she ducks her head. I kneel and wrap an arm around her shoulders. Everyone says Rhi is as lovely as Nan. For months after the funeral Pop wouldn't look at Rhi and it did something inside her. Seeing my strong cousin cry makes me defensive.

'We went to Potters' like you said. Bruises was all we got out of the trip.'

She snorts. 'Cos you weren't lookin properly, stupid girl. Used your head, didn't ya? Used ya logic and education and all that white man stuff.' She turns and spits in the fire. 'Never thought I'd see the day that Tandy's girls would turn from their own ways.'

'But, all the old fullas say not to go near that mountain. Ya want us to do things proper way, so shouldn't ya be goin off at us?' Rhi is as confused as me, but at least she isn't hurting anymore.

'Bah, old bastards thought that would keep the kids safe after what appened to me. Read it all wrong they did but wouldn't listen to me. Oh no, I'm Mad May, you know.'

The bitterness is so heavy it silences us all for a moment.

'So … you're sayin that I can go there. That Laney is there?' Laney's the only reason I'm here, I can't get distracted from that, even if it is fascinating. I can't help any of that, but I can help my twin.

Her sharp eyes collide with mine and I feel the threat in them.

'You can and she is. But so are they.'

'Who? The Potters? I'll risk it for Laney.' I stand and hold my hand down to Rhi. 'Come on, we gotta get to her.'

'You can't be serious?' Sam is up facing me over the fire.

'Ya know what they're capable of and you're still gonna go? Ya can't be that fuckin stupid!'

'What choice do I ave? The cops are takin too long, the adults won't do it without them. My sister is dyin!'

The words burst out and I admit aloud what I've been trying not to say to myself. That last dream cinched it. Laney is fading and I am desperate.

Rhi takes my hand and stands. 'You're the one said ya didn't believe in this anymore. Why now?'

'I don't know, Rhi, cos what came to the back door last night?'

'No girl, cos you know it. You feel it.' May nods at me from her seat. 'White man's logic won't help you in there, only ya instinct. Follow it to ya twin and you'll make it.'

'Aunty, you can't seriously be tellin her this,' Sam yells. 'What if she ends up dead – or worse?'

'And what wouldn't you do for your brothers, son?' May looks at him till his gaze drops.

'Well, I'm goin too!' Rhi jumps in.

'And me.' Sam's quiet reply has us all staring.

'I thought you hated me.' I frown.

'Yeah, but I don't want to see you dead and I don't mind Laney.' He shifts around on his feet while Rhi casts me a knowing glance. I roll my eyes at her.

'Do what you want, but I'm goin.' I spin on my heel and head for the car.

'Hang on, Tace, I need to get Aunty back home first!' Sam yells at the same time Rhi calls, 'Let's have a cuppa and hash out a plan. I don't wanna get jumped again.'

But I need to move. I am terrified and if I don't start now

231

I might let it freeze me in place. The look May shot me said she knows what is waiting. I feel phantom claws brush my chin and shiver. If I think about it too much I might never go back.

'Come on, Rhi, let's go. Sam, you can follow us out there if you want, but I need to go. Now.'

Stepping out of the fire's light I walk to the car and stand beside the passenger door, my back to them. Clenching and unclenching my fists, I fight my fear and my tears. I keep hearing Laney's screams. I can't leave her there any longer. A blade of grass tickles my ankle and I scratch it with my foot. When the tickling moves to both ankles, tightening a bit, I look down expecting to see grass, weeds or even fishing line caught around them.

Hands?

A wrench and I go flying backwards onto my arse. I barely choke out a sound as they yank me under the car. I try to hold on, but everything is torn from my grip. I try to kick, but they're too strong. I'm being pulled out the other side of the car into the long grass.

'Rhi!'

Yelling and running feet. Flashing light fading. Darkness and grass. Flying past. Rocks knocking out breath. Scraping. Still I'm struggling.

'Sam!'

And he's there. Grabbing my hands, pulling me. He holds on as the hands on my ankles tighten, hurting. I don't look. I can't look. Oh fuck. I stare at his face. His horror tells me everything. It feels like they're pulling me in two.

'Don't let go,' I beg.

He grits his teeth and holds. Rhi is there. Arms around Sam. They pull and pull. I cry out in pain.

'Fuck off you pricks!'

May.

The old girl runs like one renewed. Firestick in hand she dashes in. My captor lets go as the light touches us. A screech of pain, but not one that comes from a human throat.

'The fire!' May cries.

We haul arse back to the camp. Sam and Rhi have to carry me, I can't seem to get my legs to unlock.

Back in the light, they lower me down. Rhi pulls my shaking body into a hug as Sam crouches to check my ankles. They feel bruised, but I'm too scared to look. I felt something cutting.

Harsh breathing is the only sound for a while.

'She's okay,' Sam declares. 'Ya just need a bit of Savlon. I got it in the car.'

'No!' I grab him by the shoulders. 'No. Don't go near the dark.'

'It's okay, Tace, it's just there.' He points to his car, which is closer than ours. I swear I see something moving under it where the light can't reach.

'She's right, stay in the light. They're ere for er, but they'll use one of us to tempt er closer.' May's voice is trembling. She drops beside us, looking worn out.

'Are those …' Rhi's voice came tiny and afraid.

'Don't say it!' Sam hisses, jumping to his feet. 'Just don't name it. We'll wait them out, that's all.'

I'm watching the shadows, trying to see into them. Firelight dances almost playfully, stretching over dirt and grass, except for our shadows. Lifting an unsteady hand I point at Sam's shadow, long and thin reaching out beyond the light. Something moves.

I shriek as May grabs Sam's hand and yanks him to the ground. Whatever was there spits and screeches like an angry possum. A flash of movement and it returns to the shadows. A glimpse of limbs and hair is all I get. It's enough.

'Stay down!' May whispers.

We all turn and check our shadows. They're way too close to the edge of the light. Shapes shift everywhere the light doesn't reach.

Sam hunches over my ankles again, hiding his face.

'How much wood did you collect?' I ask, knowing the answer. They hadn't expected to camp the night.

His scared eyes meet mine. 'Not enough.'

'Why are they doing this?' Rhi whimpers.

My seated position is pushing something into my right bum cheek and I remember why I wanted to see May in the first place.

'I found something in Laney's room. A necklace.'

Shifting to reach the pocket, I dig around till I grab it. I pull it out, undo the tie and drop the necklace into my hand. As the pendant hits air, a howling rolls around the camp. Many voices, all of them sounding like women screaming in the dark.

'Put it away!' May shouts.

I don't ask questions, just shove it back into my pocket, not bothering to use the bag. The howling stops, but the shadows are moving faster now.

'Ya just showed them. Ya have it. We have it.'

'I'm sorry. I didn't know.'

May tucks herself into a tight ball, rocking backwards and forwards in a way I've seen traumatised people do on TV. Sam crawls over to her and wraps her in his arms. She shudders but doesn't relax.

'They come after you, they don't stop once they know, once you've touched it,' she mumbles and it becomes an uncontrollable storm of words.

Rhi slips her hand into mine.

I look up to find Sam glaring at me over May's head. 'What didja do?'

'Me?'

'She said they want ya, we all saw it. So what didja do, Tace? They don't come after people like this, not so openly and not for nuthin. So what'd you do?'

'I didn't *do* anythin. I've been at home for God's sake, bein a good girl … I mean there was Potters', but we all went there. I, I only found it, I didn't take it!'

'Neither did I, but they've been tormentin me ever since, just for touchin it. They can't torment the one who took it, he's long dead, so they go after the ones who touch it. Who know of it and don't return it.'

'That's not fair!'

'Neither is bein driven mad for sixty years!' May shouts again and all goes quiet. Even the night seems to still.

'But they said those whitefullas …' Sam's voice interrupts our match. He looks sadly at his aunt. 'They said those whitefullas did this to you.'

May's fragile hand reaches up and cups his cheek. 'They did. One of em had a wife, got her jewellery made up from local stones as a present, to show off his money. My old dad

235

tried to warn im, but he wouldn't listen. He cursed that poor woman into an early grave. But instead of takin them things back, instead of fixin his mistake, he punished Dad for bein right by stealin me. Made me touch it, wear it while he—'

Sam pulls her tighter into his arms. The devastation across his face is too hard to watch. I look across at Rhi instead.

'Laney had it, hidden in her room. But I think Troy gave it to her. Memba what e was sayin bout the necklace?'

'Stuffed it in an old safe after they were done. Put it in a lead-lined safe. Thought it would protect em. Made me put it there. After.' May gasps like she's struggling to breathe under water.

'Troy did this.' Rhi lets it hang there and I shake my head.

'Who cares about blame now? They've got her and now they want me,' I say, standing.

'Tace?' Rhi asks.

'This won't bring her back.'

I swing around to look at the traumatised woman.

'They won't give her back, not now. They don't give back what they took.'

'But I don't … I can't … what else can I do?' I yell at her, at them, at everyone.

No one will look at me. I'm staring at my future and she has no answers either.

'Do they ever stop?' I ask, hopeless.

May looks confused for a bit. 'Lately, I think. I been clearer, less scared. Maybe, they been leavin me alone. Not too sure.'

After forty years maybe it's getting to the point that she just doesn't know anymore if the monsters are in the room or in her mind.

Dropping to the ground, I draw my knees to my chest and take my first look at my ankles. I have some scratches and puncture wounds that I try not to see as claw marks. Picking my way up my legs and over my body, I find all the scrapes and new bruising that I didn't feel before. Why do these things never hurt until you see them? I brush it off as best I can, put my chin on my knees and stare out at the shadows. Betrayal sits heavy in my gut. This is my country, I am supposed to be safe. All I've done is pick up a necklace. And for that I'm to be hunted, and my twin and I are possibly eternally fucked. What kind of justice is this?

Rhi makes a little squeak and I can't look at her. This is all my fault. Pressing my forehead into my knees I try to just breathe.

'This might be a dippy question,' Sam says, 'but can't we just throw the necklace to em?'

May gives a short, sharp cackle. 'They'd take it and then they'd wait. Wait for the one who last touched it. Someone's gotta to be punished.'

I wince.

Rhi's sobs get worse and I press tighter into myself, searching for courage.

'Don't do it,' Sam says.

My head comes up and I meet his steady gaze.

'Don't do it. There's another way, you just gotta think.'

I laugh, and it hurts. 'Me? I'm the one that got us in this mess.'

He shakes his head, arms still holding a rocking May. 'No, you got caught up in it. None of it is your fault. Ya wanna blame someone, blame Laney and Troy. If it was locked in a safe then they must've stole it on one of their midnight runs. Like they were some kinda vigilante movement against the whitefullas. Like stealin their shit means somethin.' His derision and fury are plain, but his tone stays light and steady to keep May calm.

'So use that massive fuckin brain a yours, Tace, and think!'

Think about what? How we're trapped in the firelight? How they can hide in any shadow and get to us that way? Everything in my head is around shadows and light waves from science. What good is that against something this ancient? I could stand there and quote the science at them. I snort. Light waves blocked by a solid object is the absence of light ... so why aren't they crawling up our shadows right now?

My eyes land on the firestick May saved me with. It's a big one and still burning where she'd dropped it in the dirt, but it won't stay that way for long. The secondary source is casting just enough light to diffuse our shadows.

'Rhi, how long you reckon it took us to get ere?'

'Bout thirty minutes. Why?'

'So less than a hour till they get home, then another thirty to get out ere?'

Hope sparks in her eyes. 'Only twenty. I made you stop memba?'

I smile at her. 'And told me to leave a note sayin where we'd be.' I look at Sam. 'Think we can make it another ninety minutes?'

Sam grins at me and I return it. 'Don't get cocky, it's one option. Cross ya fingers ya collected enough wood and Mum is angry enough to follow us out here.'

Rhi snorts. 'Pretty sure that's not gonna be a problem.'

I notice a drop in the fire and our shadows reach higher, closer to the edge of the light.

'We got another problem.' I point at the firestick. 'That's gonna burn down fast. Once it goes, the light drops and they might be able to use our shadows.'

'We make two fires then?'

'Three.' I have all of their attention. May's rocking even seems to slow. 'We need to stretch it so it goes around the wood pile as well or we're screwed. Still think there's enough wood?'

Sam chews his lip, staring at the wood he gathered. 'Cuttin it close.'

'Not like we have much choice,' Rhi says, pointing at the shifting shapes that are gathering near where our shadows are reaching out.

I tear my gaze away and focus on the here and now.

'We have to do this real careful. Always make sure there's light to our front and our back, and never cross over each other's light. We create a ring of light with us in the middle. Ere look.'

I pick up a stick and go to draw in the dirt to show my thinking, but stop before the stick touches dirt.

Put that stick down! Don't ever draw in the dirt at night, girl.

Another rule from Nan that I've ignored since she left. My eyes meet May's and I drop the stick.

'Or not. Alright, so one person moves first to build a triangle of light. With Aunty May's firestick we just need a third point.' I point to a spot that'll do. 'Then we can start reinforcing it with more fire.'

Rhi looks at me with hope. 'Will it work?'

'If we move very carefully? Yeah, I think so. It's my idea so I'm doin it. The rest of you keep a close eye on all of our shadows.'

Glad for something I can do that doesn't involve an act of suicide, I take another firestick and slide in the direction I pointed. Too scared to stand still, I make sure everyone stays within the triangle I am creating. As I move I watch the light. I refuse to look at the shadows, the flickers of movement I can't quite make out at the edges of the advancing dark.

'Good, Tace, real good.' Rhi's encouragement stops me and I place the stick on the ground. Turning to check everything I meet two grins and one old woman who's watching me with interest.

Staying low, I move back towards them. They pass me more wood and I slowly build each firestick up till there're two small fires. Once done, I make my way back to the others.

'What now?' Rhi asks, hugging her knees.

'We wait.' I hate saying it. We're placing our hopes on something that may not happen. If the cops were too slow in talking to Mum or the paperwork took too long. Hell, if they ran into a cousin in the street and had a yarn.

A hand lands on my arm and I look up into Sam's eyes.

'Stay here.'

I nod but I can't look away from him. A single phrase has been repeating in my head and I've been fighting not to examine it. Action and doing have pushed it aside, but now there is nothing to distract me.

Sam seems to see it, and he reaches out to brush my fringe back in a soft gesture. The hint of kindness causes a fatal crack in the dam of my resistance. Tears start flowing and I hold my breath to keep it all back. He never breaks eye contact. When I can speak I have to force the words past my lips: 'They don't give back what they took.'

Rhi shoves her head into her knees, again muffling her crying. There's a harsher edge to it this time. Suppressed sobs make my teeth chatter, my whole body shaking as I fight what I am thinking. Sam's eyes turn sad, and he pulls me into his arms.

'I know,' he whispers into my hair.

A sound comes out of me then, like a wounded animal. Guttural and raw. I cry like I haven't with Dad, or Nan. Sam holds me close, murmuring comforting sounds that make no sense. Nothing can reach me in this world of pain. My heart refuses to accept what my head is saying, and they are tearing me in two.

Eventually, the tears slow. I remember myself enough to be aware of my cousin, and feel embarrassed by my breakdown. 'Thank you,' I murmur, before scooting out of Sam's arms and over to Rhi; we wrap each other in a hug. Sam pulls May into his arms and we all rest our backs together. The four of us stay close, huddling in the centre of the light, and watch the shadows. Every time the light drops low, *they* edge closer. Twin red lights dot the entire area, under cars, around trees, crouching low in the scrub, watching. The weird musty smell I'd caught a whiff of last night is suffocating.

We wait as long as we can to add the next branches to the fires. My heart climbs into my throat, my breath comes faster. Watching them come closer. Drowning in their scent.

Around and around we go till I think I might lose it.

Around and around till it feels like this is all there is in the world.

I have no idea how long we sit there like that. It feels like forever.

The wood pile shrinks. And takes my hope with it.

There is still the option to walk out there. To give them what they want. I'd sacrifice myself but save three people doing it. I can't think of Mum, I try not to think much of anything.

The necklace sits heavy in my pocket.

The first thrum of sound is like an illusion, till small flickers of light stream through the trees. The deep embankment we're sitting in means there's no way anyone from the road can see us unless they drive to the very top and look down. People come out here all the time without going to the crest. I try so hard not to get my hopes up.

When the car crawls over the embankment I sob. It's too bright to see past the headlights. It scatters the shadows, shrieks go up as light reaches unexpected places. They move too fast to see but a few sound like they're hurt.

As the car pulls up beside Aunty Mel's, I realise my mistake.
'No! Stop!'

I jump to my feet, waving like a mad woman. Rhi pulls me down by my shoulders, but we're all yelling now.
'Stay in the car!'
'Don't open the doors!'
'Fuck that, LOCK the doors!'

A combination of relief and that last comment from Rhi makes me bust out laughing, and everyone around that little fire joins me. We're laughing so hard tears are flowing down

242

every face, and if we're a bit hysterical no one points it out.

A window cracks open and my mother's voice slaps the night air.

'What the fuck is goin on?'

That sobers us up quick.

'Long story, but they're everywhere, Mum. It's not safe.' I choke on the words.

'What are?'

I lift my hand, palm out and curl my fingers into a claw, flexing them in and out a few times, just like Nan always had.

A gasp and the internal lights come on. I can see Uncle in the front, lowering his arm from the roof, and Mum beside him. They both look pale.

'How do we get you in the car?' Uncle calls.

I shrug. It feels like a sick joke. They're so close, but still an eternity away.

'Can we drive over?'

'Let's try it.'

Uncle turns the car back on and shifts as close as he can without hitting us. As we watch the chassis block the light, I spot movement.

'Stop! They're under the car!'

Uncle hits the brakes, and this time they're close enough I can see the fear in their eyes. I force myself to look away and think.

'What if we moved the triangle out and made it a circle big enough to fit the car?' Sam asks.

I smile. 'Worth a try. The car's too close now though. If Uncle backs up, we can build little fires and widen it out enough that he can drive into it.'

'Will that work?' Rhi asks, fear and hope mixing on her face.

'We have to do it real careful,' I say with a confidence I am far from feeling. 'Always make sure there's light to our front and our back and remember – never cross over each other's light. Once we have the triangle big enough we can slowly move the fires outward, make more little ones, till they can drive into it.'

'Got it,' Uncle calls. He reverses back a few metres. I can't look at Mum.

'Who wants to reinforce the fires and who wants to prep the firesticks?' I'm not about to let any of them risk moving out into the dark.

Sam drops a kiss to May's head and lets her go. 'I'm on fire building.'

'I got the firesticks.' Rhi sounds almost normal.

'I'll widen out the triangle first. Sam, don't make them too big, we have to be able to push the sides out to make it a circle.'

He throws me a thumbs up and we go to work.

Bright headlights shine over us as protection but I make Uncle turn them off. We can't see the firelight properly with those on.

It takes so long, with painstaking movements, shifting fires, building more, pushing out with our light. At some point May starts singing old rock songs and we all join in. Light and music are the best defences, Nan always said.

Old school rock and roll tunes echo around the space we've built, just as Sam steps up to tap me on the shoulder.

'We're out of firesticks, Tace, and there's no more wood.

It's now or never.'

I nod, fear gripping my throat.

He takes my hand and leads me to the corner where May still sits and Rhi tends the original fire. It's shrunk to a miniscule size while we worked, taking more and more from it to spread around.

'Uncle, we're ready. Slow but steady,' I call.

My rising fear is choking me. What if I've got it wrong? This is the moment we'll either get out okay or get taken, and there is nothing I can do about it.

Uncle's car inches forwards. As it breaches the outer rim we all release a breath.

'So far so good,' Rhi sighs.

I have a sudden awful thought and press my head to the ground, watching under the car as it comes closer. Shadows swing around the wheels as they pass the fires. My breath stops. Movement around the rims, creeping limbs and red pinpricks, then scurrying backwards as the light penetrates deeper, spreading under the car.

'Stop! They're under the car again.'

'I got it,' Sam says, pulling a torch out from the little pile of their gear.

I frown at him. 'You had that the whole time?'

He shrugs. 'One little light wasn't gonna save all of us.'

'It might now,' Rhi laughs.

Dropping to his belly near the front of the car, Sam shines it underneath and watches. The wheels get within ten centimetres of his head before he yells for a stop.

'We're right,' he calls, standing carefully because he's so close to the car's bumper he might whack his head.

A big grin breaks out on Rhi's face. 'All aboard the Thomson train, people. Last stop, safety!'

I yank the back door open and get a shock. Uncle Joe is in the driver's seat glaring at me, and Mum is now in the back, arms stretched out. 'Get in this fuckin car, Tace!'

I turn and shove Rhi in first. Total coward I know. She has to climb onto Mum's knee to make room. Helping Aunty May into the middle, Sam gets in the back while I take the front seat. All doors close and lock, and I still can't trust we're safe. Maybe because we're surrounded by silent fury.

'What about the fires?' Rhi asks. We haven't thought it through. It's too dry to just leave them burning out here.

Uncle throws a grin over his shoulder. 'Hold on!'

He hits the accelerator and flings the steering wheel around, sending us into an epic donut that many a teenage boy would envy. It isn't perfect, but it gets the job done – dirt spews out behind us. As we whip around at speed and take off out of there I stare back at the dying embers. The shadows that move past them send shivers all over me.

'They're following,' I whisper.

No one says anything for a moment.

'Someone tell me what the fuck is goin on, right now!' Mum yells and we all jump sky-high.

I take one look at Rhi and we can't help it. We both double over, laughing till our sides ache. Sam and May join us.

Uncle Joe makes it back to town in record speed. Rhi and I have most of the story out by now because we're talking so damn fast while the Millers sit silent. Probably uncomfortable with that many Thomsons in one place. Kind of like putting cats and dogs in the same car and expecting them to communicate.

We screech into our driveway and Uncle Joe orders us all out. He doesn't have to tell anyone, we know they're close. I help Sam bring his aunty in as fast as possible without picking her up and carrying her. Mum runs ahead and turns on every light in the house, even putting some Sam Cooke on the stereo at a low volume. Rhi sprints around shutting up the whole house, screw the heat, while Uncle Joe kind of flaps about 'checking things'.

All jobs done. Our strange little party meets around the kitchen table and looks at each other.

A soft scraping noise sounds at the back door and everyone flinches.

'It's the wind,' Mum says.

Feeling antsy, I do what is normal and put on a pot of tea. Pulling out mugs I don't even think about asking who wants one. If we had beer I think the adults would've preferred it right now. I know I would.

Something catches my eye outside and I turn to look. A silver shape sits out on the tank stand. Watching. I jerk back to my task and say nothing to anyone. It won't change or help things.

The adults stand around, shuffling on their feet and trying not to look at each other. Rhi and I get extra chairs from the dining room, hoping to encourage everyone to sit. No one does.

The adult Thomsons eye the two Millers and the look

is returned in spades. You can see the conflict on Mum's and Uncle's faces. These are Millers, they shouldn't be here. But May is the one exception Nan has drilled into everyone – always be polite to May Miller. And with Sam protecting us like he has, they can't be rude to him either without seeming like petty arse hats. For his part Sam looks like he wants to crawl under the table. May is the only one who seems completely relaxed, but she keeps a close eye on everyone, and a protective hand on her grandson.

I finally have enough.

'Sit!'

To my shock they do. But I'd drawn Mum's attention to me. Most of her fury seemed to fade on the drive in, but I know it's bubbling just under the surface.

'Where is it, Tace?'

Rhi and I both flinch. 'I don't think—'

May interrupts me. 'Show her, girl, she needs to see.'

'But what if …'

May's hand slices through the air, in that final way all the old fullas had, and I automatically reach into my pocket.

She turns to look at Mum. 'Nobody else can touch it; no one but you.' Her gaze is sad as she and Mum share a look. Something on Mum's face tells me what they have planned.

'Like fuckin hell I will!' I yell, yanking my empty hand out of my pocket.

'Stacey Claire!' Uncle snaps.

'Who gives a *fuck* about my language – no one else is goin to put themselves in danger. Touchin the stone, drawin them to you, none of it will save Laney!' I immediately flush,

248

horrified by what I've just said and how I've spoken to my elders. A collective gasp goes up and all eyes turn to Mum.

She looks like I've punched her, her eyes snapping shut for a few long minutes. I recognise the signs of her holding back tears, watching her is how I've learnt not to cry. She pulls all that pain inside her, closes it in, and when her eyes open again they are focused on me like a harsh light in a pitch black room.

'Maybe not, but it would save you.'

For a second I can't move, the pain is too intense. My heart keeps screaming it isn't true, wants to beg her to tell me I am wrong. That everything will be okay. Even while my brain insists things will never be okay again. I've already lost Dad and Nan, I can't do this too.

Uncle Joe turns on Mum, distracting us both.

'Al, you wouldn't?'

'What wouldn't you do for them?' Mum's soft voice flows out and settles us all down.

'That's it!' Rhi stands, shoves her face into mine and stares me down. 'You look me in the eye Stacey Thomson and tell me that your sister isn't out there?'

'They don't—'

'I don't give two fucks what they do or don't do. Answer the fuckin question!'

I take a breath. My brain tells me clearly what is real. It screams it, even when I don't want to know. But my heart tells me different. My tears dry up and I look to my big cuzzie, confused.

'You would *know* if your twin is gone, Tace. Look inside where Nan always told us to, and listen to your gut.'

'She's not gone.' My whisper is a cue for everyone to release their breaths.

I can feel Laney, I've always been able to feel her. My rational mind has fought me on this, but I've known every time I dreamed. She's in trouble but she's alive.

Rhi sits back in her chair, satisfied. 'Okay, so how do we bring her home, and get them off both your backs?'

A long silence greets her words, but she stays seated, quietly confident. Mum steps into the void and I feel hope jolt to life.

'Rhi is right, we need a plan that saves ... as many people as possible, but in the meantime,' she turns to me, fury rising, 'daughter, you will give me that necklace.'

Rhi sighs but I am too focused on my mother to notice.

Mutinous teenage attitude in full force, I cross my arms and glare. 'No.'

'Stacey Claire Thomson, you give me that necklace!'

'No.' My voice doesn't change, my stance doesn't waiver. Everyone's eyes are bouncing between me and her like it's a tennis match.

'If you don't give me that necklace right this minute—'

'You'll what?' I scream back. 'Die a slow tortured death? No. Fuckin. Way!'

'I say we give it back to the pricks who gave it to Laney.' Rhi's voice breaks our little standoff.

'Then what? Storm the caves and hope for the best?' Sam asks with a heavy dose of sarcasm, earning him a glare from Rhi.

'One thing at a time,' she says. 'If those things are too busy chasin after Troy, it gets them off our backs, and gives us time to figure out how to save Laney.'

'That's … a bloody brilliant idea, niece.' An evil grin spreads across Mum's face.

Just the other day I might've grinned too, but I actually pity Troy. Especially now I know what he'd been dealing with. My ankles throb in pain as a reminder. Still, what wouldn't I do to get Laney back? And now I have hope again I'm not about to let it go. Rational mind be damned, and all of Nan's rules too. I want my twin back!

'Easy to say,' Uncle pipes in. 'How do we get im to take it?'

'We hide it in somethin, make im think it's somethin he wants?'

'Like what?'

'Money,' Sam adds. 'Put it in somethin he can stick his hand in but not see what it is. Till it's too late.'

Uncle Joe stares at Sam for a long second. The tension climbs a bit.

'Like this?' Rhi runs to the rescue, reaching into her back pocket and pulling out a pretty little coin purse.

'No way, Rhi,' I tell her. 'Nan gave us them.'

She'd gotten them in a range of colours one Christmas and given one to all her granddaughters. They are the last thing she ever gave us.

'I wasn't gonna let im keep it.'

She tosses it to me, and I stand, turning my back on the rest of them. Bringing the necklace out of my pocket, I keep my hand clenched tight around it and the bag. I don't want to know if the howling will start again. Slipping both into the purse I snap it shut and tuck it inside my bra.

'Eyah! I want that back!' Rhi protests, knowing exactly what I am doing from my movements.

'Yep, and I don't want anyone else touchin it in the meantime. I'll wash it for ya, don't worry.'

I spin back and gave Mum and Uncle Joe the evil eye. They exchange looks that confirm she was thinking about holding me down and getting it. I dare her with my eyes to try it.

'Aunty, don't,' Rhi begs. 'It'll go down her jocks next.'

I bust out laughing, and pretty soon everyone else is too. The tension peels back a bit. Not all the way, but enough so we can breathe.

We sit, sipping our tea, lost in our own thoughts. A musty smell reaches past my head and I jerk upright. The four of us who'd been by the fire go still.

'What's—'

I put my finger to my lips and Mum stops. We're listening.

Uncle Joe hops up and goes to look out the kitchen window.

'I don't see nuthin,' he whispers. 'Wait, is that a fuckin ghost bird?'

He jerks back from the window.

A soft thrumming call fills the air. Goosebumps race over my skin.

A tap comes from directly underneath my feet and I leap away from the table, knocking my cup and spilling tea everywhere. The cup bounces and rolls on the lino as I step backwards. The tapping follows my steps so I stop. Waiting.

One giant thump comes from directly under me. I gasp and jump onto my chair. Soft scraping noises sound, like sharp nails on wood, swirling outwards to where the others sit, like they're searching for me. I burst into tears. Cupping my face I drop to the ground and run to my room, pretending I don't hear the tapping chase after me through the house. I lock both doors and throw myself on the bed. I thrust my head into the pillow, trying to muffle my wails. When the storm is over, I lie face first in my own tears and listen. There are no more sounds.

A soft knock comes from the door and I nearly jump out of my skin. 'Tace, it's me,' Rhi murmurs.

I get up to grab some tissues and let her in. Locking the door behind her I sit and clean up all the snot and salt water I've gotten everywhere.

'You okay?'

'What's happenin?' I ask between blowing my nose.

'Everyone's stayin ere. Sposed to be for protection but I think we're all just too scared to leave.' She tries to smile but it looks horrible so she stops. 'Nuthin else happened after you left. May said they were tryin to scare you out of the house.'

I flinch.

'Aunty's got mattresses and fans set up for the Millers.' She shakes her head. 'Never thought I'd see the day. Sam called his mob and told em they're campin out the river.' She leans forwards and whispers, 'Aunty won't leave me alone with him.'

This time the grin is real and I give a lame giggle. 'You're cracked.'

She winks at me and jumps on the other side of the bed. 'I'm crashin with you tonight, cuz, to "take care of you".' She does the air quotes and I laugh more naturally this time, lying down beside her.

'And if it means ya can't sneak off for some alone time with Sam?'

'I know, so obvious right?' She moves to her side and props herself up on her elbow, looming over me. 'Adults are so stupid. It's not me he was watchin on the drive home.'

I roll my eyes. 'What. Ever.'

'Come on, Tace, the guy saved you. Again! You've got the perfect excuse to call him your hero.' She bats her eyelashes and giggles.

Instead of distracting me she's reminded me of the danger. I sober up. 'What are we gonna do, Rhi?'

My flighty, bubbly cousin looks at me straight. 'We go to sleep. And wait for daylight. Then we get your twin back.'

Despite the heat, she cuddles in close and we stay like that for the night.

Day 6, Daylight

I didn't sleep a wink. Listening to every noise, jerking at every creak of the old house, plus my fear of the dreams, all of it left me wide awake. Rhi managed to get some sleep in, which I'm grateful for. Soft snores from around the house tell me others have as well. As pre-dawn light finally starts seeping in through the numerous cracks around the house, I shimmy carefully out of bed and go around opening up all the windows and doors I can without waking anyone. If I thought this place was an oven before, that was nothing compared to the torture of having everything shut up. I move around quietly in the shifting old house, every sound makes me scared I'll wake someone who desperately needs sleep.

My reward is the cool breeze that slips over my sweat-crusted skin. I start getting coffee ready. Tea just isn't going to cut it today.

I'm not surprised to find May already at the kitchen table. She's sitting there staring at her hands, not moving.

'Coffee, Aunty?' No matter what else happened that old girl has my respect.

'Tea please, bub.'

I'm getting it all ready when a soft choking sound has me around the table and crouching by her side. Only then do I see the rivers of tears flowing down her face.

I reach out and take her hands in mine. 'What's wrong, Aunty?'

She chuckles softly. 'Not a damn thing. I slept without a single problem.'

I smile up at her. 'But that's good, ay?'

She shakes her head hard, gripping my hands with hers. 'Not at someone else's expense. Not at yours and your sister's expense.'

I lean up and kiss her cheek. 'That's Laney's fault not yours. She went an mixed it with that idiot, went where she shouldn't, took what wasn't hers and this is what happens. When I get er back I'm plannin to rip out every strand of er air for all the trouble and heartache she's caused.'

I'm not angry at my twin ... not too much anyway. She's been into everything our whole lives, couldn't seem to stop herself. How do you blame someone for doing what's in their nature? I'll still be ripping her hair out though.

'How can we even think about puttin someone else through this?'

I hesitate.

'If we're goin to find where they took Laney we need to be safe to do it. He can take back what he gave.' I squeeze her hands. 'We're different from im though, cos we won't leave im in danger. Once we get Laney back, we'll figure it out. Like Rhi said, one step at a time.'

I'm trying to convince her as much as myself and she gives me a sad smile.

'You don't wanna do it either.'

'What else can we do?'

May looks straight into my eyes. 'There is one thing you could do.'

'What?'

'Don't wait for the others. You go now.'

My smile drops. I'm supposed to be with the adults on this one. Mum is already on the warpath. The little girl in me wants them to fix it so bad; my throat tightens with panic. 'Why?'

'They think they can do this and protect you, but they'll only stuff it up. You can't get in a paddock with a bull and have your focus on anythin but the big bastard.' Her thin hands grip mine harder. 'You need to go do this.'

'Alone?' I nearly choke. 'What about Troy?'

Her smile is so terribly sad. 'You don't need us, bub, and you don't need to trick Troy to do nuthin. You know where your twin is. You've always known.'

I picture the cave entrance in my dream, the deep darkness within, the tiny figure curled in the heart of the mountain that I'd walked around days before. A soft thrumming sound comes from outside and I flinch.

The old girl's eyes go to the kitchen window. I don't have to look, I know it's there.

'Ghost birds ain't bad,' she says. 'Not good neither. They warn and if it's still ere at this time then it as a message for someone in this house. I think it's ere for you.'

Nan said as much, but it didn't stop her from closing doors and windows if she saw one going about its business. But it's when they start doing weird things, like swooping people or hanging around outside a house till dawn, that a warning is clear.

A firm grip on my chin pulls me back to the present.

257

'End it. Now. This is the only way to get your twin back.'

She says the magic words; I feel my spine stiffen. I stand. Giving her another kiss to the cheek, I turn on my heel and go to Laney's room. I don't stop to change out of the clothes I'd worn yesterday, the ones I'd slept in and been dragged around in. I pull Laney's old softball bat out of the cupboard and stay there for a second, drinking in my twin's room. I lift the coin purse out, remove the necklace and lay the purse on Laney's pillow. I don't want Rhi to lose it. Necklace secured back in my bra, I go in search of Uncle's keys. Mum's keys would've been easier, but I needed a proper four-wheeler for that last bit of road, and Mum's old Corolla wouldn't manage it. They're easy to find, lying beside the couch where he'd bedded down last night. His mouth is wide open and he's snoring softly. I feel bad but I take them keys. The old girl is waiting for me by the back door, Sam's torch is clutched in her hand. She passes it to me, squeezing my fingers.

'You can do this,' she whispers.

Making it out to the car, I go over the basics in my head before even putting the key in the ignition. I know starting it will wake them, but they have no other cars at the house that can follow me and there's no way the cops will be out this early. I'd been bush-bashing with Dad as a kid so I know how to drive on backroads. Still, I won't have much time before they figure something out.

I'm already out of town heading for the Potters' place when I realise May never said Laney or I will get out of this.

258

I keep my brain focused on directions the whole way out, even as I bounce my way over that shocker of a track. I'm so scared of getting lost or stuck, or doing something wrong, my whole focus is on driving. I need to go slow for this bit but my heart keeps demanding I hit the accelerator. Mum and Uncle won't be far behind, just a run up to Aunty Mel's place to grab her car and they sure as hell won't have to be as careful. As I drive, the light and heat increase, but I'm so cold inside I want a jumper. The hour-long trip feels like it takes half the morning.

I tumble out of the car, trying to find a way to tuck the torch in so I can have my hands free to use the bat. My hairband turns into a handy tie that wraps the torch up in my shirt. Picking the bat up, I swing it a few times to get a feel for it, then stop stalling.

Walking through bush is an everyday thing for me, it should feel natural, like home. But the coolness of those trees enfolds me and I am reminded that this place isn't home. It's taboo. And I am going to break that today.

Shivering, I move up the mountain. I ignore the insanity of following directions from a dream. I climb for a good fifteen minutes, looking for easier paths the entire time but finding none, when I realise I'm being followed. Soft little scrapes, the odd rustle. At first I think it's rock wallabies, maybe snakes, heading in the other direction when they realise I'm close. But the sounds always come from behind me. My steps pick up the same pace as my heartbeat.

I feel it up ahead. A heaviness pressing on me, a warning to turn back. The trees are leaning in, grabbing at my clothes, trying to tell me what I already know. This is no place I want to go. Want to and need to are very different things.

No thoughts are allowed to come except those that point me towards Laney. I won't turn back, I won't let her down and I will get us both out. The noises following me are keeping pace. If it was Mum or Uncle they'd have yelled at me to stop. It's daylight, it can't be them. I don't want to know what's back there.

Two boulders loom ahead, and above them I can see the entrance to a cave. My instincts scream and I know I've found her. Climbing up isn't that hard with this one, there are spots between the boulders like steps. They are far shorter than a normal human would need. I pause at the entry, switching on my torchlight and readjusting everything. Deep breath in and out, I grip the bat with both hands and raise it. Breath in and out. I step into the dark.

The hair on my gunu-gunu is on end, goosebumps bloom everywhere on my skin, every warning instinct I have is screaming for me to run. A damp, musty smell fills my nose, reminding me of unwashed fur and earth. I force my breaths to stay slow as I move sideways, bat at the ready.

I walk carefully like that for at least ten minutes, maybe more. The light behind me is no more, with all the twists and turns the cave takes. And always it slopes downwards. I can't help marvelling at the smooth rock floor and walls. This isn't natural, they're honed by years of passage. I'm making sure to marvel so I can't think what might have caused that.

A scrape of sound behind me and I turn, swinging hard. A hand shoots out and catches the bat.

My torchlight flickers over a sneering face and I'm shoved backwards. It forces me to let go of the bat as I land on my back, all the air leaving me in a rush. By some miracle the torch is still tied to my shirt. It shows Dan Potter standing above me, gloating while he taps my bat against his palm. The wind has been knocked out of me and I lie there, struggling to breathe.

'Just couldn't stay away, could ya?' He squats down beside me, leering while the light casts crazy shapes all over his face. 'I knew you'd come here for somethin'. Is this where you've been hidin' that thievin' sister, ay?'

'How did you …' I gasp.

'Heard your car.' He smirks. 'Guess ya aren't as smart as ya thought.'

He reaches out and brushes my fringe off my forehead. The mirror to what Sam did, but where that made me feel safe, this just makes me sick. 'Maybe if you ask real nice, I'll let you go after I'm done.'

I scramble away from him on my hands, scraping them over rocks, totally uncaring of the pain. He stays crouching, laughing like this is a fun game. He doesn't have to chase me, the light tells him exactly where I am. As much as I don't want to do it, I reach up to turn it off. I see him stand and take his first steps towards me before the light blinks out. It is pitch black now and I force myself to lie still. Waiting for my eyes to adjust.

'Now, now, Stacey,' he tuts. 'Don't you know I love to hunt?'

A soft footfall tells me he's moving forwards. If I stay where I am he'll find me. If I move he'll hear me. At least my breath is back now. My hands clench on rocks and I resist the urge to peg a heap in his direction. Instead I take just one and carefully slide it over the floor to my right.

'Hah!' He leaps in that direction and I slide more rocks harder to the right, picking that second to roll to the left. I'm pulled up short by a pair of legs.

Frantic scraping in the dark to my right and a familiar smell tells me it isn't Dan. I roll back the way I've come in a total panic.

I hit Dan's legs and manage to bring him down with me.

'Fuckin' bitch!' He grabs at me and gets hold of some of my hair. I keep right on rolling, feeling it wrench from my head. It hurts but who cares. I've heard another voice in the dark. One I know.

I keep moving, listening to Dan scramble along after me. 'Get back here, you little slut!'

He's as blind as me. I can't get up and run for fear of wiping out on the walls or a low-hanging stalactite. I hear the voice again and my heart leaps. So close!

'Gotcha!' A click and a stream of light cuts through the dark.

Dan is only a few metres behind me with a pen-torch in his hand. One of those tiny LED things that still manages to be intense. I get up and run, but too late.

Grabbing a bigger fistful of my hair he rips my head back, wrapping his other arm around my chest. I struggle against him but he's a full-grown man who does physical labour for a living; I'm a scrawny, bookish teenager.

He drags me down to the ground, forcing me under him till he's straddling my hips, his knees trapping my arms at my sides. He leans in and brutally shoves his mouth on mine. Pushing till my teeth split my lip and blood pours into my mouth. He bites down on my bottom lip till I am forced to open my mouth so he can shove his vile tongue inside. I whimper and try to bite him, but he rips my head further back. He digs the torch into my jaw right at the hinge joint. The pain is unbearable.

A groan in the dark makes him pull back. It draws both our eyes and Dan brings the light around to the source. A small ledge drops about a metre down from where he has me. There lies a thin figure, curled in a tight ball. Her hand covers her eyes and she groans again like it hurts.

'Laney,' I gasp.

'Tace,' she whispers, so quiet but I still hear her. 'Run.'

A soft growl comes from just beyond her. A shifting in the dark that is all too familiar, the horror inside me builds higher.

'What the fuck is that?' Dan swings the light to get a better look and the growls become enraged shrieks. He finally gets scared. Too late. He leans backwards, releasing my head and arms. I fumble in my bra and pull out the necklace. The chain is so long I slip it right over his head without a problem.

'What the—'

The shrieks turn to screams. Dan goes from crouching over me, staring at the necklace in shock, to flying through the air. His torchlight flickers crazily against the walls. I stay utterly still as I feel air rushing over me, shadows deeper than the dark. I catch glimpses of fast-moving images in the flickering torchlight as Dan strikes wildly around him, keeping the torch in his fist.

Dan swinging at the dark. Light. Inhuman screams. Laney. Dan. Light. Screams. Laney.

I'm up and moving, leaping down to the ledge. Pure adrenalin pouring. Pulling her up I try not to wince at how hard it is to lift her, she's almost a dead weight. Her entire body is shaking and I can hear her breath coming fast and hard. It feels like she might be going into shock. This will be my only chance. Focus!

Laney. Dan running, falling. Laney looking at me, dazed. Dan.

'Run!' she whispers.

'That's what I'm doin,' I growl back.

Lifting her enough to get her arm over my shoulder, I half lift, half drag her back up the ledge.

Dan punching out at the black, his back against a wall. Deep scratches appearing over his exposed skin. Darkness flows down his skin, a deep red when the light moves over it.

The movement of the torchlight is slowing, but I can see the way back. Laney locks her legs and tries to help me. It's not much but it'll have to be enough. I move as fast as I can, refusing to think about the screams behind us.

'Help! Don't leave me!'

I'm not a killer, and there is no righteous justice here. I did this. I close my ears and focus on Laney. She is the bull in the paddock, my only goal. I'll deal with what I've done later.

The shrieks and scuffling are getting louder. Dan is still fighting.

'Stacey! Help!'

I'm crying and I don't know why. He was going to rape me. God help me, the longer he fights, the better for us.

We've made it past one of the many curves in the tunnel, blocking the horrible flashing light. The dark closes in. By some miracle Sam's torch is still tied to my shirt. I have to pause to turn it on, fumbling the switch. The screams became wordless, pushing me faster. Laney's quiet sobs force me to harden up. It will all be for nothing if I can't get her out. His struggles bounce off the walls around us like an accusation.

As far as we've come in that short while I can still hear the screams turn to gurgles. Hear the struggles lessen. Quieten. Stop.

Soft tearing noises. Oh God, please tell me he isn't feeling that. Sharp snapping in the dark.

Another growl and a shuffle tells me we're next.

I turn while supporting most of Laney's weight, aiming the torchlight down the cave. Our backwards progress is much slower and harder going, but the light is enough. It fills the cave wall to wall and floor to ceiling, keeping them back. I can only pray there is nothing between us and the cave's entrance.

It felt like such a short walk in, but I'm tiring fast. The bruises and pains of the last few days weigh me down, the new ones hurting worse because of it. Laney must've passed out because now I am flat out dragging her. I am failing. I know it and so do they. Their growls of fury became purrs as they follow, stalk, wait.

'Tace!'

I am so close to losing it I even hear Mum's voice.

'Tace! Keep coming!' And Uncle's?

A spike of electricity leaps through me and I almost lose my grip on Laney. I don't dare look; what if it isn't real?

What if I turn and move the light? Tears flood my sight and I blink them away, trying to keep my gaze fixed on the shifting dark. Sounds of pounding feet bounce off the cave walls.

'We're almost there, keep comin!'

I stay on my feet, but only just. I'm shaking so hard. Strong arms reach under Laney's arms and her weight lifts. Softer arms wrap around me from behind. I pick up the smell of Mum's shampoo over the horrifying musty smell and shudder.

She presses her lips to my ear and starts a litany of whispering strength. 'Don't turn around, baby. You got this. We're almost out. I'm here. You can do this.'

We stare at the pinpricks of red light. Their purrs turn back to growls. Furious shrieks. The baleful eyes follow us the whole way out to where the sunlight leaks through the cave entry. I still don't turn. Refuse to give them my back till I am out in full sunlight. Even then I check my shadow won't reach the cave entrance before I finally let myself turn away.

Mum releases me long enough to grab me by the hand and make a run for it. Sunlight and steep terrain or not we have to get out of there. I see Uncle ahead of us, carrying an unconscious Laney over his shoulder. He'd waited to see we were out and then took off. Mum has to drag me through the bush. We keep stumbling, falling and tripping. The light hurts everything and I can't see. She never pauses.

Bundling into the back of Aunty's car with Mum, I realise Uncle has Laney in there too, draped half over his lap, checking for injuries. Sam is at the wheel. I get a look at Aunty Mel and Rhi waving at me as they fly past in Uncle's car. May is looking over the front passenger seat, grinning at me.

'Good girl,' is all she says before Sam hits the gas.

Sam floors it out of there, past the Dodge parked to one side that makes everything in me crumple. I collapse into Mum's arms sobbing.

She hugs me close, wrapping me tight in one arm, while her other hand rubs Laney's leg.

'It's okay,' she whispers. 'It's okay.'

But she doesn't know. It will never be okay again.

A Few Days Later

Light-filled rooms with bright white walls stretch out around me. Sitting in the hall I rub at the stains on my hands. The door opens and a nurse steps out. She's one of the white ones from around here, but a good one. There's no judgement, she just smiles and motions me in.

I go straight to Laney's bed, climbing up beside her and cuddling close. Our faces on the same pillow, I lift my right hand and she lifts her left. Palm to palm, we weave our fingers together.

Tucking our joined hands between us, I close my eyes.

'I knew you could see me,' she whispers.

I crack one eye open and raise the accompanying eyebrow.

She smiles. 'I knew you were with me, those times when you were dreaming. I could feel ya beside me.'

I open the other eye and frown at her, but she just laughs. 'Mum told me.'

I shake my head and close my eyes again.

'You know it's been a while now. Are you planning to never talk again?'

I keep my eyes shut.

The doctors want me to go to a trauma psychologist in Bundaberg. They say I'm punishing myself for something. I know what, but they won't believe me so why bother?

When they did a search of the place for 'whoever' took Laney, they found Dan's car, and the real panic set in. They're still searching those hills for him like they hadn't for Laney, even went into the cave yesterday after Uncle agreed to show them where it was. They couldn't beg, bribe or force any blackfullas into that cave though. When they did go into it there was no sign of Dan and the white people didn't see nothing in there.

'Nuthin they don't want to see,' is how Aunty Mel puts it.

The cops decided Laney must've gotten trapped in the cave and I'd somehow found her. Some weird twin connection is what the lead detective said. They'd tried to question me for a while but gave up when all I did was cry. The first few times it was genuine panic and guilt, but now I'm at a point where I see a blue uniform and I start crying just to make them go away.

Rumours flying around town are that I killed Dan. His parents came over to our place to scream abuse a few times. They can't prove anything, but it's all too convenient – a black girl is found and a white man goes missing. Not that anyone is drawing 'untoward conclusions' as I heard one of the detectives put it to the media. Course, now it's a white man missing there are police, searchers and journos everywhere. Mum says they'll clear out as soon as something else happens.

Conspiracy theories and gossip are running wild. People have even asked me if Dan is the one who took Laney. Doesn't matter what the rumour is, I'm the villain. They all figure if I'm innocent then I'd be talking. Couldn't argue with them there. Hell, if they knew what I'd really done they'd lynch me. Laney told everyone she doesn't remember much, but I'm pretty sure she's lying. There's something in her eyes when she looks at me now that wasn't there before.

We're still sisters, still twins. She's alive and that's my only comfort.

'Rhi's been comin past too, told me all about what ya been up ta.' She giggles. 'Damn, Tace, I wish I'd been around to see ya rebel side come out.'

I poke my tongue at her.

'She also told me some ome truths about Troy. You were right, he is a dickhead.'

Her attempt at a joke falls way flat and the hurt is there for anyone who knew how to listen. My free hand comes up to pat her cheek. I never want to be right if it hurts her.

'Never mind, we've already started plannin my revenge. And now that my sister is a total bad-arse rule breaker, I expect ya to help.'

I give one deep nod of approval and she laughs.

'What about ya love life? Now that we're sort of buryin the hatchet with the Millers, maybe you could ask Sam out?'

I snort. Sam isn't around. He'd called the house a few times, but let it go when I wouldn't talk to him. We hadn't exactly left things on good terms the last time I saw him.

The Miller–Thomson truce is a brand-new shiny thing that could be tarnished with a few harsh words or one incident, I suspect. With Aunty May now officially the elder of their mob, rumours are that she and Pop are talking and that might be enough to rein in our two families. I'll reserve judgement – grudges aren't called that because they're easy to give up, on either side.

'Still not goin to talk, ay? Well, I've decided I'm good with it,' Laney says.

A suspicious eye cracks open.

'I mean, if ya can't talk, then ya can't talk back right? No sarcastic comments. No bitchiness to deal with. My life just got that much more peaceful.'

My middle finger comes up and I scratch my nose with it.

'Ay, is this how we'll communicate now?'

The other eye opens and I give her the foulest look until she throws up her hands.

'I'm just warnin ya I intend to take full advantage when I get out tomorrow.'

I roll my eyes. Reaching up I shut her eyes and close my own. I am sleeping a lot lately. Nobody has mentioned school yet and I'm not in a rush to go back to Cassie and her shit. I spend so much time in bed now they might have to change *my* name to Laney. The only good news is she's coming home tomorrow. They'd kept her in here to assess her mental wellbeing as well as get her back to full health. Almost a week with a little water, and what was probably raw grubs and bugs to keep her breathing, and she was not in great shape.

I'll be glad to get her home, mostly for her, but also to get Mum off my back. She can hover all over Laney for a while. I thought she'd been over-protective before this; that was nothing compared to now.

I am anticipating some intense fights between Mum and Laney very soon. You can't cage a Thomson woman unless she wants you to.

A gentle kiss on my forehead makes me sigh.

'Love you,' she whispers.

I squeeze her hand and we lie together like that.

The door creaks and I jump. Reminding myself again that I am in a brightly lit room during daylight hours. I look up to see Sam holding the door open for Aunty May. She's out of her nighties and old jeans these days, replacing them with long skirts, bright blouses and a wide-brimmed hat set at a jaunty angle. Her eyes sparkle under that brim, alive and clear in a way that makes me glad to see her. I hop up to greet them.

'Hello, niece,' May exclaims, opening her arms so I can come in for a cuddle and kiss. 'It's good to see you.'

'Niece?' Laney chokes.

'And here's the famous sister.' May pulls away and moves over to Laney, leaving me to face Sam.

My guilt stops me from meeting most people's eyes, but I try a hesitant nod, turning away before he can respond. I escape around the hospital bed, bringing the only chair in the room over so May can sit. She settles herself down and watches us both. Sam comes and stands beside her so I walk back around the bed. Now that Laney is safe I feel much more awkward around him. So weird.

'Tace, didja tell ya sister all about your adventures?'

I look to Laney who answers for me.

'She's not speaking, A ... Aunty?'

'It's not a question girl, it's a fact, now that me and your sister have been and healed up old wounds between our mobs.'

I cock an eyebrow.

'And you can cut out that sarcasm, Miss Muffet. Me and your grandfather will heal it together.'

I lower my eyebrow. I did have hope, just not a lot of confidence.

'Not talkin ay?' She eyes me closely. 'And why not?'

I refuse to look at her, choosing instead to stare at my sister for help.

'It's what happened in the cave—'

I elbow her in the side, forcing her to stop.

'Should I ask Sam to leave?' May asks.

I hesitate but shake my head.

'But we can't talk about it.'

I nod.

'Well, this is a really friggin annoyin way to talk!'

'Tell me about it,' Laney mutters.

I glare at her.

'Ya not still worried by them things, ay bub?' Aunty May asks, her hand coming up in the familiar claw clenching move.

I'm glad she doesn't name them, even in broad daylight I can't shake the feeling they are close.

'It's done now, girl. Finished.' Her hand flicks out and across. 'They got what they wanted. If we stay away, don't break another rule, we should be just fine.'

It's the 'should' that keeps me awake at night. No one knows anyone who's escaped them so there is no real way of being sure. Pop and Mum had a big fight about it. She insisted he smoke out the house and he did it. But he grumbled the whole time about useless gestures.

Laney lies back on her pillows and falls into an 'I'm sick and frail' pose that is so obvious it's see-through.

'Sis, could ya get me a drink of water? I'm still so thirsty.'

I glare harder at her, but her dehydration worries me so I grab her water jug and go out into the hallway to fill it with the good cold filtered stuff. It doesn't take long. As I turn, carefully balancing the water, I almost run straight into a broad chest. My eyes flick up and Sam and I stand there for a while, just looking.

He reaches out and brushes my still-healing lip, making me wince.

'Sorry. Did Dan do this?'

I can't look at him, or answer. And I can't tell him to move. I am stuck between a Miller and a water fountain.

'So yes. Did he hurt anything else?'

The fear in his voice forces me to look up. I shake my head, making sure I hold his eyes. A rush of breath leaves him and fans over my face. It smells like mints.

'Whatever happened, Tace, it's not your fault.'

'Course it's her fault,' May's voice comes from behind him.

'Aunty!' Sam is so shocked he takes a step back so me and the old girl are looking right at each other.

'It's your fault he got taken cos ya put that necklace on im, didn't ya?'

I flinch, and May steps closer.

'It's your fault cos ya chose to save ya sister and yaself.'

Flinch. Step.

'It's your fault cos he followed ya into that place.'

Flinch. Step.

'It's your fault cos he was gonna hurt you and instead e got hurt. And part of you is glad it was im and not you.'

Tears flow down my face and it feels like she's flogging

274

into me with each accusation. Everything I've told myself comes out of her mouth.

'It's your fault ya didn't die there, too,' she whispers into my face.

I start to sob uncontrollably and she bundles me in close, holding tight till the storm is over. When I'm calm she pulls back, smoothing her calloused hands down from my forehead to my chin, brushing tears away as she goes. She cups my jaw and looks deep into my eyes. Only Nan has ever done that.

'Ya gotta stop torturin yaself. He made is choices and you made yours. Some ya can blame yaself for, but others are all on him. And, bub, I'm so glad you're here.'

Her sincerity touches me deep, in that infected place where I hold Dan's cries for help and the sounds of his horrifying death. They'll never find him inside that cave, and racist or not, no one deserves to die like that. Or to be left wondering what happened to their son.

The entire time May watches me, following all the thoughts that cross my face. She seems satisfied by whatever she sees because she kisses me softly on the cheek and lets go of my jaw.

'Good girl. I gotta get goin. When your sister is out you come see me and we'll ave a nice cuppa and a yarn.'

I smile for the first time in days.

Order given, May struts down the hall towards the exit. Sam stops beside me for a moment and smiles.

'See you soon, Tace,' he promises before following his aunt.

People will still call her Mad May. That'll probably always stick. Makes me wonder who the mad ones are in this town.

I have a feeling they're all in for a shock. The thought makes me chuckle.

I wake screaming in the middle of the night, sure there is something in the room with me. Certain that something has me.

Mum comes running, wrapping me tight in her arms while I sob on her shoulder. After the storm turns into sniffles, she bundles me into bed with her, making sure to keep the lights blazing. It's the only way I can relax now. I refuse to talk, to tell her about my dream, even when she begs. I know she'll take all the blame for herself because that's what she does. I don't want her to feel the way I do.

Neither of us sleep. I'm too scared and I think Mum might be afraid to in case I have another nightmare. We stay awake, hugging each other.

Into that sad, desperate place the faintest trace of a scent comes wafting. A familiar one that grows stronger and stronger.

Imperial Leather soap, White Ox tobacco and talcum powder, with hints of fire smoke.

Mum gives a weird combination of a sob and a laugh.

I'm crying again but for far better reasons. The unconditional love enveloping me loosens my throat.

'Night Mum, night Nan. Love you,' I whisper.

Mum's arms tighten hard around me and I feel her shuddering breaths on my neck. I know she's fighting tears, because of the way she's holding her breath. She's so focused on not crying that she doesn't hear the soft thrumming call that draws my eyes to the window sill. The ghost bird sits staring at us, before turning and flying into the night. Gone as quietly as it came.

For the first time since this all started, I feel safe. I fall asleep with Mum's arms and Nan's presence surrounding me.

Author's Note

This book grew out of my Masters, where I had the opportunity to sit down with some of my aunties and talk about the history of our town. I asked for and received their permission to write about our community, culture and spiritual beliefs, as long as there were no real people, families or historical events. It breaks my heart to say we've lost all but one of those aunties since then. I owe them everything.

As the project has evolved, so too have my characters, and while I have strived to meet my aunties' expectations, my family has pointed out to me that I have inadvertently written about some family members. Thank you to my mother and sister for being okay with that. Having just lost my own grandfather, I was unable to write the grandfather in this story any other way. I have received permission from most of his children to write him into this work.

The creatures in this story are ones we believe exist and are not named for two very specific reasons: I don't want them to be misappropriated, and I have deliberately fictionalised some of their characteristics so my representation of them is no longer accurate. People in my community will understand what I have stayed true to and what I have fictionalised.

Acknowledgements

I'd like to thank the Queensland Literary Awards, the State Library of Queensland, and the Copyright Agency Ltd for this entire experience. It has been a true adventure. And particularly to the judges of the David Unaipon, Melissa Lucashenko and Jared Thomas, who gave such valuable feedback. I would like to thank the Anne Edgeworth Trust and the ACT Writers Centre for helping me travel home to sit down with my elders. And thanks to Varuna the National Writers' House and all the amazing staff there – the space and time to write that you provide is invaluable. I was only able to attend Varuna with the support of an artsACT grant. Thank you all so much!

I have a passion for feedback and there have been many people who've given generously of their time and offered their valuable thoughts. Thank you to Kerry Reed-Gilbert, Kim Johnston, Samantha Faulkner, Ross Hamilton, Donna Hanson and Carol Major. Also to Rhonda Black for her brilliant advice, and Grace Lucas-Pennington and Megan McGrath – if I hadn't seen you ladies speak I wouldn't have sent my manuscript in to the David Unaipon.

A special thank you to my supervisor, Tony Eaton. I have learnt so much about writing from you. Thank you so much for everything you do.

I wrote the first draft of this book at Capital Pancakes in Canberra. Thank you to the patient staff for letting me sit there for hours on end and fuelling me with delicious food and coffee.

I'm beyond grateful to the entire team at UQP for their time, patience and energy, especially Kristina Schulz, Vanessa Pellatt and Madonna Duffy. Thanks to Jody Lee and Margaret McDonell for editing and proofreading.

Thank you, Aunty Rosie, and all the other aunties who gave of their time, knowledge and energy. I wish you were all here to see this.

To my partner Ben, none of this would be possible without your love, encouragement and patience. To Garry and Trish County, your support and enthusiasm is contagious. To my Uncle Billy and Aunty Linda for the help when I came begging for a place to write out of the heat. To my sisters, Lyndsey and Brooke, and all my nieces and nephews – you are my inspiration. To my amazing mother, Odette, you are my hero.

Lisa Fuller is a First Nation Wuilli Wuilli woman from Queensland, Australia, and is also descended from Gooreng Gooreng and Wakka Wakka peoples. She won a 2019 black&write! Writing Fellowship, the 2017 David Unaipon Award for an Unpublished Indigenous Writer, the 2018 Varuna Eleanor Dark Flagship Fellowship, and was a joint winner of the 2018 Copyright Agency Fellowships for First Nations Writers. She has previously published poetry, blogs and short fiction. Lisa is an editor and publishing consultant, and is passionate about culturally appropriate writing and publishing.

Lisa is a member of Us Mob Writing, the Canberra Speculative Fiction Guild, the First Nations Australia Writers Network, and the Canberra Society of Editors.

Ghost Bird won the Griffith University Young Adult Book Award in the 2020 Queensland Literary Awards, the 2020 Readings Young Adult Book Prize, and the Norma K Hemming Award. It was also an Honour Book for the 2020 CBCA Book of the Year: Older Readers and was shortlisted for the Aurealis Awards.